It felt like fate. When Luther placed his forehead to hers, their breaths intermingling, she didn't resist.

"I've been through my own hell, too, Kit. Nothing like what you've faced, but I've seen things most people would never imagine. It can be lonely in that place of dealing with your own reality."

"Yes." She sighed out her response and her body swayed toward him. Tired of fighting her desires, she placed her gloved hands on either side of his face and forced him to look into her eyes. "Thank you for letting me know I'm not alone, Luther."

His answer was immediate and not of the verbal variety. When his lips touched hers, she was still looking into his eyes and saw something deeper than curiosity or commiseration. Before she could begin to figure out what it was, his lids lowered and she followed suit.

* * *

We hope you enjoy the Silver Valley P.D. miniseries.

* * *

If you're on Twitter, tell us what you think of Harlequin Romantic Suspense! #harlequinromsuspense

Dear Reader,

My Silver Valley P.D. series for Harlequin Romantic Suspense has been a wonderful, sometimes scary and always romance-filled ride. *Stalked in Silver Valley* is book nine and we find Kit, a survivor of domestic violence at the hands of her ex, a Russian Organized Crime operative, working side by side in an undercover op with Luther, a trained secret agent. As they combine formidable forces to finally bring down the menace of ROC in Silver Valley and the entire Northeast, Kit and Luther discover they have more to offer one another than professional expertise. While they are both professional enough to keep their mission the priority, they find keeping their hearts shut down from their mutual traumatic histories becomes impossible in the face of their immediate chemistry and deepening emotional connection.

Kit was a victim of human trafficking and domestic violence. If you or anyone you know is currently suffering or has suffered from either situation, please seek help. There are a myriad of organizations waiting to help you. You are not alone.

Peace,

Geri

STALKED IN
SILVER VALLEY

Geri Krotow

HARLEQUIN

ROMANTIC
SUSPENSE

HARLEQUIN®
ROMANTIC SUSPENSE™

Recycling programs
for this product may
not exist in your area.

ISBN-13: 978-1-335-75943-6

Stalked in Silver Valley

Copyright © 2021 by Geri Krotow

This edition published by arrangement with Harlequin Books S.A.

For questions and comments about the quality of this book,
please contact us at CustomerService@Harlequin.com.

Harlequin Enterprises ULC
22 Adelaide St. West, 40th Floor
Toronto, Ontario M5H 4E3, Canada
www.Harlequin.com

Printed in U.S.A.

Former naval intelligence officer and US Naval Academy graduate **Geri Krotow** draws inspiration from the global situations she's experienced. Geri loves to hear from her readers. You can email her via her website and blog, gerikrotow.com.

Books by Geri Krotow

Harlequin Romantic Suspense

Silver Valley P.D.

Her Christmas Protector
Wedding Takedown
Her Secret Christmas Agent
Secret Agent Under Fire
The Fugitive's Secret Child
Reunion Under Fire
Snowbound with the Secret Agent
Incognito Ex
Stalked in Silver Valley

The Coltons of Grave Gulch

Colton Bullseye

The Coltons of Mustang Valley

Colton's Deadly Disguise

The Coltons of Roaring Springs

Colton's Mistaken Identity

Visit the Author Profile page at Harlequin.com for more titles.

To Victims of Domestic Violence and
Human Trafficking

You are seen. You are not alone. There is hope.

Chapter 1

The sky over Silver Valley, Pennsylvania glowed with the orange and pink hues that indicated autumn had arrived. Kit Danilenko had missed the sunset since she'd worked late today but was grateful to see what remained of the display. How many days, months and years had she dreaded the end of each day?

Burrowing into her pale blue peacoat as she walked to her car, she breathed in deeply and exhaled the remaining whispers of the life she'd fled, making a conscious decision to embrace who she'd become over the last couple of years.

Kit loved the end of the day, after she'd put in a good eight, twelve or sometimes eighteen hours at the Silver Valley Police Department, where she helped solve high profile criminal cases, mostly involving Russian Organized Crime, ROC, due to her language ability. Thanks to extensive therapy and medical support, she was able to dive deep into the cases without experiencing the PTSD flashbacks that had haunted her right after she'd turned in her ex, a former Russian Organized Crime operative. Being able to work at SVPD to bring down ROC's local operatives was a dream come true after receiving her degree in criminal justice.

The drive back to her apartment was no more than five minutes, but put her into a new mindset nonetheless. It was always a treat to know she was going to a safe place, the home she'd built for herself. The one-bedroom flat was a stark contrast to the nine-bedroom mansion she'd been imprisoned in by her ex, for the better part of six years. Now her new home was exactly how she liked it.

The hands-free phone system lit up with the caller, but nonetheless she spoke with caution into the voice-activated microphone.

"Hello?"

"Kit, it's Claudia." Her boss. "I don't have anything for you tonight, but Colt is going to introduce you to an agent who you'll be assigned to work with as soon as we have any leads on our main target." Claudia Michele was the retired two-star US Marine Corps General who ran Trail Hikers, the government shadow agency that bolstered US law enforcement at home and abroad. Although they happened to be headquartered in Silver Valley, their reach was global. Kit did language and communications work for them, too, sometimes getting pulled off her SVPD work to do so.

"I'm ready whenever you need me, Claudia."

"I know you are. I wish I had more for you right now, but we're all waiting."

"I know."

"I'll be in touch." Claudia disconnected. Kit was thrilled that someone like Claudia, and her entire organization, had confidence in Kit's abilities. Claudia and Trail Hikers had been involved in the op that eventually took down Kit's ex, and Kit had worked alongside TH personnel before she ever knew they existed.

Most of the SVPD didn't know about TH. Whenever they saw an unfamiliar face in civilian clothes come into the station, and especially Colt's office, that person was assumed to be a federal agent. Kit had been stunned that she'd been asked to apply for a position so quickly after joining SVPD. But since Claudia was married to Kit's other boss, SVPD Chief of Police Colt Todd, the two had both witnessed how far Kit had come from the dregs of an abusive, forced underage marriage to working through her mental, emotional and physical trauma. The couple had given her the building blocks to continue with the degree she began part-time while still married to Vadim Valensky, the notorious ROC human trafficker.

With Vadim behind bars for good, Kit's life had morphed into something beyond her wildest dreams.

The car dashboard lit up again, followed by the mechanical bell ring. She recognized the ID this time.

"Hi, girlfriend!"

"Hey." Annie Fiero-Avery's voice filled the car and Kit smiled. Her closest friend since leaving her ex, Annie knew her every secret. Mostly. "You home yet?"

"Almost. In the car, waiting at the second stoplight."

Annie's warm laughter rumbled over the speakers. "It is rush hour in Silver Valley, you know. I called because Josh has an assignment tonight, and I wondered if you want to meet for herbal tea or a decaf in the café later?" They both avoided caffeine after lunchtime.

"That sounds wonderful." Kit wouldn't break her date with the sofa for just anyone—but Annie was always her top choice.

"I'm not ruining any fun plans you might have?"

"Stop. I don't have plans." Kit tried to sound exasperated but she understood Annie's motives. She'd witnessed Annie's happiness firsthand when Annie married Detective Josh Avery in the catering barn owned by Coral, who had remarried her ex, Kyle King. Her friends were so happy in their relationships, and Annie in her marriage to Josh, that she thought Kit would find happiness with the right person, too. Annie was always hinting around the subject. "You know, just because I'm finally feeling myself and enjoying life doesn't mean I have to add a man to it."

"Not *a* man, the *right* man. When it's time. I'll see you at the café in a couple of hours, then?"

"Sure thing."

Kit waited for the phone to disconnect automatically as she sat at the prolonged light. Looking past the long line of cars and to the intersection, she saw there was a small fender bender being cleared to the side of the road. Another reminder to check the hot sheet before she left the station. She could have kept working for another fifteen minutes. Her fingers were on the stereo button, about to hit Play, when a chill skipped across her nape.

"Dang it." She let the words out quietly even though she was alone in her small sedan. For the third time in as many days, she had the feeling of being watched. Not security camera, eye-in-the-sky kind of surveillance. This was the same basic instinct that had served her well when she was married to her ex, a human trafficking monster. The gut feeling that never let her down always told her if Vadim's drunkenness would be the sloppy, pass-out-on-the-sofa kind, or would morph into the rage that led to physical abuse.

Kit checked her rearview and side mirrors, noting that two cars behind her was a black SUV. Unremarkable in Central Pennsylvania, where swiftly changing weather patterns, combined with varying terrain, made the vehicles practical and not just another sign of suburbia. She'd noticed a particular SUV yesterday, and the day before, with the same stickers on the rear window, indicating that the owner had a family. They were stick figures dressed in varying athletic gear, the mom in tennis, the dad with skis, one girl with a soccer ball and another with ballet shoes, making it the least likely vehicle to be following her. Except it kept appearing in her rear view mirror, like now.

Traffic moved at a snail's pace due to the minor accident. She maneuvered into the right turn lane, slowed down and waited for the SUV to pass, doing the same thing she did yesterday after getting the creeps in this exact location, the last traffic light before entering Silver Valley proper, the town's historical district.

She slowed down further to match the traffic flow, and came to a full stop right before she had to make the turn home. The car behind her beeped, but she didn't want to miss her chance to see the SUV's rear window.

At the precise moment she was forced to begin the turn, the SUV sped through the intersection, a reckless move that would normally have her noting the license plate and handing it over to one of the SVPD officers. Instead, she kept her gaze level, straining in the dimming light to see if it had the same stickers on its bumper.

The SUV's windows were darkened, something she'd discovered yesterday, so she didn't attempt to make out the driver or to see if there were passengers.

She searched for the unmistakable white stick figures, and her stomach sank when she found them. If it wouldn't put civilians at risk, she'd have whirled back into the traffic and followed the car. Instead she had to make the turn and take a different way to her apartment.

Kit racked her brain. She could let her colleagues at SVPD know, but without a license plate number they weren't able to do a whole heck of a lot. Plus, she didn't want to appear unprofessional—they'd ask her why she thought she was being followed, and while SVPD officers all extolled the importance of gut instinct, it had to be followed with cold, hard facts. Had she been at risk? Had the vehicle's driver ever attempted to put her in a dangerous position?

Simply thinking this SUV was following her wasn't enough, and Kit knew it. Her times leaving the station varied, so that took away the chance of her and the SUV driver having the same schedule. But Silver Valley wasn't so large that it would be unusual to see the same drivers on the road from time to time. Improbable, yes; impossible, no.

She was about to park in the lot behind her apartment building, but not before she drove by the row of lots that stood behind all of the buildings that lined Main Street in Silver Valley. The mostly historical structures had served other purposes a century ago, from the local police station to a bank to the original fire brigade. They'd been converted to meet more modern needs, but Silver Valley had done a good job at preserving the town's and Central Pennsylvania's architectural heritage.

A black SUV wasn't parked in any of the nearby lots, and Kit let out a long breath. It was normal for her to feel unsettled every now and then; she'd survived a prolonged traumatic event, as her therapist reminded her when she got down on herself for not being "completely" over the fallout from her abusive marriage.

Kit parked her car in its usual spot, determined not to let her quick-trigger alarm run her life. As soon as she pulled in, she felt at home. Her new familiar. And safe from the suspicious SUV and everything else.

The back of the three-story brick building blocked any view of the remaining sunset. Aromas of pizza and coffee tickled her nose. The local coffee shop was in the building next to her apartment, and the Italian restaurant sat across on Main Street and down a block. She allowed herself one takeout per week of the authentic Neapolitan fare.

Sometimes she wandered into the coffee shop after work, but tonight she wanted nothing more than to curl up on her sofa and cuddle with Koshka, her beloved feline.

She walked alone from the lot, across the access street and to her building. Her footsteps fell silently on the cobblestone path.

A loud clanging made her jump and she whipped around to face the sound. A man stood near the trash and recycle receptacles behind the coffee shop, emptying glass bottles and aluminum cans into the bin. She hadn't noticed him walking up, and his sudden appearance jarred her—until she made out his face.

"Brad! What are you doing here? I didn't recognize you in civilian clothes."

SVPD Officer Brad Norris grinned and held up a hand in greeting. "I'm heading over to Mario's for a slice of pizza."

"Oh, meeting your family?"

"No, Marcie's got them out and about, running errands."

"Okay, well, I'll see you tomorrow, then."

"Yeah, see you tomorrow."

She walked around to the front of her building and entered through the main door, climbing the three floors to her apartment. Brad Morris was the nicest guy and one of the first officers to befriend her when Chief of Police Colt Todd had hired her as an unsworn employee. She'd met Brad's wife at a charity gala and wanted to kick herself for being so riled by his appearance behind the café. Maybe she needed to call her counselor and ask to start her therapy sessions weekly again. They'd gone to once per month over the past six months, but it was possible her brain was acting up and going into hyperalert status again. The long hours on the ROC case might be stressing her.

Chief Todd and his wife, Claudia, were vigilant with her. Even though Kit was young enough to be their daughter, she didn't see them as parental figures, though, but strong mentors who'd not only helped her get out of an abusive home life but trusted that she'd healed enough to be a part of their organizations.

Kit had never been happier to work for law enforcement to bring down the source of pain for too many innocent victims. Another positive was that she had her own safe place to call home. She'd hit the jackpot.

With all her recent good fortune, she needed to shake this sense of being followed, targeted. Her new life left no room for a PTSD flashback.

Undercover Agent Luther Darby drove from his sometimes home, nothing more than a small condo in Newark, New Jersey, to Central Pennsylvania and wondered if he was kidding himself.

Was it really this close to the end for East Coast ROC ops, and for Dima Ivanov and Ludmilla Markova? After years of tracking the organized crime ring, its own evil nation of sorts, he wanted to believe it was true. Wanted to think he'd never have to go deep undercover again, to get so close to the enemy that he could be taken in by them. Well, one of them, in particular. The wife of one of the big bad guys.

They're both dead. Let it go.

His phone rang, the Caller ID flashing across his dashboard. Claudia Michele. It was as if he'd summoned his boss and director of the Trail Hikers, the lethal agency that got called in to back up all types of LEA, law enforcement agencies, when the stakes were too high to risk more highly trained agents.

"Claudia. I'm on my way."

"I know." Of course she did—Claudia tracked each and every TH operative worldwide from her vaulted office at TH Headquarters on the outskirts of Silver Valley. "I thought we'd use your drive time to do some prebriefing."

"Roger that."

"We're still not clear on Ivanov's movements but

there have been some cell phone hits that match his previous patterns."

"Who's he talking to?"

"That's what's strange—it looks like it's Mishka Valensky, Vadim's son."

"Vadim, the human trafficker?"

"Yes. He's out of commission of course, locked up for good. But his son evaded any charges."

"Why would Ivanov want to talk to the son of a man who blew it in ROC's eyes?"

"They're both desperate and want an in with ROC. Mishka's probably looking to get back in with ROC, which will be nearly impossible after his father's incarceration. Especially with the subsequent dismantlement of Vadim's human trafficking ring. Ivanov's disenfranchised himself with most of the ROC hierarchy since he let Markova steal his funds. He'll do anything to get back in."

"But?" He knew his boss, and her determined tone indicated she was fitting some of the jigsaw pieces together.

She sighed over the connection. "*But* is right—Markova is our *but*. She's beyond intelligent, and combined with her KGB training decades ago, there's a good chance we didn't recover information on all of Ivanov's accounts that she stole."

He whistled. "Meaning Ivanov might have resources to take over his gangs again and get East Coast ROC back on its feet."

"Precisely."

"Crap, boss, that's a blow. I thought I was coming into Silver Valley to bring Ivanov in." Markova was a given if they got Ivanov, he'd figured. Not so much now.

"As we know, there are no coincidences with ROC. Ivanov hasn't kept Markova alive without very good reason."

"When was the last sighting?"

"This morning, at a rest stop outside of West Virginia."

"And last week was Tennessee. They're coming back to roost." Why else would two known head honchos of a criminal syndicate risk coming back to the scene of their biggest crimes?

"That's my conclusion, too. It appears Ivanov is going to attempt a meeting with the remaining ROC skeletal crew, which we have to prevent."

"If he reestablishes himself as the kingpin, the East Coast ROC will spread like wildfire again." Luther's chest tightened at the thought of losing all the ground they'd gained. ROC was operating on a thread at the moment, and so close to being destroyed on the East Coast. Finally.

"You and I have the same conclusion as several of our analysts." Claudia's frustration matched his, probably more, since she'd overseen not only all the undercover operations against ROC and countless other criminal groups through the world, but was responsible for intelligence collection that only the shadow organization could conduct.

Trail Hikers employed a large contingent of intelligence and communications experts. Many were regular civilians who held down average jobs as their cover, living and working in Silver Valley and the surrounding Harrisburg area. But on days off, evenings and weekends, they sacrificed their time and in some instances risked their lives to help bring in the worst kind of terrorists and other criminals.

"If your analysts concur, then we're on to something. Where do you want me to go, ma'am?" Claudia kept things on the informal side with her agents, but Luther could get only so chill with the retired two-star US Marine Corps General.

"Keep the plan we've already established. Get settled, learn the area. There's a few days, maybe a week, before you have to head into the woods with the comms expert. You'll meet her tomorrow, at the police department."

"Roger."

"I want you to know that she's been through a lot to get to this point, and we're fortunate she's agreed to work for us. She's been through a tremendous ordeal and is still climbing out of ground zero from injuries suffered while living with an abusive husband, an ROC operative."

"Copy that, Claudia." No one got to work with TH without being tested in fire. He appreciated his boss's willingness to cut him in, so that he could be best prepared to meet the comms person.

"And Luther?"

"Yes, ma'am?"

"It's good to hear you sounding yourself again."

Heat rushed from his chest to his face. He'd only talked to Claudia once during the mission debrief about his op, where the woman he'd invested too much in had been killed. He knew the Trail Hikers staff psychiatrist and psychologist had spoken to her, too, as he'd given them permission to share whatever they needed to, to prove he was okay and ready to get back in the game.

"It's…it's good to be back." What more could he say but the truth?

"Safe travels, Luther." Claudia disconnected, and he was left with his thoughts. He purposefully refused to enter the dark passages in his brain that took him back to the day when he'd found out his lover was a liar and a cheat, committing the worst betrayal the entire time they'd been together. He'd witnessed her murder that same day.

Nope, not going there.

It helped to have a high stakes op to center his thoughts. Ivanov and Markova, the former FSB agent-turned-ROC operative, were as high as it got. Add in that Markova had been trained by FSB's precursor, the KGB, and the danger couldn't be much worse.

No way in any scenario was Ivanov going to come in easily, or quietly. There was always a chance the man would kill himself before allowing law enforcement a chance to arrest him and interrogate him for the last remaining details of his operations.

Luther wanted to get all of the heroin, fentanyl and meth that Ivanov had trafficked to this country off the streets, permanently. They'd already stopped most of the human trafficking, or at least it had moved out of Central PA and on to the West Coast. It was like herding felines but at least the LEAs were beginning to run the show when it came to ROC.

Except Markova—she was the unknown. Not that they didn't know her capabilities. Luther had spent a full week reading the files on the woman who'd been at the top of her game as a Russian FSB agent and basically defected to ROC and won her way to the States. Markova had been trained by the best former Soviet KGB operatives. She was deadly with a capital *D*. And now she'd manipulated Ivanov, had him eating out of her palm if what he, Claudia, and dozens of analysts believed to be possible and true. Even though Ivanov had taken Markova with him unwillingly, according to the intel reports, there was no way she'd still be with him unless there was something in it for her.

Markova wanted to be the next ROC kingpin, Luther was fairly certain.

Luther tried to relax in the leather seat of his Jeep as he turned onto Interstate 81 and continued to close the distance to Silver Valley. It might be his last time to think alone, if previous anti-ROC ops were any measure. But when bitter memories of his last, disastrous op flooded his mind, he wished he were already fighting Ivanov, one-on-one. That last op-gone-bad in New York had resulted in the woman he'd foolishly trusted being murdered in cold blood before him. Images of her cruel death still clung to the recesses of his mind. It was like the groundhog game at the State fair. Just when he thought he'd cleared them, another popped up.

Your job is to bring in Ivanov.

Keeping the focus on Ivanov and Markova went a long way to helping Luther remain in the present, and sane.

Also accepting he'd be single for the rest of his undercover agent career, if not for his entire life made jobs like this so much easier. He wouldn't have the weight of someone he cared deeply about hanging around his neck.

* * *

"Thanks for meeting me." Kit smiled at Annie Fiero, the SVPD police psychologist. Also the part-time manager at Annie's grandmother's yarn shop, where they'd met while Kit was still with her ex, Annie was Kit's most trusted confidante. They sat in front of the gas insert fireplace at their favorite Silver Valley coffee shop, located on the medium-size town's historical Main Street. The Harrisburg suburb enjoyed the benefits of small-town living with access to most big-city resources. Kit had thought she'd leave Silver Valley at the first chance, after being brought here against her will nine years ago. But the community had embraced her in unexpected ways these last couple of years, and she'd decided to stay for now. It felt like home.

"No, thank you for suggesting this." Annie stretched, her burnt orange turtleneck coordinating perfectly with her tights. "We can't have real girl talk at the station, and Josh is home more nights than not."

"No, we can't." Kit sipped her Earl Grey steamer, known locally as a London Fog, and let herself relax. She loved her job at Silver Valley Police Department, where she worked as an analyst and language expert. But having a quiet break from the heavy pace was priceless.

"What's going on, Kit?" Annie's sharp gaze reminded Kit that her best friend, a police psychologist, was at heart a therapist.

"You can't help yourself from seeing how everyone else is doing, can you?"

"Nope. Just ask Josh. I drive him crazy. When he

got off his shift last night, I practically grilled him for any evidence that he was having the start of PTSD."

"Has something happened I should be aware of?" As an unsworn member of SVPD, Kit was still involved in very deep undercover work and dangerous missions, but she wasn't always in on the latest operations.

"No, nothing that you don't already know. ROC." Annie made an ugly grimace as she uttered the acronym.

Kit nodded. "We're not going to get a break until Dima Ivanov and Ludmilla Markova are captured."

"Don't you think it's fitting, in a way, that LEA has been so focused on taking down Ivanov these past couple of years, and now, as we're closer than ever, Ludmilla Markova is just as much of a threat?"

"You mean a woman? Yeah, it's poetic, for sure. ROC doesn't value women, except for as commodities in the sex market." Kit knew firsthand, as she'd been forced into an underage marriage right after falling for an au pair scheme that originally brought her to the States.

"Let's talk about you, Kit." Annie stirred her caramel latte, her brows knit together. "You've been a little more antsy than I've seen you in quite a while."

Kit sent up a silent prayer of thanks for this woman sitting across from her. Annie had not only helped her escape an abusive, forced marriage, she'd seen to it that Kit received the best medical support available to help her heal from the extensive trauma she'd received at the hands of her abusive ex.

"I have the feeling I'm being watched again. And before you ask if I'm still going to my group therapy sessions, or if I've stopped doing any of the self-care practices that got me better in the first place, the answer is yes on the therapy and no, I haven't let go of my meditation. I feel stronger than ever, and further from the woman I was when we met."

"Okay. What triggered these feelings?"

"It's not a 'trigger' event, Annie. I mean it. If someone were following or watching you, how would you feel?"

"I'd get that itch at the back of my neck, maybe a clench of fear in my gut. If I'm really in danger and see it, I feel a wash of cold run down my insides—probably the adrenal rush."

"Exactly. That's how my anxiety attacks have presented—as if there's real danger, but there isn't, of course. This isn't the same." Kit got tired of having to prove she was healing, getting stronger all the time, but she didn't resent it. More than anyone else, she understood that PTSD and her resulting anxiety and depression could rear their ugly heads at any time. It was a blessing to have the knowledge and self-awareness she'd learned through years of therapy. A double gift was having a friend like Annie, who'd never hesitate to let her know if they saw something change in her behavior that she'd missed.

"Tell me."

"I can't put my finger on it. That's how I know it's not something triggering me. It's random—I think I saw the same car following me after work, three days in a row. But I can't prove anything—I haven't even caught a good look at the plates. Then there are the odd times I'm at the grocery store and I swear there's a guy who sits at the bakery counter, near their little coffee shop—you know where I mean?—who just happens to be there when I walk in. I don't buy my food at the same exact time or day each week."

"He could be a regular, someone who's there every day."

"True. It's just that I know a regular when I see one." She motioned to the front room of the coffee shop, where a group of men sat, laughing and watching the muted television screen. "They're locals. I don't know any of them personally, but I can tell. And I know they're safe."

"You do have a good instinct for safety." Annie validated that Kit hadn't lost her sense of self permanently in her marriage to an ROC operative. "Could it be Vadim's son?"

Annie asked about Mishka, Kit's ex's son, who was closer to her age than Vadim. Kit had confided in Annie about how Mishka had made overt passes at her while she was still living with and married to Vadim, his own father. Mishka was an only child, who'd been spoiled by his criminal father.

"I've been wondering if Mishka's put his men on me. When he didn't go to jail last year, with Vadim, I was worried I'd see him sooner than later. But he's left me alone. I'd hoped changing my last name and getting a new life, completely different from the circles ROC runs in, made a difference. But now…"

"My suggestion is to let Colt know tomorrow at work and tell him to inform Claudia." Annie referred to their boss, Silver Valley Chief of Police, Colt Todd. He and Claudia made a formidable team, between SVPD and TH. Kit and Annie worked for both, depending upon the law enforcement needs of the area. Their jobs with SVPD were public knowledge, unlike any work they did with TH.

"But what do I tell Colt? I told you I don't even have the license tag numbers. He'll think I'm losing it again."

"Hey, that's not fair. He's not like that. Colt understands more than anyone that mental health isn't a moral imperative. He might have concerns that you're not feeling as strong as you've been—just tell him what you told me. It might end up being nothing, but haven't we all learned that there are no coincidences when it comes to ROC?" Annie's brows raised and her expression reflected what Kit knew. ROC wouldn't leave Silver Valley or abandon its grip on East Coast heroin distribution without one last big fight.

"I'd put my sanity on the fact ROC is too busy staying alive to come after me." Kit had provided the needed intelligence and then testimony to put her ex behind bars for the rest of his quality years. "But after living with Vadim and seeing them from the inside, I know they live for revenge. It's very important to them to leave no enemy behind."

"And that's why you need to tell Colt." Annie looked at her phone. "I should let you go. We both have to report in early tomorrow."

"Thanks, sweetie." They stood and Kit hugged her friend.

"You're amazing, Kit. A force of nature." Annie pulled back and grabbed her bag. "I'll see you in the a.m."

"Good night."

Kit took her time gathering her few items, needing an extra moment to herself. Annie always helped her

feel more grounded, stronger. Which was why Annie's acknowledgment that she might be on to something with her sense of being watched set off an alarm
in Kit.

Silver Valley fought a war with ROC as the illicit
organization gasped its last breaths, with Kit stuck in
the middle of it all.

Chapter 2

Luther looked around the small flat the next morning as he sipped coffee. This was going to be his home until he completed what he'd been working on for the last three years of his FBI career and the first two years of undercover ops with Trail Hikers. He'd managed to set up state-of-the-art surveillance equipment in a matter of an hour last night, turning the humble apartment into a fortress.

Normally posted to Manhattan, he was grateful he'd been able to convince his boss and Trail Hikers Director Claudia Michele to let him participate in the culmination of nonstop tactical and strategic operations against ROC. Since the remaining ROC hierarchy had continued to use Central Pennsylvania as the East Coast logistical headquarters for heroin distribution, there had been an uptick again in overdoses and drug-related crime. Even with the government seizure of billions of dollars of Ivanov's offshore accounts, the weakened infrastructure continued to run. As Claudia and he agreed in their conversation last evening, if Ivanov regained control of ROC it would be disastrous for millions of innocent civilians and a huge blow to LEA who'd sacrificed so many man-hours, and sadly, lives, to the cause.

It became increasingly difficult for him to track Ivanov's movements from afar, since the shamed former head honcho remained on the run. Which landed him here in Silver Valley, Pennsylvania. The picturesque town wasn't far from the banks of the Susquehanna and he could almost convince himself that he was on vacation with such beautiful surroundings. Except for the body armor, two handguns and blade he was attaching to his body in various holsters. He kept an impressive arsenal even for a former FBI special agent, all courtesy of Trail Hikers. ROC was a formidable opponent, and there were precious few agents left with the training he had, combined with the knowledge of years of intelligence work in the field. Luther had to be prepared to engage ROC henchmen at any moment, as he had done before in the unrelenting fight between law enforcement and the criminal adversary.

He left the tiny second floor apartment out a back door after making sure all his locks and sensors were set. If anyone broke into the apartment, an app on his phone would immediately alert him. As he quickly descended the wrought iron fire stairs he scanned the back parking lot that opened onto an access road behind Main Street. There were few people visible, and little traffic. The sun was still low on the horizon, and it was just past six in the morning.

Crisp and clear air promised spring in the Cumberland Valley, edging out the frigid winter. New York City was definitely milder in climate, but Luther had been raised in Maine, where he'd learned to adapt to the four seasons as easily as he became adept at hiking since a young age.

He'd missed the family summer get-together at his parents' Maine home, due to Ivanov's disappearance and ROC's resurgence in Silver Valley, which directly fueled the East Coast heroin trade. Luther didn't mind doing his share of the workload; he'd known when he'd signed on with the exclusive Trail Hikers Agency that his time was even less his own than it had been as an FBI agent.

He spotted movement in his peripheral vision and froze at the bottom of the stairs. A male figure carrying a large black plastic bag hadn't noticed him—a good thing. It took Luther a few heartbeats to recognize the branded T-shirt and cap the man wore from the local coffee shop, in the building next to his apartment building. Luther had made note of it last night when he drove into town just before midnight.

"Hey, how's it going?" The barista tossed a large bin of recycling material into a blue bin.

"Good, thanks." Luther was used to the anonymity of New York and its seven million citizens; Claudia had warned him that he wouldn't move around the town of Silver Valley with as much ease. She'd been correct. Of course, the experienced intelligence operator was rarely wrong.

"You new here?" The barista smiled, crinkles around his eyes belying his trim youthful figure.

"Ah, yeah." Man, he wasn't used to having to make small talk, not unless he wanted to in order to nab a suspect. Luther forced himself to relax and appear like any other civilian who'd gotten a recent job transfer.

"Great. If you're looking for a job, we're hiring." The man pointed his thumb over his shoulder at the coffee shop's back entrance.

"Thanks for that. I've got one already, but I'll keep it in mind." The aroma of roasting coffee mingled with fresh baked goods in the cool air and his sweet tooth flared. But he had to be at the Silver Valley PD station in ten minutes.

"I'm Kyle." The man held out his hand and Luther shook it.

"Luther. I'll stop in after work for a cup of coffee."

"You won't regret it."

Luther watched the man until he went back inside before he walked across the access road to his car. It was probably unnecessary, but he didn't want the barista to know which vehicle was his.

Once in the car, he backed out of his parking spot and then turned to make his way to SVPD. Again, he caught a motion in his peripheral vision. The same barista had returned to the Dumpsters to deposit more recycling and gave him a quick nod of recognition. Luther held his hand up in a brief wave.

Yeah, Silver Valley was going to take some getting used to.

"Kit, can you come in here for a minute?"

Kit looked up from her station laptop and stood as soon as she saw Police Chief Colt Todd next to her desk.

"Yes, sir." The veteran cop wasn't one to put on airs,

but he normally didn't interrupt his officers when they were in the middle of filing a report. Colt knew how precious the hours of a shift were. They'd all been pulling extra hours at SVPD. The department consisted of forty-odd officers, a handful of detectives and support staff, providing around-the-clock protection to Silver Valley. Kit was officially one of the support staff, as she was an unsworn officer, but Chief Todd treated her like all the other uniformed officers. He said that just because she didn't carry a weapon or usually accompany officers on patrol, she wasn't any less part of the team.

Kit appreciated Colt's empowering view but often wished she could do more than translate ROC documents, at times handwritten in cryptic Cyrillic, or aid in interrogating a Russian-speaking suspect. But her scars from Vadim were deep, and while her bruises had healed and she had few permanent skin markings from his beatings, her mental health was another story. It had taken months of therapy, which she still attended, along with a very skilled psychiatrist helping her with medication to ensure her brain had the best chance of recovering to a normal chemical balance. She also attended a support group for survivors of domestic violence and had recently stepped up to help run a weekend retreat for the local area. Since she'd graduated college, she found she did best when her weekends were occupied with service work. Living alone was a treat after years of Vadim's suffocating behavior, but her therapy and group sessions had taught her that isolating wasn't the answer to her recovery, either.

Kit made a few quick notes in the documents she'd been studying so that she could pick up after her meeting with Colt. Some days it seemed the fight against ROC never ended.

Central Pennsylvania had been devastated by the heroin epidemic, but Silver Valley in particular had taken a hard hit when ROC decided to make the town their headquarters for heroin distribution.

Kit saved the work she'd completed and cleared her desk before she searched for her small notebook. She knew ROC all too intimately and had made it her personal objective not to rest until they were eradicated from Silver Valley. Preferably off the planet.

She closed her laptop and took a second to pause before she stood and walked through the bay of desks and down the corridor to Colt's office. It was still a thrill to be a part of Silver Valley PD. They'd done so much for her not too long ago, and she'd known she wanted to give back, from the minute they'd arrested her abusive husband.

She'd left more than her surname behind when Vadim Valensky had been incarcerated. He'd been locked away after being found guilty of drug and human trafficking. Kit had lost everything materially it seemed, including the house she'd come to view as a prison, but gained her priceless freedom during the ensuing investigation and Vadim's conviction. When the government claimed the house and sold it at auction, she'd cried tears—of relief. It was the last shackle tying her to her life as the wife of an ROC henchman.

Now, to dismantle ROC. She suspected Chief Todd wanted to see her because of the work she'd begun with the SVPD team that was assigned to keep tabs on the latest ROC information.

"Sir." She waited for her boss to motion her inside his office.

"Shut the door and then take a seat, Kit." He motioned to the sofa against the wall and closest to his desk, where a man in black utility pants and a long-sleeved black athletic shirt stood. Her pulse quickened, and she tensed. Except…this didn't feel like her anxiety. Anxiety didn't make her think about how attractive a stranger was, how if she met him under other circumstances she'd want to know how his full lips felt on hers.

Oh, geez. This was so not the time.

"This is Agent Luther Darby. He's with TH." They were using all of their combined manpower to douse ROC's sinister reach into Central Pennsylvania.

Kit reminded herself she was used to working with men, Luther was no different, and automatically reached her hand out to shake the agent's hand. He engulfed her hand in a huge grip, palm to palm, and a sensation of warmth ran up her forearm. Definitely not anxiety-related. But why, of all the men in Silver Valley, did her hormones decide to wake up for someone she had to work with?

She swallowed and forced her gaze up to his face. Luther Darby's expression was neutral, his stunning silver eyes unreadable, but the energy emanating off him was unquestionably lethal. Add in his height, at least a half foot taller than her five foot six, and his muscular build, and he was almost too much male in one person.

Relief eased the tightness in her abdomen. He was just a whole lot of testosterone, that was all. It could be any man with such a formidable presence.

"Pleased to meet you, Kit. Luther." A gravelly voice added to his edginess.

"I'm...I'm, K-Kit." Cold sweat poured down her back, trailing under her bra strap, and she was grateful she had a suit jacket over her blouse. "I mean I'm Officer Danilenko. Unsworn. Call me Kit." They ended their physical contact, the touch only lasting as long as necessary to define it as a handshake. *Get a grip, girl.*

A spark of curiosity lit Luther's eyes, evaporating his guarded, all-business mask. He nodded before abruptly turning his attention back to Colt. As soon as he did, a hot flash hit Kit, but it wasn't from hormones as she was only twenty-six. Both the cold sweat and hot flash were familiar symptoms. Great. Now her hormones were being doused with adrenaline.

Crap. This was the worst time for her PTSD to decide to ring the alarm.

"Kit, all okay?" Colt's familiar voice grounded her in the moment. She looked at her boss, touched the corner of his desk, cool and smooth under her fingers.

"Yes, I'm good, thanks." She smiled at Luther and at Colt, used to managing the milder symptoms of her anxiety far better than unexpected sexual desire. There was no need to broadcast every time her brain chemistry hit a blip. Colt knew about her struggles with mental illness since it was all a part of her records, and she wouldn't have applied for the job without full disclosure. Still, she didn't know Luther and her mental state wasn't any of his business. Unless they were going to work together in any kind of potentially dangerous situation.

She addressed Colt. "What's going on, Chief?"

"Shut the door, Kit. Why don't you both sit down."

Colt sat behind his desk, and she watched Luther sit on the sofa.

Kit closed the door, then chose the cushion farthest from Agent Darby. She suspected he was FBI, but didn't bother asking. If she needed to know, Chief Todd would tell her.

"I'm finding myself both happy and concerned to have you here together. First, it means we're that much closer to wrapping the ROC case. Second, we're facing down the worst criminal scourge that's ever hit Silver Valley." Colt had started talking before Kit even sank down into the worn leather seat.

She fought the urge to look at Luther Darby, to try and decipher the man she'd only just met. Superstition and spiritual stuff wasn't something she relied upon on a daily basis, but if she did, she'd have to define what was happening to her as fate. There was something heavy in the air, as if fate were trying to tell her that this man was going to play a big part in her life.

It had to be work related. Men, and personal relationships with them, had been pretty much off-limits as she'd healed. And if she were to pick someone to have a relationship with, he'd have to be in a safe profession. Accounting or teaching, whatever—anything but law enforcement. Kit was done with trauma-drama in her life, save for work. She'd had enough to last a lifetime.

Chapter 3

Luther tried not to grind his teeth, but what the heck was going on? He wondered if the pressures of the ROC case had blinded Colt to the point that he couldn't see how green and timid Kit Danilenko appeared. Luther had no problem working with a rookie, but for the final, most important part of this case—not so much.

Worse, a surge of an emotion he had zero time for rose in his gut, filled his chest with heat. He had a reflexive need to protect Kit. He didn't know the woman, for heaven's sake.

But she'd be a beautiful woman to get further acquainted with. He ran his hand over his face, giving himself the split second to re-center, get his thoughts out of his crotch.

"That's why you're the best man for the job, Luther. I wouldn't pair Kit with just anyone." Colt's words jolted him from his mental ire, and he immediately felt a flood of remorse. He'd missed what Colt had said.

"I'm sure you wouldn't be here if both Colt and Claudia didn't recommend you." He aimed his comment at Kit, who sat a bit straighter. The wariness in her blue eyes had turned to defiance. He swore he saw sapphire sparks in her large irises.

"Obviously."

Yeah, he'd interpreted her take on him accurately.

"I mean, we're in the middle of ending the most influential crime ring in the US since the Latin American drug cartels came on the scene. It makes sense that we've both got the training it's going to take to finish it up." Luther tried to clean up how he'd spoken to her but wanted to groan with frustration. He sounded like an idiot.

"You're not going into anything more than a surveillance mission, Luther. Kit's the SVPD surveillance expert, and her TH training makes her one of their best, too." Colt resumed control of the meeting and Luther took his cue. But he didn't stop checking out the partner he'd be working with for the next several days, according to Claudia.

She was small, but he wouldn't think of her as petite. She grasped the arms of her chair with slim but capable hands, and he noted there was no ring on her left hand. Not that he was interested in her marital status, or lack thereof.

He forced his attention to Colt. "Any op against ROC can become more than what we planned for." He knew it firsthand and had almost died in several stakeout ops that had blown up into full-on shoot-outs.

"As Colt said, I'm experienced with surveillance,

and being mostly behind the scenes. If it grows into something larger, we can always call in backup. This isn't my first op, Luther." Kit spoke as if she were siding with Colt, making it clear she didn't expect their op to be more than a snooze fest.

"First or five hundredth op, each should be treated as your only op." His words were sharper than he'd intended but he couldn't ignore the thrill of seeing how she reacted to them. To him. Her cheeks flushed and her breath hitched, making the curve of her breasts—

Stop. Now. He needed an extra long workout today.

"You're both right." Colt cleared his throat. He didn't look comfortable playing mediator, and Luther wanted to kick himself for putting his new colleague in this position. "It should be a fairly straightforward mission once you're in the field."

Colt's reminder that they'd be alone, in the middle of nowhere, wasn't what Luther needed, not with Kit sitting right next to him, with his libido sending definite messages about how attractive Kit was. All he'd been through in the botched affair with an ROC mob wife apparently hadn't taught him a dang thing. Already Kit's eyes distracted him, and earlier a glimpse of her legs caught his attention when she walked in.

Luther didn't do distractions.

"I'm confident Kit and I have the experience between the two of us to do whatever the mission requires." Maybe if he said it aloud fifty times, he'd get his head back on the mission and off what Kit's presence was doing to his dick.

Kit hadn't gotten involved with anyone since Vadim's arrest. Even in her very unhappy marriage she'd never had the urge, or opportunity, to even consider cheating on her husband. Men were an enigma to her, on so many levels. Why wouldn't they be when she'd been brought to the States from a small town in Ukraine, under false pretenses as a teen, and within a month was married to a man three times her age?

Luther Darby, however, was different. Her palm still tingled.

Stop. It's the anxiety.

But she wasn't feeling all doom and gloom, the way her panic attacks hit her. And she hadn't had one in a very long time. Her attitude toward life in general, had improved greatly in the past year. Never better, in fact.

"ROC plays for keeps, that's a certainty." Luther's low voice shook her out of her self-analysis. It was oddly reassuring since he was someone she'd just met.

"They take no prisoners." The words slipped out and she risked a quick glance at Luther. Colt knew her story, but to this agent she was no one but another colleague. The desire to show him she was competent surged.

What did her friend, and Annie's grandmother, Essie, who owned Silver Threads yarn shop, always tell her? The astute septuagenarian's words echoed in her mind as she tried to focus on Colt's speech. *"Soul recognition is the most powerful force on Earth, maybe even in Heaven, too."*

A tiny snort escaped her lips and Colt looked at her as he spoke, probably wondering what the heck she was thinking. She gave her best listening expression and mentally chided herself for getting distracted by a man she'd known all of seven minutes, tops.

"We've already got the best of the best working all

aspects of bringing ROC down, but there's a gap." Colt shuffled the papers in front of him. He had a computer like everyone else but still preferred to print the intelligence reports to aid in his analysis of the information on the computer. "As you both know, Dima Ivanov remains at large, and we believe Ludmilla Markova is with him."

"If he hasn't already killed her." Kit wished she could take the words back. Why did she have to say everything that came into her mind? Seemed the intensive therapy she'd gone through while getting her criminal justice degree had unleashed her inner bigmouth. Being free of the fear-induced repression living with Vadim had caused was welcome and necessary to her survival. Offering her opinion all the time, especially when not asked, was another thing.

"Why do you think he'd kill her?" Luther's query took a lethal slice to her theory. "I think he needs her alive to get what he wants."

Kit shrugged. "It's what ROC does. They eliminate anyone who poses a threat. We can't be sure, but it's pretty clear from what we've learned from the prison guards and other inmates that Markova was running her own drug distribution ring from prison. A kind of anti-ROC. She added meth and cocaine to the heroin, which she cut with fentanyl. Ivanov is not one to put up with a double-crosser, and one who's built upon a business he took years to establish." Her voice didn't waver, but she wondered if Luther heard the slight accent she'd been unable to drop no matter how much she studied English. She was perfectly fluent and had lived here for almost a dozen years. Yet when she was nervous or tired, her Ukrainian accent came through.

"You can't make assumptions with ROC. That's what gets officers and agents killed." Luther was suffering no fools, and somehow she instinctively knew he placed her in the "fool" category. What was the man's story?

None of your business. She needed to talk to Annie or her therapist about this.

"There will be plenty of time to discuss your theories on the case over the next month." Colt interrupted them, a bemused expression on his face. Kit had noticed that Colt's handsome face had become more deeply lined as the ROC case ground on. Silver Valley had lost too many people to heroin ODs, and the demands on SVPD and all law enforcement agencies were overwhelming on the best days.

"You said there was a gap in our op?" Luther quietly prompted Colt, and Kit had to admit he did it in a respectful manner without any of the arrogance she'd witnessed other, invariably less capable, men emit.

Colt ran his fingers through his silvering hair. "Yes. The latest intelligence indicates that Ivanov is holed up not very far from here. We'd assumed he'd left the state after we recovered the data Markova had stolen from him. We're still not certain if Ivanov knows what she stole." Colt referred to last summer, when SVPD and FBI had discovered that Markova, a former Russian FSB agent and now the right hand to Ivanov, had stolen key overseas account information from the ROC kingpin. It appeared Markova was looking to either take over ROC herself, or make a break from it with the billions she'd be able to take from Ivanov. But the FBI and the Treasury Department, along with Homeland Security, had frozen all of the accounts that Mar-

kova's stolen data revealed. It left ROC and especially
Ivanov incredibly vulnerable.

"It doesn't make sense that he'd stay anywhere near
Silver Valley." Luther spoke, and Kit took the chance
to check him out. He sat back, his black slacks tightly
stretched against his lean thighs. He'd crossed his ankle
on his knee and his hand rested on it. A very strong,
capable hand. Because he'd rolled his sleeves up, she
saw the controlled strength in his forearm, another
stamp of his masculinity.

What was going on with her? This had to be the
insta-lust that Annie spoke about with the other girls
when they all had Friday night Girls' Night, after the
knitting circle. It shouldn't shock her so much, as Kit
was twenty-six and had sexual needs. Her therapist
insisted she would eventually be comfortable with a
man after the years of abuse. But wouldn't that happen
more slowly, over months? Not this intense awareness
of the man sitting on the sofa next to her.

"Kit, what do you think?" Colt's query jolted her
out of her confusion. Heat rushed to her face, and she
knew her pasty white skin radiated beet red.

"I…ah, I don't think we can be sure about anything."
At Colt's raised brow, she shook her head. "Sorry, I
drifted there."

"Luther's point that Ivanov would most likely move
heaven and earth to get far away is valid, but the reports that came through last night and early this morning have him in an area approximately twelve miles
from here, in the middle of the Cumberland Mountains.
It looks like our worst fears."

Kit gripped the chair arms. "Ivanov is going to force
the meeting with the remaining ROC hierarchy?"

"That's what Claudia thinks, and I agree." Luther interjected. "It appears to me that Ivanov must still have hidden accounts, resources that the FBI and Treasury didn't seize. Or maybe Markova's the one who has them. It would explain why she hasn't made her escape—even with Ivanov's cruel streak, she's well trained and would have no problem killing him."

"You think they're planning for Ivanov to regain control of ROC, with Markova as his second, instead of only being his best operative?" Kit reasoned aloud. "That makes sense to me."

"Do we have an exact GPS loc?" Luther pulled out his phone and started tapping in notes.

"No." Colt shook his head. "If we did, I wouldn't need you two for the assignment." Colt turned to the large chart on his wall that depicted the entire Susquehanna and Cumberland Valley area, in the middle of which sat Silver Valley. He pointed to a small valley. "The report caught a burner phone's signal here. There are at least forty or so hunting cabins, but it's impossible to know which one he's in, if any. For all we know he was just passing through."

"Men like Ivanov don't casually pass through a remote hunting location." Kit couldn't hold back. "You are planning to go in and apprehend him, right?"

Colt's eyes widened. "No, no, nothing like that. We can't take any chances with either of them. Which is why I need your expertise in comms and you need Luther with you. FBI will do the eventual arrest, with a lot of backup from us, S.W.A.T. and other LEAs." Colt's gaze moved to Luther and the men exchanged some kind of silent message. Kit shifted in her seat, knowing that as an unsworn officer she wasn't always privy to all the details of such a sensitive case. And she certainly wouldn't be part of the actual takedown, when it was planned. It didn't make her desire to be fully cut in on all the information any less, though. Not for the first time she silently damned the mental illness that limited her participation in taking Ivanov and ROC down once and for all.

"What do you need from us, Colt?" Luther spoke with familiarity. Kit assumed he and the police chief had worked together before and ignored her feelings of being left out. Another fallout from her trauma, needing to be in control of everything. She was a professional colleague, not some young girl whose friends were purposely cutting her out.

"We need constant monitoring of the area. We're looking to determine if Ivanov is there, and if he is, which cabin he's in. We want to know if Markova is with him, and if she is, is it willingly or is he holding her hostage?"

Luther nodded. "Although it's hard to believe Markova would stay anywhere unwillingly. Her prison break last winter was a feat only the most highly trained FSB pro could pull off." As she observed him, Kit was struck by his outward calm and professionalism. It reflected in his eyes, too, but she still detected that hint of guardedness toward her and possible concern that she was his competition. Maybe he was an agent used to working on his own and thought a local police officer, especially an unsworn one, was a pain in the butt.

"What do you need me to do, sir?" She spoke up, wanting them both to know she'd do whatever tasked with.

Colt paused and looked at her. She had the distinct feeling he was reluctant to tell her. He'd shown signs of being a bit fatherly toward her when SVPD had rescued her from her ex, but had displayed nothing but pure professionalism since she'd been sworn in.

"Kit, this is where your expertise with the Russian language comes in. Luther has rudimentary language training but your skills are impeccable. Luther is going to be running the op, and while you're fully capable of handling all and any sticky situations that arise, I want you to fully focus on keeping Luther informed on whatever Ivanov and Markova, if she's there, are saying."

"No problem. Will we be using the unmarked comms van?" She'd been trained in how to operate the equipment in the back of the nondescript white van that was SVPD's workhorse and communications headquarters during undercover and other operations. It was her favorite place to be during an op, where she knew she was helping as much as anyone else in her position, freeing up a sworn officer to knock down doors.

Colt scratched his head. "Ah, no. You will have the top equipment with you—" again, another quick glance at Luther "—and Luther here will bring you up to speed on any of the tech you're not familiar with. But you'll both be staying in a hunting cabin. I need you to go undercover as hunters."

"Perfect timing with deer season opening next Monday." Luther referred to the Pennsylvania State holiday that was ten days away and took place the Monday after Thanksgiving. Schools were out to encourage children to spend time with their families. Indeed, many hunted, and many more spent the day doing early holiday shopping.

"As long as you're sure I won't become a liability to Agent Darby, I'm in. We have almost a week to prepare, unless you need us out there sooner?" She wasn't authorized to use a weapon in the line of duty. Not until she was completely cleared by her psychiatrist. Truth was that she enjoyed being unsworn, a nonuniformed SVPD employee, more than she'd ever imagined she would.

"That should be fine. You both need time to get to know one another. I'll leave you to work out your abilities between the two of you."

"I have zero undercover experience. But if you want me to hole up in the cabin and monitor comms, that I can do." She spoke up to make sure Luther knew what he was getting into, working alongside her.

"You're being too modest, Kit." Colt looked at her for a long moment, and when she remained silent, he spoke to Luther. "Kit was a key player in bringing in Ivanov's top henchman in Silver Valley just a little over two years ago. Without her courageous actions we might be fighting a lot more than Ivanov and Markova at this point."

"I'm impressed." Luther's compliment was like receiving a special treat from a teacher, back in her hometown in Ukraine. It was always nice when someone saw her for her intelligence and capabilities and not as a piece of meat, like Vadim had.

Save it for the therapist.

"I don't have a weapon, you should know. I'll be dependent upon you if there's any kind of shoot-out." She smiled, trying to inflect the American humor she so adored, but it was hard to tell if Luther caught it.

"I'm a fast draw." His reference to Western cowboy culture infused her with a sense of well-being, and she laughed.

Colt spoke up. "You'll be safe, Kit. Luther is tops in this business, and he'll have a small arsenal of weapons. My hope, of course, is that you won't be needing anything but the comms gear, and that you'll sit tight while the FBI arrests Ivanov and Markova."

"How many federal agents are in the area?" Luther kept tapping notes into his phone.

Colt shook his head. "That's just it. We'd normally already have their full support but they've had to send help to the northwestern part of the state."

"The white supremacist cult?"

Colt nodded. "Yes. It's bigger and badder than the one that tried to take over Silver Valley a few years ago, and LEA statewide has their hands full with it. We're going to have to commit several SVPD officers to it soon, but I was able to buy more time in order to get the last of ROC out of here."

"Thank goodness for Trail Hikers." Kit was in awe of the agency that had helped bring Vadim to justice and give her life back. Not to mention providing her with a job that gave her life purpose and a deeper meaning. An ability to give back to the community.

"You sound like you've worked with TH a bit, then?" Luther's question was for her.

"Yes, during the op that Colt already mentioned, and as needed for different cases more recently. My language ability and understanding of cultural references is my specialty."

"It sounds like we'll be well matched, then. I can read Russian and speak it conversationally, but some of the more subtle references to Pushkin go over my thick skull."

Kit laughed. "If you even know who Pushkin is,

you're doing okay." Pushkin was to Russian language and storytelling what Shakespeare was to English.

"Who the hell is Pushkin?" Colt looked like the one who was left out of the conversation, and Kit sat up straighter as she briefly explained Pushkin's significance to Russian culture.

"Okay, well, I'll let you worry about that." Colt's mind was on bringing down ROC without losing any officers, not Russian literary history. "Do you have any questions for me?"

"How long will the operation take?" She needed to make sure she filed her current reports before she left and make arrangements for someone to watch Koshka, her beloved tuxedo cat. Another great thing about getting rid of her ex—she could have whatever pets she wanted in the tiny apartment she rented in downtown Silver Valley.

"Undercover means as long as it takes." Luther answered, and when she looked at him, his eyes were clear but she saw a shadow that made her mental hackles spike again. Did Luther Darby resent her presence in this operation?

Chapter 4

Luther fought against his impatience as he locked gazes with Kit Danilenko. He'd worked as an FBI agent for ten years and an undercover agent for Trail Hikers the last two years. A case took as long as it took. It didn't go by any preconceived timelines, no matter how much experience an agent had. He should know—he'd worked on cases from Moscow to Mumbai, Afghanistan to Alabama. They'd all played out differently and over varied lengths of time, from a few days to months on end.

He didn't want to have to explain anything to Kit—time spent on anything but taking down their ROC targets was wasted. Why now, in the most important case of his career to date, was he being assigned a damn unsworn? Frustration warred with common sense. He didn't doubt her language abilities and knew he needed them. But to go into the woods where Ivanov lurked with anyone but another officer capable of handling weapons wasn't high on his list of desirables. Not when they were running against the clock with Ivanov's planned attempted takeover.

"I understand that undercover can take weeks, months, even longer. I want to make sure I plan appropriately." Kit raised her chin, emphasizing her high cheekbones, and he saw the flash of defiance—aimed directly at him—in her deep sapphire eyes. Her moon-pale hair was pulled back into a professional French braid but he imagined it was long, straight and silky when down.

What the hell was he doing, thinking about how her hair would feel in bed? *In bed?* He let out a long sigh. It'd been so long since he'd had time to even think about going on a date, or better, bedding a woman, that he was easily distracted.

Dating colleagues wasn't necessarily off-limits, but one he was working with in an operational capacity—most definitely forbidden in his mind.

Focus on her uniform. The problem was that her "uniform" was a white blouse, black jacket and black dress pants. Plain enough, and appropriate for an un-sworn official. But he sensed that Kit Danilenko was attractive no matter what she wore, because even in this otherwise nondescript suit it was impossible for her to hide her feminine curves. Which he'd noticed the minute she'd walked into Colt Todd's office. Tight but curvy ass, the kind a woman who knew her way around a gym might have. Full breasts that her button shirt did little to hide. And under that blouse he'd bet she had a tiny waist, with tight abs to match.

Fuuuudge.

"The deal is this, folks. I want you in place well before hunter's Monday, and it'll have to be over Thanksgiving. Sorry to bust your holiday plans, but this is critical. You'll head out to the area no later than early next week. Since Luther has a Jeep, you'll use that, to prevent the risk of the station's unmarked cars being a giveaway to ROC. We can't underestimate their operational intelligence at any point. Plan on being there for at least two weeks, but realistically I hope to hell it's not that long. It might take a while for Ivanov to show his face again, though. In the meantime, narrow down where the cell phone hits are coming from, and if you can do it, where he's staying. Determine if Markova's with him, on her own or otherwise. See if any other ROC are there. You know what's expected." Colt looked at Luther, and he nodded at the law enforcement veteran. Luther respected Colt immensely, not in the least because Colt's wife, Claudia, was the director of Trail Hikers. The woman was as much of a powerhouse as Colt, even more so in reality.

"How…how big are the cabins?" Kit licked her lips and Luther forced himself to return his gaze to the notes on his phone. This could end up being a very long two weeks. If she was as good as he suspected, because Claudia and Colt wouldn't send anyone less into the field to conduct surveillance against Ivanov, it wouldn't be more than seventy-two hours. He'd done enough of these types of missions in the past.

None with a woman as mysterious as Kit.

"Most are one room, with bunks or several twin beds. They're made as places to drop off food and clothing while you spend all day in the woods, hunting.

You'll both need full hunting gear, rifles, you know—all that makes you appear as the average Central Pennsylvania hunter." Colt's explanation kept Luther's thoughts from going totally into the sexual fantasy realm. "But I'd suggest that, unlike a regular hunting trip, you go light on the Yuengling." He smiled as he spoke of locally brewed beer that was a nationwide favorite. "Although you might need a break here and there. There's no telling how long it may take."

Great. So not only was he going to be working with an unsworn, but Colt thought they were going to be indefinitely in a one-hundred-square-foot room.

"Have you ever fired a weapon?" He was compelled to ask the question. It was fair, but the guarded look in her eyes had an effect he never expected.

He felt like the lowest form of dog crap.

"I've fired weapons before, yes. But as an unsworn, it's not in my job description." Claudia's words came back to him. The part about Kit still climbing out of ground zero. Kit might not be an operational agent with his experience, but he didn't know half the hell she'd lived through, could only imagine it. She deserved his respect.

"Kit's not authorized to use a weapon in her administrative position here, Luther. Although since she's with you, I wouldn't expect her to have to." Colt Todd's meaning was clear. Kit was to work comms, period. She'd translate the nuances Luther might miss in any conversations or activity they monitored. He'd protect them both if need be.

Luther nodded. "Got it."

"Now that you've 'got it,' where do I meet you?" Kit's gaze was still on him, and he gave her points for not losing any sense of authority because of his query. His awareness of her was on hyperdrive even as he mentally acknowledged she was his law enforcement partner for the next several days or even weeks.

This was absolutely ridiculous and grossly unfair. Why, when he finally met a woman who turned him on so elementally, did she have to be not only an operational partner but such a young one?

She's at most only five years younger than you.

"Ah, we'll exchange contact information, and I'll text you when and where. It's got to look like a legit hunting gig, so let's have you drive to my place and leave your car there, then we'll head out."

"Sounds good." He detected a very slight accent, but in actuality, Kit sounded and spoke like any other American. She was definitely talented with languages, because he had trouble with foreign language speakers when they slipped into local dialects and accents. American English had many variations, and not just in the expected places like down south. He'd noticed that some of the Central Pennsylvania locals still relied upon more "country" idioms, saying *fixin' to do* instead of *I'm going to* and using *needs* plus the past tense of the verb, like *my car needs cleaned* instead of *needs to be cleaned*. He found the less grammatical expressions comforting after so many months working in and around New York City and its fast pace, matched by hurried conversations.

"Okay, folks, why don't you stay here and work it all out. Feel free to use my office as long as you need. I have to go meet my wife for lunch." Colt stood and shrugged into a blue blazer, his holster hidden by the oversize garment. "I have the utmost trust in both of you." Colt leveled a glance at Kit.

"You okay with this, Kit?"

She smiled at her boss, the connection between them palpably full of mutual respect.

"Yes, I'm fine with all of it. Thank you so much for this opportunity, Chief." Kit sounded as if Colt had told her she'd won the lottery. Discomfort tugged at Luther's conscience. When was the last time he'd been so grateful for his job?

Before you got burned by Evalina.

He brushed aside the errant thought. Yeah, he'd all but died at the hands of an ROC wife last year, in the bowels of the worst part of Brighton Beach. So what? It didn't have to affect this case, or his feelings toward Kit Danilenko. She wasn't a mob wife anymore, at least. Never had been, not willingly, from what he'd pieced together between his and Claudia's earlier discussion and meeting Kit.

Kit's initial nervous energy upon being called into Colt's office and meeting Luther was dispelled at the reality of having to prepare for an undercover operation. Only a year ago the possibility of working an op one-on-one, alone, with a man might have been impossible. She had to give herself credit for how far she'd come, thanks to her therapist and all the other work she'd poured into her recovery. As she took measure of Luther, she had to bite the inside of her lower lip to stop from grinning. Not once had the thought that Luther might be a physical threat to her occurred. It was the tiny bud of attraction that was the surprise reaction to the man. And her sexual desires weren't something she'd explored since gaining her freedom from Vadim and beginning her new life at SVPD, so she forgave herself if her body wanted to have a crush on Luther.

She ignored any fluttering wings in her gut at the sight of the man and focused on what she needed. Information.

"What kind of equipment will we use to hear their conversations? Colt mentioned TH technology, which I'm familiar with but not as much as SVPD gear. Do I need training on anything new?" She had experience with SVPD's and Trail Hikers' undercover vans but technology quickly changed, and different equipment could have slight but significant abilities.

"Claudia said you've already worked with the listening unit I'm bringing. It's on a portable rack that fits on a back seat." He told her the model number, and Luther's voice was low and intensely masculine, but in a nonthreatening way.

Kit recognized the comms unit. She'd used it when they'd staked out a couple of ROC operatives last month. She nodded. "I'm familiar with it."

"If we need to be in place by next week, we'll have to get our supplies sometime before this weekend. Then we can get together and go over what we've gathered." Luther tapped into his phone.

"Are you making a shopping list?"

His long, adept fingers stopped and he looked at her. "As a matter of fact, I am. We'll get the hunting gear at the sporting goods store and the groceries at another spot."

"Okay. There are several groceries sprinkled across town. Are you familiar with Silver Valley?"

"Briefly. I moved into an apartment last night."

"Where?"

"Downtown, on Main Street."

Her interest piqued.

"That sounds like where my place is." Kit felt like she was having an out-of-body experience, watching herself have a conversation with such a powerful man without any sense of danger. She'd never tell someone she'd just met where she lived, or even intimate where her place was.

Yet she imagined having a long cup of coffee while telling Luther her life story. *Odd.*

"There are are a lot of small units and rooms for rent downtown." Luther dismissed her comment, clearly distracted by his list making as he stared at his phone.

"Back to the supplies, why don't you get the hunting gear and I'll get the groceries? Send me the list you have so far. I'll take care of the rest. Any food concerns or allergies?" She picked up her phone from where it rested on top of her notebook and asked him for his contact information, which she used to send him her info.

He gave her his number and then responded to her other question. "I have no allergies, except maybe poison ivy."

"You've reacted to it before, then?" She'd seen enough of the noxious vine growing on the property she and Vadim had lived on when she'd been an unwilling partner in his life.

"I have. Last summer when I was working an op I got it all over my back. It wasn't pleasant."

She wondered how he'd gotten it on his back and not elsewhere, imagining him lying shirtless on a lawn or forest floor but quickly banished the vision. Not something she wanted to process here in front of him. They had work to do.

"I know what it looks like, and I'll do anything around it for us if needed. I've never reacted to it. But sounds like we'll be inside for the most part, right?"

Luther shook his head. "No, actually we're going to need to play the part of average hunters, so getting out and about will be part of our cover."

"You mean yours—I'm going as your support. I'm not really an agent."

"But you are, for this op, right?" Luther leaned back, his eyes sparkling with interest. "You've never hunted before, have you?"

"No." Images of people being shot when she was saved by SVPD and Trail Hikers a few years ago flashed through her mind. She'd never fire a weapon at an innocent animal. "It's not my thing. But I understand that for a lot of families, the one deer they get over this weekend feeds them for a good part of the year."

"That's responsible hunting, yes. And I'd hope that in the middle of Pennsylvania, that's the norm."

"As compared to?" She wasn't sure what he was getting at.

"Trophy hunting. Paying top dollar to be able to shoot down an endangered species."

"Oh." Her gut sank as memories flooded her. Vadim had had rhino tusks displayed in their house like badges of honor. They'd always disgusted her. "Yes, I'm familiar with that. And aren't they usually overseas?"

"Most, yes." Luther leaned forward on his knees. "Are you okay? I didn't mean to upset you with talk of trophy hunting."

"You didn't." She lied. Luther wasn't a proven entity yet, no matter how much all indicators showed he was a trustworthy person. Just because he was a valuable agent who did his job well and was trusted by Colt and Claudia didn't mean he was someone she could trust with her personal reflections. "I, um, am familiar with trophy hunting. It's abominable. And nothing like a good hunter, male or female, helping keep the deer population down and providing for their family."

Luther appraised her, and she saw something in his eyes that looked promising, hopeful. "We're on the same page there."

"Do you hunt?" She tried to imagine him in the woods, tracking a deer.

"No. Not a hunter, but I do appreciate my solitude in the woods, or mountains. I don't get a lot of time to do that, not with this job."

"I understand. Since I've worked for SVPD and TH, I've learned to grab my free time where and how I can." For her, that often meant a night curled up with a sweater that she was knitting, while watching a streamed program about house organizing. A sigh escaped her lips. How long had it been since she'd made it to the local yarn shop's knit and chat? Too long.

"That's the life of law enforcement." Luther stood and she followed, aware again of how much taller than her he was. She put him at six-two. "Why don't we meet up on Sunday, after you get the groceries and I get the gear? Oh, I'm going to need your sizes for the hunting camo clothing."

"I'm a small in most things, a medium will work, too. I have plenty of jeans and outdoor leggings I'll bring along, and I have hiking boots. Should we meet here on Sunday to see what we have and figure out how to pack it all in a Jeep? We'll have the conference room to ourselves, unless something big breaks."

"No, if we're going undercover we need to do it from the get-go. Which means either you come to my place or I to yours. We can sort our supplies like any other hunters would."

She swallowed. No man had been in her apartment, ever. But this was work, and Colt trusted her. If Colt recommended Luther, she had nothing to worry about.

"I'll text you my address. See you Sunday." Before she lost her nerve, she walked out of the office and into the ladies' room. Kit needed a quiet moment alone to check in with her emotions, to make sure she wasn't setting herself up for an anxiety or PTSD flare.

But as she sat on the sofa she and several other female officers had commandeered for the restroom, she knew that her PTSD wasn't what was igniting in reaction to Luther's proximity. It was something far more pleasant, albeit unwanted.

Chapter 5

Kit slid into her favorite booth at Silver Valley Diner and asked the waitress for a soda water with a slice of lime. Luther wasn't here yet, but she was fifteen minutes early for their lunch meeting.

It seemed a little odd to be having lunch during the week with a man she worked with. She and her SVPD colleagues usually ate in the station break room, working on different cases together as needed. If she were having lunch with any of them, she wouldn't be feeling this sense of anticipation, she was certain. She grabbed her phone out of her bag in an effort to distract herself from her nerves.

"Hey. Thanks for saving me a seat." Luther's voice could turn on a neutered gnat. Kit reminded herself that she was an adult woman with at least a tiny fraction of self-control.

"No problem." She waited as he settled and opened up the large, flip-style menu. This had been his idea. *Let him talk first.*

He shut the menu after barely glancing at it, and his gaze met hers. She'd not been able to get his gray eyes out of her mind since they'd met a few days ago, and still, the intensity of his presence gave her pause.

"I suppose you're wondering why I asked you to meet me here."

She shrugged, trying to appear detached from the chaotic swirl of emotions he unleashed. "I figured you wanted to talk about our trip, although we can't go into too much detail here."

"Yes, but more to act as if we're friends getting ready to go on a real hunting trip."

"Okay." She thought it was overkill, but Luther was a full-time undercover agent for TH. It was only fair to give him the benefit of the doubt.

He grinned, and she saw how this grim agent could turn on a dime into a formidable, irresistible flirt. *Keep it to business.*

"One thing about an undercover—" he lowered his voice "—is that it's important to play the game right from the get-go. There's no telling when the stakes will become life-or-death. This way we're prepared no matter what."

She sipped her water, let the carbonation fizz on her tongue. Would kissing Luther make her tongue feel the same?

"I get it. But you're not expecting this to turn into anything that intense, are you? Besides the hours of work in front of a screen? It could end up being beyond boring. I'm sure you've run into long hours with nothing to show for it."

"I have."

The waitress sidled up, and Kit didn't miss her side-long glances at Luther as she took his drink order, then both of their meal choices. It was laughable, how attractive he was, and even more intriguing, he didn't seem to take it personally. Luther exuded confidence rather than ego. And he'd earned a higher level of self-esteem, based on his level of expertise, from what she observed.

"You always order breakfast for lunch?" She'd done the same, picking a Belgian waffle to his meat lover's omelet.

"Almost always. I could eat eggs at every meal, with a steak thrown in now and then." The waitress dropped off his iced tea and he thanked her. Also a gentleman. Not that Kit was keeping score on how good a man or potential hookup Luther was. Her last thought made her swallow. She'd been listening too much to Annie about needing to get out into the dating scene.

"Me too, but I like my carbs. Pancakes, waffles, crepes."

"You don't look like you eat a lot of carbs." It wasn't a leering remark.

"I obviously can't eat them all the time. Exercise is definitely one of my outlets in life."

"Are you a runner?"

"No, although I do it when I have to, like for the department's PT tests. Even though I'm unsworn, I like to get out there with the officers and do my best. I'm more a gym class person."

"Yoga?" His brow rose and she couldn't help laughing.

"You're really trying to stereotype me, aren't you?

I do a variety of classes. Yes, yoga's one of them, but not my main focus." Actually, meditation had gotten her through many of her rough spots the last couple of years.

"But?"

"But?" This man missed nothing. "I was thinking about meditation, which I started doing at the end of yoga classes, as most do. I liked how good I felt after, relaxed, even energized. So I researched different types, and now meditation is part of my, ah…mental fitness routine." There. Let him think whatever he wanted. Kit wasn't one to hide the effects of the trauma she'd been through, though she was careful who she shared them with.

Luther's fingers drummed on the table once, twice, then he picked up his straw's wrapper and began to wind it around his thumb. "I meditate, too."

"You do? I mean, of course you do. More than anyone I'd think you'd need to be grounded and focused for your work."

"You got it." He leaned back and smiled as the waitress placed large, oval platters in front of each of them. "This is fantastic, thank you."

"Would you like a refill on your tea?"

"Yes, thanks."

As an afterthought the waitress looked at Kit. "More soda water?"

"Yes, please." Kit allowed a smile as she buttered her waffle and drizzled it with one of three all-natural syrups that the diner kept on the tables. She knew this wasn't a date—it was work. But she couldn't help the joy bubbling up from her midsection.

Maybe Annie was right. Kit needed to get into the dating scene. It was time.

Too bad Luther was the wrong dude.

"You like your maple syrup." Luther tried not to stare at everything Kit did. Her motions were full of grace, her posture almost regal. He knew she'd survived some bad years, according to Claudia, but it didn't show in the completely poised woman sitting across the table from him.

"It's a treat. I don't eat lunch out during the week, usually, so why not go for it?" She kept looking at him and then looking away when their eyes met, her long lashes sultry against her pale skin.

"We're going to be on a much more limited diet out in the woods, so enjoy this." He dug into his omelet and couldn't remember the last time he'd really tasted his food. Or enjoyed a meal companion so much. "How long have you lived here?"

"In Silver Valley? Or the US?"

"Both."

"Well, this town is all I've known since coming to the US, actually. I was sixteen when I came over." He noticed she didn't say *immigrated* and didn't press her on it. He could put two and two together quick enough. Reports of her trauma, and her participation in putting away her ROC ex, spoke volumes. He'd guess she'd been trafficked over here, originally. A discussion for another time, when Kit was ready.

"You've never left Pennsylvania?" He couldn't keep the incredulity out of his tone, and Kit was quick to laugh.

"Of course, I've been to New Jersey, where my parents and sister have settled. I go see them every so often. And I've taken the odd trip here and there. I was in Florida last year with a few of my girlfriends."

"Other cops?"

"Well, Annie is the SVPD psychologist. You may know her or her husband, Josh, as they both work on the same team we do." He respected that she dropped classified information in a way no one but he would get. "Annie's grandmother owns the local yarn shop, and they have a pretty active knitting group. We all go on day trips here and there, to the shore, New York City, Philly. Last year they planned a weekend at Disney that was so much fun." Her entire face lit up as if she were five years old. He wondered about her childhood, if it had been as hard as her adolescence.

"There are benefits to small-town living, that's for sure." He tried to keep regret out of his tone.

"Silver Valley's more of a medium-sized town, and with Harrisburg less than fifteen minutes away it's more like one sprawling metro area."

"I've noticed. I know I've only been here less than a week, but you're right. The towns all blend together, punctuated by shopping areas or different parks."

"Are you a runner?"

"Not in a formal way but I do use it to keep in shape."

"If you're looking for a park, Adams-Ricci is a nice place to run or walk. It's about a one-and-a-quarter-mile loop, all paved, and it's not completely flat."

"Nothing's flat around here. A nice change from New York."

"Do you live in the city, then?"

"No. I keep a condo in Newark. It's a little more affordable and gives me some space from the city."

"I wouldn't call Newark any kind of suburb." She smiled and sipped her water. He ignored how pretty her ruby lips were, puckered around her straw.

"Anything's less hectic than Manhattan." He didn't want the focus to be on him, or even Kit. His plan had been to keep it light, figure out how they were going to work together.

"You said we needed to keep up appearances, but I feel like you have other motives for this meeting."

Kit's acuity was like a gut-punch to his ego. He'd thought he was so smart. The shock of her awareness turned into a rush of heat, right between his legs. Nothing more attractive than an intelligent woman.

"I do. I've figured out over years in this kind of work that if I can have an enjoyable meal with a colleague, it's a good indicator of how we'll work together in the field." He met her sapphire gaze with intention. What he didn't expect was the smoldering heat she seemed to emit.

"I don't know. I've had calm enough meals with people who turned out to be impossible to live with." Her ex had to be the subject of her observation. Again, he let it lie. Kit's past was none of his business, unless it was going to affect their mission, and Claudia and Colt had already determined it wouldn't.

"Ah, but living and working together are very different, aren't they? I work with so many incredibly talented folks who I'd never want to share a house with. Bunking down during an op is one thing, when there's an objective goal. But having to live with someone for the sake of it, day in and day out…no thank you." He knew he sounded bitter, but so be it.

"What, ah, is your definition of *bunking*?"

At her cautious expression he wanted to put a sock in his mouth. He'd let his tongue run away and made Kit uncomfortable. For reasons he refused to get worked up over, keeping Kit at ease around him was paramount. He wanted her to always feel safe, secure.

"It's not what I'm guessing you think I mean." He leaned in, needing to get this right. In his urgency he reached out and rested his hand on hers. She didn't move hers away, which gave him a thrill he'd have to look at later. "I don't make it a habit to get involved, emotionally or physically, with women I work with. I'm usually in the field alone, or with other men, and by *bunking* I mean just that—camping out, roughing it, as long as needed to accomplish a mission. You're safe with me, Kit."

She tilted her head and stared at him. "What do you mean when you say it's not a habit? You have slept with female colleagues?"

He leaned back, breaking their contact but noted that she never blanched from his touch. In fact, her hand remained atop the table. "Yes, but rarely. And it's never happened unless it's a mutual agreement. Something that happens in the field and stays in the field."

How on earth they'd ended up talking about whether or not sex was okay for either of them on this mission was beyond him. To her credit, Kit didn't balk.

She nodded. "Okay, we're clear on that. I think we'll work well together. I'm not looking for physical intimacy with someone I work with, so that takes it off the table. We're colleagues, period."

"Yes." He knew he lied with every fiber of his being. Because his erection wasn't the only evidence of his desire for Kit. The keen disappointment when she set her boundary—a fair, smart one—was something he'd rarely felt. And he hadn't even been asking her to go to bed with him.

It was there, between them. The attraction.

He deliberately remained quiet, hoping she didn't see his thoughts in his expression. When he looked back up at her, she looked shaken, her gaze on something over his shoulder. He turned to look in that direction but only saw the diner's door close, the bell jingling as it shut. Turning back to Kit, he measured his words.

"Who did you just see, Kit?"

She blinked, shook her head and refocused on him. "No one important."

Okay, so she didn't trust him yet. He'd change that by the time they finished their fieldwork. It wasn't lost on him that he had a primal need to have Kit completely trust him.

Another first for him, with a woman he barely knew.

A few days later Luther surveyed the sporting goods store as if it were another mission on his long list. He checked with the notes he'd taken at SVPD, ensuring that the hunting camouflage pants and jacket he'd picked for Kit were the right size. Maybe he'd been hasty to insist on splitting their shopping. It'd be easier to have Kit pick out her outfit.

Annoyance tugged at his conscience. He was giving far too much thought to a work colleague, no matter how attractive. Kit had made her position clear at the diner, and it was best for both of them.

The last clothing he'd bought for a woman had been the waterproof jacket he'd snagged on the run, to keep Evalina from getting hypothermia while they endured hours in the sleet in the Mohawk Valley in Upstate New York. The plan had been to extricate her from the ROC web she'd been part of for ten years, since she'd married one of the ROC top dogs. Well, that had been his plan, anyway. He'd never planned on being sold out, led to what was supposed to be the site of his execution. When Evalina took a bullet during the final standoff with the man he was charged with taking down, it'd been too late for regrets. Both she and her husband had died that day. Was he headed into similar emotional quicksand with Kit?

He didn't think so, since Kit's situation was completely different. She was out from under the ROC's hold and had passed myriad security clearances to be able to work for SVPD and TH.

Still, his heart had been crushed by Evalina.

Luther shoved the emotional fallout of his poor choices with women aside. He trusted the Trail Hikers; if Claudia and Colt said Kit was the best for the job, then she was, and he had to ignore the voice trying to remind him that getting involved with another ROC spouse was by definition bad news. All he needed to keep in mind was that Kit was his colleague, here to complete a mission. A brief partnership in the midst of the chaos and sometimes hell that working against ROC could be.

"Can I help you find something, sir?" A bright-eyed young clerk with the badge of the store proudly displayed on his chest stood before him. Damn, he must have drifted off while placing items in the cart.

"No thanks, Riley. I'm good."

"We're here to help." The teen seemed buoyed by the use of his first name as he looked at the contents of Luther's cart. "Maybe you need a new hunting rifle to go with all that gear?"

At this Luther stifled a laugh. If the kid knew what kind of arsenal he had on hand, his enthusiasm might turn to shock.

"Ah, no thanks. I have my grandfather's old rifle, in fact. Serves me well." This part was true; he'd brought along Granddad's beloved weapon for the op, to keep up the appearance of being nothing more than a hunter.

"So you're one of the old-fashioned kind. That's cool." The way the kid said *cool* let Luther know that he thought he was anything but.

"Thanks. I'll let you know if I need anything, Riley." He'd learned to use names not just out of politeness and courtesy but also as a memory aid. Luther never forgot a face but sometimes did misplace names.

"Sure thing."

Luther finished up the shopping as quickly as possible, and once in his Jeep he checked the dash clock. He was due to meet Kit back at her apartment at dinnertime. Odd that she lived so close to the tiny flat he'd rented. Yet he got the appeal of an apartment in the tiny historical downtown of Silver Valley. With the cute diner, restaurants and coffee shop only steps away from the upper story apartments, it was ideal. The only thing missing was a decent grocery store, but there were several within a five-to-ten-minute drive.

He had two hours before the meeting with Kit. Just

enough time to check in to Trail Hikers headquarters and read the latest intel on ROC and most important to him, Ivanov and Markova.

The quaint buildings of Silver Valley became interspersed with large distribution centers and the usual big-box stores as he made his way through the town. This was the epicenter of logistics for most of North America and certainly the Eastern Seaboard, which is what made it an ideal spot for ROC to center its heroin ring.

He tried to let the natural beauty in before he had to read about ROC at TH headquarters. Silver Valley was situated in the base of a valley that was surrounded by the Appalachian and Cumberland Mountains. He'd seen and completed missions in "real" mountains, out west in the Rockies and as far east as the Urals of the Russian and Asian Steppes. But none struck him as picturesque or soothing as the blue-toned hills that embraced the Susquehanna and Cumberland Valleys.

His turn signal clicked a flat monotone as he waited for a green light to turn left onto the technology parkway that led to the nondescript office building where TH operated. It was no use; he couldn't stop the swell of anger at how ROC had invaded this perfect slice of the planet, wreaking havoc on innocent lives and families. Did anyone else in this town feel the omnipresent sense of evil that meant ROC was still here, waiting to spring into full operations again?

As he made the left turn, another thought flitted across his mind—a wish that Ivanov was already in prison, or dead. Anticipation of completing the mission always gave him a sense of peace—Luther knew that what he did for a living kept very bad people from hurting the average very good citizen. But this mission was different, and not just because he was getting ready to help bring in the kingpin, the crux of the ROC's lethal operations.

He realized he was looking forward to working one-on-one with Kit Danilenko.

"I told you to stop it with the cell phone." Ivanov snarled at her, his formerly handsome face twisted with the rage of being cornered, the knowledge that the end of his criminal empire might be near.

"It's a burner. Just like all the others." She held up her tote bag that was full of at least a dozen more disposable phones she'd purchased at several different discount stores in Central Pennsylvania, using credit cards with a myriad of false identities that she was able to adopt at will. "No one is going to find us from one cell phone intercept." She'd called into her offshore account he knew nothing about, right under his nose. She'd surreptitiously corralled money from his account into hers, slowly siphoning off Ivanov's funds. He thought she had access to the one remaining secret account of his that the FBI hadn't seized. She withdrew cash only when he asked her to do so, to keep them in groceries and under a roof each night. Ivanov trusted her and she let him think he could. It gave her leverage, kept him from hurting her. And her from killing him and escaping. In reality, Markova had realized that in order to truly disappear without anyone chasing her, she had to become the head of ROC. She knew how to evade American law enforcement—hadn't she escaped her own FSB? But as long as she was seen as Ivanov's second-in-command, she would be resented

and hated by the remaining East Coast ROC. They'd
kill her as quickly as Ivanov.

Her plan was to let Ivanov think she was with him
to support him, give him the money to resume his
place as the head boss. But she'd kill him the minute
they had the meeting with the remaining supervisors
who'd managed to keep at least the drug sales going.
Human trafficking had been halted, but she'd get that
going for them again, before she disappeared for good.

Above all else, Markova wanted her freedom from
any authority, for the rest of her life.

"You don't know that you won't be intercepted. The
FBI is all over us. I'm wanted in every state." Ivanov
kept his handgun in his belt and she saw him rest his
hand on it, as if the silent visual threat would keep her
from doing what she wanted. What he couldn't hide
was the way his hand trembled. Shook, actually. He
was trying to quit the vodka again and it wasn't working, judging by his distillery bad breath and the yellow
tinge of his skin. It was pathetic how easy it would be
to exterminate him on the spot.

Not yet.

"Actually, I do. It's my job to know all about communications." Markova was a former FSB agent,
trained by the best the KGB had to offer. Her leaders
and instructors had been at the top of their game during
the Cold War and passed all their knowledge onto her.
Escaping Russia and the clutches of the Kremlin had
taken her years of planning, yet she'd managed to do
it. She'd promised Ivanov she'd help him bolster ROC
on the East Coast, and she knew his goal had been to
become the head of all ROC in North America.

That was almost a decade ago, and in that time she'd

orchestrated her escape from ROC and all of this life she'd learned to hate. Markova had been so close to executing her plan, until Ivanov caught her at her own game.

But he didn't know everything. She only had to survive this time with him, convince him that she had something he could use—money—and she'd disappear, never to be seen again. Not as Ludmilla Markova, anyway.

"We're too close to evasion to let a stupid cell call betray us. Why did you have to phone now, anyway?"

"I checked on the balance of the account in the Cayman Islands. You'll be glad to know that your one billion has turned into almost one-point-three since last month. I've got only the best investors working it."

"I need to double that by next month. I can't do anything from here. We have to have the meeting before the rats figure out how to take total control." Ivanov's breath stank as it reached her nostrils. They sat in a small beat-up SUV that they'd bought with cash from an auto dealer in Harrisburg. Her head was cold since she'd shaved her hair and dyed her eyebrows. It made wearing various wigs easier. Ivanov had refused to go to such lengths with his disguise but he kept a brimmed cap pulled low over his face and his white beard made him look almost like a grumpy Santa Claus. It also showed his years, and the strain of running his nefarious network of humans, weapons and drugs.

"You will. Here." She handed him the large foam cup of hot coffee she'd just purchased in the doughnut shop. Ivanov was a rough, nasty man but a baby when it came to some creature comforts. His coffee was one of those.

"You got cream?" He suspiciously sniffed at the brew as they stayed put in the parking lot.

"Yes, and sugar." She gritted her teeth, shoving down the urge to slap him or worse. Only a little more time and she'd be able to escape. With the millions she'd stashed for herself, in a Swiss account and not the Caribbean, she'd be able to place herself in her own witness protection program. Her life on the run, the constant need to check her back, would be over.

But not while Ivanov and his key henchmen were still alive. Markova had to play along if she didn't want to find herself dead before her great escape.

"We need to disappear again, boss." She hated calling him "boss" but he loved it, still thought of himself as her superior. She had to stay in the game a little longer.

Games were her forte.

"I'm not ready to go back into those woods and play American pioneer. I'm no Johnny Appleseed."

"I didn't know you knew American history, Dima."

Bright sparks across her vision hit right before the pain from his fist to her temple radiated over her skull. Her head bounced against the passenger window and she quickly looked around the parking lot to see if anyone saw his assault. That was all they needed—to be taken in for questioning over something so stupid.

"Bitch, don't question me. Ever. Do you want to go back to the cuffs?" He referenced the hand and ankle cuffs he'd kept her in for the first week they'd been on the run. That was months ago. Right after the shoot-out in the cemetery headstone factory. After seven days she'd convinced him that she still had a good portion of his money hidden in the Caribbean account, far from the computers of the Treasury Department. Ivanov had lost billions when the US government had frozen his funds and all known ROC accounts. He blamed her for revealing the passwords and account numbers to the authorities, because they'd dug up the valuable information where she'd buried it, at that barn that was now rebuilt.

Her fingers itched to light more matches, to burn the new barn to the ground like the original. Maybe after she was able to escape Ivanov and ROC, she'd give Silver Valley one last kiss goodbye. No evidence this time, though. The burned-out barn would be enough of a signature.

"Answer me, Markova. Where will we go that's not those boring woods?" Ivanov's voice was cajoling, as he often was after he hit her or slammed her against a wall. Relatively light abuse after the kind of training she'd endured. The hardest part for her was not striking back. If she seriously harmed or killed Ivanov, his remaining goons would be after her, as would law enforcement. She was good, excellent even, at evading one or the other. But things didn't go as smoothly when both sides were after her. She'd learned that the hard way last year.

"You've lost the ability to hide in plain sight. Too many of the top dog wannabes are looking for you, and you're dead if you go back to New York."

"Brighton Beach is my home." He sounded like a petulant child. Which, after all these months of being his captive, she'd learned he was, emotionally. He might have the intelligence of an adult male but not the psychological fortitude.

"Not anymore, not if you want to live and continue to be the head of ROC on the East Coast."

"I'll never be happy until I get the top ticket." Ivanov had shared with her that he was the only man who could run all of the North American ROC properly. She'd refrained from voicing her opinion.

"Kovkofsky is never going to give up the West Coast lead position, and you know he wants you dead so that he can take over East Coast. I have the latest information from the phone calls I've had to make, Ivanov. We have no choice but to go back to our campsite."

He held the coffee cup very gingerly for a man who was capable of so many different types of torture and murder. Markova felt a thrill of competition in her gut. She was meaner and better at killing than Ivanov could dream of. She'd show him, when the time was right. And remind him of each time he'd hit her, every time he'd belittled her abilities.

"Fine, but I want a nicer place."

"That will be too suspicious. Right now the local folks think we're bird-watchers, maybe hunters. We pay the rent in cash. Anything fancier requires a credit card, which is no problem, but it also raises our risks by too much." She'd told him repeatedly that cash and low profile living was the way to their survival.

"I want to kill that bitch that I see with SVPD and the FBI agents. At all the shoot-outs we've had with them. The one with the gray hair."

Markova knew who he meant. The woman, some kind of federal agent, she assumed, who was always conferring with the SVPD Chief of Police, Colt Todd. She knew his name well enough.

"Fine, that can be arranged. After we're back in hiding, away from all these people."

"And I want the SVPD Chief dead, too. When I am back in full measure, I need to have sent a clear message to Silver Valley law enforcement. They let ROC run their town or we'll kill them all."

Chapter 6

Luther entered the passcode and waited while the biometrics technology scanned his face, left retina and hand. The large outer door to Trail Hikers headquarters opened without a sound, the pneumatic hinges the best money could buy.

He walked through two more security zones, taking time to enter the appropriate identifying information, and finally into the main reception lobby. He approached the tall counter-style desk and nodded at the receptionist.

"I'm Claudia's next appointment, I believe."

She tapped her computer screen and nodded. "Yes, you are. Follow me." He was escorted to an area behind the bulkhead that boasted Trail Hikers, Inc., in large black letters against a fabric panel. He knew it was all for show—the panel was really a bulletproof barrier protecting the CEO from potential lethal attacks. As far as Luther knew, Trail Hikers had never been compromised nor its mission blown, but in the Information Age of constant hacking and computer vulnerabilities, it was only a matter of time.

"Here you go." The receptionist entered her information into the scanning device next to the CEO's office, and he did the same. Once the system corroborated their inputs, the door slid open, revealing that it was actually not solid oak but six inches of steel encased in three-inch wooden panels. Nothing but the best was on-site at TH headquarters.

As soon as he stepped over the threshold, the door slid shut with an impressive tiny click, not unlike one of his cupboard doors closing. Immediately he was aware of the silence, save for the light clicking of fingers on a keyboard as Claudia Michele, CEO of TH and retired two-star US Marine Corps General, worked at her bay of computers.

She looked up from her desk, and he felt the cool blue gaze as much as he saw it from across the room. Her silver bob accentuated her still-youthful face and intelligent gaze. As he drew closer, he noticed lines on her skin that hadn't been there just months ago. ROC ravaged all who went after it. And ROC was only a sliver of the worldwide ops that Claudia was in charge of.

"Good afternoon, Luther. Take a seat. I'm finishing up some last-minute orders."

Luther complied, sinking into one of the plush yet functional chairs in front of her contemporary glass tabletop. Claudia shoved her keyboard to the side.

"Would you like a drink? Water, coffee, tea? There

are energy drinks in that small fridge over there, too."
She motioned at a very chic yet efficient kitchenette
that occupied a portion of the far wall to her right.

"No, thank you. I'm in between gathering equipment for the stakeout and going over our provisions
with the SVPD employee I'm working with."

"Yes, Kit Danilenko. What was your first impression of her?" Claudia seemed to assume they'd only
met in Colt's office.

"I had lunch with her the other day, to follow up on
our initial meeting with Colt." It was important Claudia
knew he wasn't making a knee-jerk judgment. "She's
intelligent, misses nothing if the way she hung on to
every word Colt said is a clue. But she's also…" He
searched for the best adjective. Kit wasn't shy, as that
implied naivete. She had an innocence about her, but
that wasn't something he wanted to let Claudia know
he'd sensed. "Guarded. As if she doesn't quite trust
everything, or everyone."

Claudia flashed him a quick smile. "Excellent assessment. She's unsworn because of some medical issues that she's still working on."

"You mean mental health, I assume? Not that it's
any of my business, unless she's prone to getting ill to
the point of not working."

Claudia shook her head. "No, she's past that place.
And you're right, for now it's none of your business.
But I'm not bound by HIPAA, and since you're working so closely with her, you need to know that she's
been through a hell of a lot."

"So Kit's why you called me in here?" He'd been
hopeful there was new intel on Ivanov or Markova.

"Yes. And no, there isn't anything more on Ivanov.

He's hiding from ROC as much as us, with all of his accounts frozen."

"I have to believe Markova is his ticket to financial solvency. Otherwise why keep her alive?"

"We don't know that she's still with him, or alive. It's a day-to-day question. They were last sighted together almost two weeks ago, and that was a shaky witness. He might have another ROC agent or accomplice with him. Markova might have been fed to the wolves already."

"True."

"Back to Kit. You know the basics on her, and it sounds like you're getting to know one another more as you prepare to go in the field." Claudia maintained her professional demeanor, but Luther felt a tug of guilt, as if Claudia knew he was too interested in Kit. Crap.

"Basically, she escaped an abusive marriage to Vadim Valensky, a local ROC thug. We only care about it at our level of operations because of how the ROC's many spiderweb threads interconnect. Kit's a solid entity in that she cooperated with authorities while still at risk from her ex, and on top of that she'd begun criminal justice studies at HACC." Claudia referred to the local community college, Harrisburg Area Community College. Luther knew Harrisburg was the nearest largish city to Silver Valley, less than twenty minutes away.

"Sounds like she wanted to be a cop."

"She did, and does. But once she graduated from Penn State she'd figured out that working through the years of what she'd endured wasn't going to happen overnight. She didn't want to risk being away from law enforcement for such a long time, so she figured out that her language abilities lent well to her being an unsworn agent. SVPD is filled to the brim right now with sworn officers and detectives, so it all worked out for her. Colt needed the language and cultural expertise she brings to the table."

"Forgive me, Claudia, but I'm not getting what this is really all about. You're filling in a few details, but nothing that's going to affect how Kit and I work together in the field." He knew that he was their single weapons expert, and the one who'd be firing anything as needed. If they did their job right, they'd be out of the hunting area before the takedown occurred, but one thing about ROC he'd learned to depend upon: nothing ever went as expected.

"I'm vouching for Kit. In the most professional, unprofessional way. If you need her to handle a weapon, I've no doubt she'd do it with aplomb. Legally she still can't be a sworn officer and I'm not certain she'd even want to, now that she's enjoyed over two years of solid, dynamic work with us and SVPD. She's healed, Luther. The woman I met when Vadim was taken in is lightyears from who she is today."

"I've known folks who go for years with their mental health issues under control, well managed. Yet one instance can trigger a chain of biochemical events that leave them in a rough place again."

"Speaking from experience, Luther?" Claudia missed nothing, and she knew his file, too.

"Perhaps." He wasn't hiding anything from Claudia or his employer, the US Government via Trail Hikers. He'd suffered from PTSD after his stint in Iraq, when the National Guard unit he was assigned to spent a year in the country. An armored vehicle he'd been rid-ing to a remote post had hit an IED. His concussion hadn't been as bad as many TBIs his teammates suffered from, but the emotional and mental damage had been done. It took him three years of intense counseling to get through it, and his main employer at the time, the FBI, had fully supported his rehabilitation. "I haven't had an episode since the last one, right after I got back from the war."

"But we all fear a rebound, something we can't foresee triggering it, don't we?" Claudia spoke as if she, too, understood the suffering he and so many other troops went through.

"Yes, that's always there. But you and your superiors trust I'm good enough to serve in this job."

"We do. You are." She looked away, as if there were a window in the wall instead of the global map that indicated TH operation sites. When her glance returned to him, Luther saw a softness in her usually professional demeanor. "Take care of yourself out there, is all I'm saying, Luther. Kit can take care of herself."

"Roger." They discussed the ins and outs of trying to remove ROC's sticky tentacles from the East Coast and hopefully the rest of North America. Afterward Luther drove back to his apartment, the back of his four-wheeler loaded with enough clothing and hunting gear to last them a month if need be.

He'd heard Claudia, and trusted her. So why was he feeling uneasy about working with Kit?

It's yourself you don't trust.

Kit sat in one of the two easy chairs in front of the fireplace at the coffee shop. There were a few chain coffee shops in the surrounding Harrisburg suburbs but she didn't care for the busier atmosphere. The warmth and friendliness of this café had wrapped its arms around her more than once after a long day, and most especially in the early days and months after her divorce. She munched on the tiny gingerbread man that had been served hanging from the edge of her latte. It was one her favorite seasonal drinks, and they'd just brought it out this week before Thanksgiving.

"You're quiet for someone who couldn't wait to meet." Annie sat across from her. "I figure it has to be about something really juicy since you can't discuss it at the station."

Kit nodded. "It does. This is my second lunch hour away from work in two days, so you know it's um, exciting. I think I'm having some um, different kinds of feelings about my partner for an upcoming op."

Annie's eyes narrowed. "I heard we had some developments in the ROC op. You're involved? As an interpreter?"

"Basically, yes. But it involves going undercover for a day or two. Maybe a week."

"Where? Or wait, don't tell me. Oh, no—you're going to miss our Thanksgiving!" Annie frowned but didn't belabor it—she worked at SVPD and TH; she knew that ops came first. "Do you need anything from me, clothes or otherwise?"

"No, I'm good. I'm even taking some knitting with me because you know how stakeouts are. They can get long and boring."

"Except for the person you're working with... Is it the dude I saw you walk out of Colt's office with last week?"

"Wow, I didn't even see you then." Heat rushed up

her throat and enflamed her cheeks. She'd really become way too invested in Luther Darby, considering the short amount of time she'd known him. "Yes, and we have been talking each day, texting, and met at the diner for lunch yesterday. All about business, of course." Mostly.

Annie laughed. "You answered my question. First question is—why him, why now?"

Kit swallowed some of her gingerbread latte before answering. "The last several months I've been noticing men more, I suppose. You know, in that way you say is perfectly natural. But it's not anything I've followed through on. It seems too much effort. You know, to first get to know someone, make sure they're not another abusive man, then to have to spill my guts about my past…" She looked out the window at the snowflakes that drifted past. An early snowstorm was predicted for Thanksgiving weekend. "I don't feel like I have the energy to do all of that, just for a date."

Annie leaned forward and briefly touched her wrist. "You don't have to do all of that, Kit. Checking out a guy, making sure he's safe, that's something we all have to do. As for more than a conversation or coffee date, there's no reason to tell anyone your past. Not until you're ready ."

"You'd know about that more than I do." Kit's frankness didn't put off Annie—they were pretty much best friends. Even with Annie and Josh becoming a couple, Kit hadn't lost the first friend she'd made since being trafficked to the US from Ukraine, as a teen.

"Mmm. You know, Kit, it doesn't matter why or what—we all have a past. Sure, some of our histories are more traumatic than others, and yours is at the top of that."

"Except it could be so much worse. I had a loving family and decent childhood. I made stupid decisions once I turned sixteen."

"And that's not uncommon, no matter where you grow up. But you paid dearly for those choices. It's natural to be hesitant to do the work to have a life partner, or in your case, make that first date happen after such a long haul of recovery."

"It's thrown me, is all."

"What's that?"

"The physical attraction. I can't think of another reason why I was so fascinated by this LEA officer's hands while Chief gave us the details of our op." And while he played with his straw wrapper earlier.

Annie giggled. "Oh, I can think of reasons, trust me."

"Stop." Kit couldn't stop laughing, though. Annie's humor was infectious as was her joie de vivre.

"We've talked about needing to trust yourself again. What does your therapist say about this?"

"I haven't had time to talk to her, not since we've been assigned together. And besides, this is just the start of me even thinking about dating, right? I'm not about to get close to someone I'm working with, not on such an important op."

Annie shrugged. "Hey, chances are that yes, this is just the first guy to legitimately rev your engine since you got your life back. There will be plenty more. But, life can be far more interesting and surprising than we're able to imagine."

"Meaning?"

"Meaning that I think it's always a good idea to keep an open mind. Sometimes the people we're thrown together with at work become our family."

"And spouse." Kit winked at Annie, who'd fallen for Josh Avery, the SVPD officer and Trail Hikers undercover agent who'd helped her get Kit out of Vadim's clutches. Together, with Kit's information, they'd taken down Kit's ex and stopped ROC from trafficking young and underage women into Silver Valley.

"Yes, and stepdaughter." Annie's contented expression elicited a pang of longing that Kit had never felt before. She'd spent the last few years getting her own life together, so that the prospect of having to share it with another person, much less entertain the thought of children, hadn't been on her mind.

"I have to admit I don't like all of the emotions that being attracted to one man causes."

Annie's grin was understanding. "You mean how your mind future-trips to a happily-ever-after?"

Kit knew her eyes widened, her blush deepened. "Yes! What is that?"

"It's just biology. Hormones have a way of throwing all of us off-kilter." Annie tapped on her phone and stood. "I've got to get back to work."

"Have you been busy at the station?"

"Yeah. Domestic violence victims seem to never be in short supply. But our community outreach to the local churches and community college has made a big difference. We're getting women to report and agree to go to a shelter before their situation escalates. You had a lot to do with that, Kit."

Kit knew that Annie wanted to give her credit for speaking up publicly about what she'd been through, to encourage other women to step forward and stop the abusive life they'd become a part of. But she wouldn't have been able to do any of it without Annie's help.

"If you hadn't noticed the bruises on my face and neck in the yarn shop, I might still be with Vadim." She shuddered. "Or more likely, dead."

"But you're not. You're here. You've followed your dream of becoming a law enforcement agent, and don't scrunch up your face. In case you haven't noticed, I'm not a sworn officer, either. We both give support to the force that they need. Not everyone is meant to carry a weapon and bust down doors."

Annie's frankness made Kit laugh. She stood and hugged her dear friend. "I'll see you back at the station whenever we get back."

"You will." Annie hugged her back. "Thanks, girl-friend."

"For what?"

"For being you."

"You're okay with watching Koshka?" She knew her companion for the last couple of years would be in good hands.

Annie nodded. "Of course. I adore that smarty-pants."

A giggle escaped Kit's throat. "She sees you coming a mile away." Koshka always jumped up on Annie's lap the minute she sat down in Kit's apartment.

"We'll be just fine while you're gone. And so will you, Kit."

Kit sure hoped so.

"Did you tell Colt or Claudia about your possible stalker?"

"No, but I will. It's been nonstop for me between my caseload and preparing to go in the field."

"Have you had any more incidents?"

"No, except I did see Mishka at the diner yesterday."

Annie put her coffee down. "Wait—you didn't even call me! What did he say?"

"Nothing. He ignored me, after he gave me a really hard stare. That's it."

"That's creepy."

"He's always been a creep, no question. He picked up a to-go order and left, nothing to report."

"Let's hope it stays that way. Still, tell Colt." Annie picked up her coffee and stood to leave. Kit followed, preoccupied with the memory of seeing Mishka yesterday and how she'd not reacted. She wanted to believe it was a measure of how far she'd come, but was it because of Luther sitting across from her?

She made a silent vow not to get too reliant on Luther's strength.

It's too late.

Kit made her way up the steep stairs of her century-old apartment building, silently cursing the planet-killing plastic grocery bags as they cut into her forearms. She'd bought too much for it to all fit into her reusable bags and had hung the plastic bags on her arms to avoid multiple trips up and down the stairs. Living on the top floor was appealing most of the time, affording her a view of the sunrise and sunset over downtown Silver Valley, from her front room and back bedroom windows.

The two long flights of stairs also gave her some

decent exercise on a daily basis. But lugging pounds of food upstairs wasn't fun, no matter how fit she was .

She crested the last rise and stepped on the landing. And froze.

Luther stood in front of her apartment door. The only light was a single overhead bulb and the quickly failing daylight that shone through the high, small window at the opposite end of the hallway. The twilight glowed around Luther, emphasizing the long lean mass of muscle that defined his physique. He leaned against the corridor wall, his phone in hand as if he'd been passing the time while waiting for her. His gaze was on her, as he'd probably heard her footfalls since she'd entered the building.

"You're early." It was five forty-five and they'd agreed on six.

His dark brow rose, and in the dim light she couldn't see what emotions reflected in his eyes.

"Hello to you, too." He quickly consumed the space between them in a few long strides. Grasping several of the bags, he took them from her.

"Sorry. I like to have things planned to the minute, too much so. It's good you're early. I'm planning to go to the Friday night knit and chat at the yarn shop, at seven." He walked with her to her door and she immediately noticed how natural it felt.

"No apology necessary. I get it. Our line of work necessitates exact timelines." He faced her at the door. "You're in good shape, Kit. I've only got half of what you're hauling up here and it's heavy." Just as he had in the diner, he complimented her without sounding like it was a slimy means to get closer to her. Not something she'd experienced in her marriage.

She didn't reply as she shoved her key into the lock. Hoisting a bag onto her hip, she turned the handle and pushed open the door. "Come on in. You can put everything on the counter."

She felt Luther's presence behind her, his footsteps quiet but definite. The door clicked closed behind them, and she knew he'd taken care to check it—the hinges were rusty and prevented the door from closing on its own.

A sense of pride filled her as she tried to see her home from his viewpoint. Cream tones on the living area walls yielded to bright sunny yellow in the kitchen, where a skylight positioned over the entire room spilled remaining daylight onto the granite counter. She dumped her bags, and Luther added his by hers while she flipped the switch, immediately illuminating the clean, cheery atmosphere she'd striven for when she'd decorated the apartment two years ago.

"Nice place." His appreciation seemed sincere as his gaze took in her knickknacks, the potted herbs and the floral monthly planner attached to the refrigerator with magnets. "You're supposed to be going to the yarn place at seven?" In this light she could see his eyes, and their dark depths yielded to deep, deep blue with specks of gray.

"Yes. Every Friday night that I'm not working. It's a fun place to hang out." She looked at her watch. "We've got plenty of time to get our work done."

"I still can't get over the fact that you knit." His incredulity struck an old chord, a tight wire she'd thought she'd clipped and thrown out. She crossed her arms in front of her and looked up at him, refusing to break eye contact.

"What's your problem with fiber art?"

"Fiber…art?" He ran his hand over his face, and if she hadn't met him while he was a cool and put-together agent back at the station, in Colt's office, she'd swear he was trying to regroup. Backpedaling, to recall one of her favorite American expressions.

"Do you think that I'm supposed to be working 24/7?"

"No, none of the above. You impressed me as all business, though, back at the department and at lunch the other day. Of course you have outside interests, but I associate knitting with my grandmother. I know it's more popular again, and I'm not slamming you."

"Good to know. What are your hobbies?" If she was going to allow her hormones to have their first outing since her hard-won freedom from the enslavement of her abusive marriage, she may as well know something about the man who'd awakened that part of her.

The sexy part.

"Ah, well, I enjoy hiking, rock climbing. Skiing when I have more time. But the last few years have been short on recreation."

"Because you're working on ROC?"

He looked at her as if sizing up an opponent. What on earth? How could she pose any kind of threat to him, the seasoned agent who'd won the approval of Claudia Michele and Colt Todd? Kit knew that only the best were assigned to the ROC takedown. All of SVPD worked on the resulting crimes—drug dealing, high-end retail thefts, money laundering, prostitution from the human trafficking that had finally been halted.

"Yes. Ivanov in particular. I'm one of many who'd give their left nut to have him in jail."

She laughed. "I can't say I'd give one of my ovaries to catch Ivanov and Markova, but I'm willing to do pretty much whatever it takes."

The mission to dismantle ROC by eliminating Ivanov was left to only the best of the best.

Kit knew this because, so far, she hadn't met anyone with her Russian language ability. Not in the Harrisburg area, anyway. There were thousands of Russian-speaking Americans in the Susquehanna Valley but not so many with her background of having been trafficked and then escaping, followed by becoming a law enforcement employee. And Luther had to be the best TH had to offer.

"I need to get these organized, the cold stuff in the refrigerator." Kit grasped at any distraction from his gaze, her reaction to his nearness too much of a distraction.

"This looks like enough food for a month." Luther grinned as he methodically unpacked the bags, handing her the perishables and stacking the nonperishables on the counter.

"It's not all for our trip." She opened her freezer, a drawer at the bottom of the appliance, and dropped in several bags of vegetables. "I figure I'll be tired when we get back and I was low on food. This way I won't have to go to the grocery store right before I get back to work."

"Do you always think ten steps ahead?"

She paused and looked at him over her shoulder. "Yes, I suppose I do."

"That sounds like the makings of a good agent to me."

She slowly straightened and faced him. As she opened her mouth to reply, a shadow passed over Luther's face. Over the entire kitchen. The words she'd meant to say came out as a loud scream and she pointed.

Luther looked up just in time to see the man with the gun pointed at them through the skylight.

"Move!"

Luther acted on pure instinct and years of experience. He simultaneously shoved and lifted Kit up and out of the kitchen area, the sound of bullets shattering the skylight piercing the dusky quiet. He motioned toward the door as he pulled his weapon, and Kit bolted for their escape, opening it and running into the corridor with him on her heels.

"Go downstairs and into the coffee shop—have someone call 9-1-1."

"Where are you going?"

"No time to explain. Just go."

Her firm request took him by surprise. Other agents usually followed his orders without question. Footsteps sounded over their head, and he ran down the hallway to the other end of the building. Where the steps to the roof were. He'd checked out the entire building before he'd waited at Kit's door.

Halting abruptly at the foot of the stairs, Kit barreled into him.

"Downstairs, now!" He bellowed at her before he began the climb to the roof. To his relief she turned and ran back down the hall toward the main apartment stairwell. It allowed him to refocus and aim his gun in front of him as he prepared to open the door onto the roof.

His Glock .45 cocked and ready to fire, he opened the door slowly. The winter air hit his cheeks and then his lungs as he came out and did a full 360 sweep of the top of the building. The shooter was gone, the broken glass of Kit's skylight the only evidence he'd been there. Until a movement caught his eye and he saw the figure, dressed all in black, on the next rooftop.

"Stop! Police!" He began a full pursuit, bracing himself for what he had to do. It wasn't more than a six-foot gap between this building and the next, but if he missed it—no, he wouldn't. His rock climbing skills proved worthy as he leaped across the gap, landing on his feet on the tarred roof. He ran to the back, to where the fire escape provided a quick escape for the assailant.

But as he reached the edge of the roof and looked over, he saw the shooter disappear across the street, on the other side of the railroad tracks that ran through downtown Silver Valley.

"Son of a puppy." He pulled out his phone and hit the speed dial for SVPD. Detailing where he thought the shooter might be headed, he heard sirens already on the way.

But just like him, he was afraid the units were too late. The shooter had gotten away.

He put the phone in his back pocket and holstered his weapon, climbing down the fire escape, which landed him in front of the back entrance to the coffee shop. When he'd picked the apartment flat he had, he'd had no idea he and Kit were in the same building. Now that he knew they were, he'd thought he'd make sure she was safe throughout all of this op. He hadn't planned to tell her he was in the same building, not yet. Luther was a man with many targets on his head—the price for being a good agent.

But the shooter had been over Kit's skylight, and

when Luther looked up, they were pointing their weapon at Kit.

Who was after Kit? And was it going to jeopardize the overall mission to bring down Ivanov and Markova?

Chapter 7

"Did you see his face, Kit?"

"No. He was wearing a hood and all I saw was that gun. I know it was a Sig Sauer .22. Vadim used to make me keep one when he was out of the house, and I had to verify it was unloaded and hand it back to him whenever he came home." She hated that Luther sat on the sofa across from her and Colt and Claudia. They'd left the evidence collection for several other SVPD officers and were debriefing in a small flat across from her apartment. She'd ascertained it was the place Luther temporarily rented. He certainly was a covert operative—she'd never realized anyone had filled the space since the previous renters left two months ago.

"Have you ever been targeted like this before?"

She met Luther's gaze as she fought against the churning in her gut. "No, not since my divorce, months before, actually. And why do you think I'm the one the shooter was taking aim at? The window shattered right above where you were standing." She didn't want to talk to him about Mishka, or about any part of her past. She'd have to mention it to Claudia, though. And Colt.

His dark brow rose, as did one side of his mouth. "I've been in this town less than forty-eight hours, and I utilize the best counterdetection skills I have. To include technology."

She knew he meant that he had all of his cell phone signals scrambled and switched out SIM cards regularly.

"Wait." Claudia spoke, and they both returned their attention to her. "There's a good chance that this is another one of ROC's diversion tactics. Last month they made it look like they'd set up human trafficking again, and both TH and SVPD dedicated bodies to the case."

Colt nodded. "Only to find out that it was a false alarm. In the meantime, ROC managed to get another million dollars' worth of heroin onto our streets and the entire Harrisburg metro area."

Kit remembered the catastrophe, and how much Colt and Claudia had berated themselves for falling for the criminal organization's bait. She and the other SVPD employees had been just as upset. It was infuriating to be duped by the lowest of the low.

"It could be a warning about going into the woods." Kit thought aloud. "If they have any idea that we're on Ivanov's tail."

Claudia shook her head. "No, it's not that. As Luther said, he's taken all necessary precautions. He hasn't left any indications that he's on to Ivanov's whereabouts.

The two of you never met alone together, for this op, before recently, correct?"

"Correct. Just earlier today at the station, and at the diner for lunch." Kit looked from Claudia to Colt. "If this is about Luther and I going undercover, there's no one who knows about it." A memory tickled her conscience. "I mentioned that I was on an op to Annie at coffee earlier, that's it. And when we were at the diner, I saw Mishka. Vadim's son."

"Mishka's been given enough warnings to know that if he even appears to be communicating with his father again he'll be behind bars. I don't think he'd risk it—he's worth more to ROC on the outside. It could be random." Colt looked at all of them. "And I'd be willing to accept it as such, but not when it's your apartment, Kit."

"My apartment?" But as soon as she asked, she knew exactly what he meant. "You don't think Vadim still has people coming after me?" Her ex had been prosecuted to the fullest extent and was serving a life sentence in a federal prison out of state. The earliest he'd be eligible for parole was in twenty years, and the chances of him living that long after such a hardcore ROC lifestyle was slim. An alcoholic, Vadim had shown signs of being near the end of his disease process. Only by having to be sober in prison was he still alive, she figured.

"Not Vadim. The chances of it being him, running ops from a federal pen, are slim. But we always knew that the higher echelons of ROC might come after you. You're solely responsible for the dismantlement of their entire trafficking ring from Ukraine to Silver Valley."

"Solely? Hardly. The excellent work of Annie and

SVPD are what saved those women." And her life, too. "And they don't usually go after LEA. Why me, why now?"

"You're an easy target, unsuspecting with all the other activities ROC is involved in at the moment." Luther's quiet assessment was detached, void of emotion. So why did it stir up resentment in her?

"Wait a minute—are we getting to a place where I don't go on the op with you? Because I'm too much of a risk?"

"No, you're still going. It's safer to have you out of Silver Valley for now. We'll do what we can to find out about the shooter." Claudia's determination reflected in her voice. "There's no way they know you two are working together. In fact, I'm thinking that if it was a way to scare you, Kit, the shooter may not have noticed Luther, and if they did, they don't associate him with LEA."

"That's true." Kit rubbed the tops of her arms.

"Cold?" Luther's query cut through her racing thoughts.

"Yes, but I'm not in shock. Relax." She saw the way he looked ready to leap to her aid. What would he do? Throw a blanket around her? "I may not be an operational officer but I'm no shrinking violet."

"'Shrinking' and purple flowers aren't something I'd compare you to." Luther looked amused and she quickly glanced at her two bosses. But they were oblivious, in a quiet conversation, whispering with grim expressions. It tugged at Kit's heart that ROC was affecting the couple. They were professional titans in their own rights, but also a married couple who clearly adored one another. As a cop or any type of LEA it was tough to come home and force the day's work out of your head. It had to be especially difficult when you both worked for the same department or agency. Kit knew that Annie and Josh sometimes had trouble keeping work at work. Claudia and Colt probably did, too.

She looked at Luther to find him gazing at her bosses, a puzzled frown on his face. So it affected him, too.

"What are we going to do moving forward?" She needed to know if it was still a go at 0-dark-thirty tomorrow, or if she was to continue her regular police work as if nothing had happened.

"We're going." Luther spoke up, his voice resonating in the small space. Even with the open floor plan and generously sized kitchen, his apartment was still very modest, similar to hers. The thrum of the officers collecting evidence in her apartment sounded across the hallway, and drowned out Colt and Claudia's conversation.

"I don't think you can make that decision unilaterally, can you?" Her reward for the pointed question was a piercing stare.

"Ah, I am used to making my own decisions, but if it makes you feel better…" He turned toward Claudia and cleared his throat. "Ma'am." Claudia stopped mid-conversation with Colt and faced them .

"Yes?"

"If it's still okay with you both, we'll take off early tomorrow, arriving in the AOI by ten." Luther spoke with such authority it was hard to fathom a reason to calculate just how long this was going to take in inclement weather.

"AOI?" Kit had learned it was always better to ask for clarification than worry about appearing ignorant.

"Sorry—military speak for Area of Interest. I was in the National Guard for a bit."

"Thanks for explaining."

Claudia nodded, her eyes clear. "I concur with your decision, Luther. Kit, are you on board with what's expected of you? Luther will provide you any protection you need, weaponswise."

"Yes." Although she wasn't feeling the expectations they placed on her shoulders were so much about her language skills as regarding her need to completely trust this man whom she barely knew. But wasn't that part of police work? Building strong bonds in a short amount of time, dependent on the mission?

The rub was that she didn't need the attraction she felt toward Luther distracting her from the mission. But that wasn't something she'd discuss with Claudia. Not now, not ever.

"Good." Claudia spoke with a tone of relief. Had she really been concerned that Kit would refuse to go with Luther?

"Can I speak with you alone, Claudia?" Kit felt better speaking to her Trail Hikers boss about whom she thought the shooter might be. She didn't want Colt's fatherly instincts flaring, not when she was about to go on such a possibly dangerous mission with Luther.

"Sure thing."

They sat on a double bed in Luther's bedroom and it was all Kit could do to ignore how much her body reacted to his scent, which was everywhere. Pure man, but clean and strong, not heavy with booze or cigarettes.

"What do you need to tell me, Kit?" Claudia's eyes were full of concern, but the woman was a shark when it came to solving crime and keeping her agents safe. Even a non-weapon-holding agent like Kit.

"I'm worried that Mishka, Vadim's son, is stalking me. I've been feeling watched lately, and I've caught him downtown near me a few times over the last month or two."

Claudia's mouth melted into a grim line. "This is something that would have been a good idea to tell me or Colt sooner, Kit."

"I know. But I hadn't seen him since the trial, and when I did recognize him I figured it was a coincidence. At least the first time."

"There is no such thing as coincidence with ROC." Claudia's concern appeared to outweigh her disappointment that Kit hadn't said something sooner.

"I'm sorry, Claudia. It might not be him, but it was pretty clear that the shooter aimed for Luther. And I've... I've never had a man in my apartment before. If it is him, it makes sense he'd go after Luther."

"He has no clue who he aimed at." Claudia's lips lifted in a wry smile. "I almost feel sorry for the jerk. Luther could take him out with one hand, given the chance."

"I'm sure he can."

"You go on your mission with Luther. As I said, it's better to have you out of sight for the time being. We'll keep an eye on Mishka, although both TH and SVPD are strapped for manpower." Claudia sighed. "I'd really hoped to have ROC out of here by now. Only this last big fish to catch and we'll have done our job for the East Coast."

Kit thought about how nice it would be to live in Silver Valley and have it like everyone said it was before ROC tainted it.

"I'm here to do whatever it takes."

Mishka Valensky pounded his sofa in frustration, in the process knocking over the empty Baltika 7 bottles he'd placed on the cocktail table. His father, Vadim, had been unable to find out where Ivanov was holing up, as Vlad, Ivanov's son, refused to give out an inch of information.

Mishka needed to know where Ivanov was. He had to see the bastard in person. It was the only way he'd convince him that he wasn't as stupid as his father, that he could be trusted to run whatever part of ROC Ivanov needed him for.

But he needed Kit by his side to seal the deal with Ivanov. Unless he convinced Ivanov he had her under his control, Mishka's name was as good as mud because of how Kit's testimony helped put his father away. Much of the hearing had been closed, and no one knew, save for the jury, what Kit had said about Vadim, Ivanov or ROC. Mishka didn't think she was smart enough to really grasp what an important figure Vadim had been, and she'd been motivated to save those girls his father had stupidly hid on his own property. He could convince Ivanov of this, if Kit was by his side, where she belonged.

He'd been so close to getting to her, convincing her to come with him, and now… Nothing.

It'd been satisfying to watch the fear dance over her

face when she saw him at the diner. He'd gotten overly excited, though, and risked too much, too soon.

Because of his stupidity Kit had disappeared right after he'd tried to shoot the freaking bastard who was in her apartment. It was the same man she'd been with at the diner. He had no idea who the man was, but he knew it spelled trouble.

According to his contacts, Kit hadn't had a man in her apartment the entire time she'd lived there, since moving out of the mansion his father had built for her. Remembering how she'd never appeared comfortable or grateful for how hard his father worked made Mishka want to sit her down for a hard conversation.

He put his feet on the low table and tried to force himself to relax. The boys had the shop for this afternoon and tomorrow, since they weren't expecting a lot of business the day before Thanksgiving. He looked at the empty pizza boxes next to his foot and kicked them aside, making the rest of the bottles hit the floor with a thud. This piece of crap apartment was a far cry from the luxury his father had kept them all in for many, many years.

And because of Kit, it was all gone.

Mishka knew he should hate her and want to take her out like any other enemy of ROC, but Kit was different. She hadn't had a chance, coming from Ukraine. She wasn't pure-blooded Russian like his family. He was certain that with the right man she'd come around and see the truth and where her loyalties should lie.

With him.

His phone lit up and he saw it was his father, who was allowed one call per week. They had to talk in code and save the important information exchanges for when Mishka visited the prison and could see his father's facial expressions, make sure he was following Vadim's instructions properly.

"Da." They only spoke in Russian, to make things harder for any of the prison guards who might listen in.

"Son, you coming up this week?"

"Yes, of course. What do you want or need?" He wasn't allowed to bring Vadim a whole hell of a lot, but sometimes with the right size bill one of the guards they trusted would allow a jar of *cherny ikra*, black caviar. Vodka too, as long as there was enough for the guard and his friends.

"Nothing. Just time with my son." That meant at least the vodka. Vadim had been struggling lately, as every channel he and Mishka had used to keep their ops running enough to bring in some money to the pawnshop had dried up. Vadim believed that Ivanov was in trouble, possibly done running ROC. From the news reports Mishka read over the last year, the ROC East Coast honcho had disappeared. That would leave Vlad running the show, never a good option. Vlad was crazier than Ivanov. There'd be no room for Mishka in an organization run by Vlad Ivanov.

"I'm fine. Everything's fine, my father. Have you heard from anyone in the family since we last spoke?"

"Nyet." Vadim's voice was thick with frustration, and Mishka imagined his father's hands shaking from alcohol withdrawal. The amount of liquor he smuggled in was a fraction of what Vadim had been consuming on a daily basis before his arrest.

"That is disappointing, Father." Annoyance roiled his gut, and he stood, pacing in the tiny room while holding the cell to his ear. "I can't do my job well if

I don't have all the right training." Their code for "I need more information." Like where the hell Ivanov was holed up.

Because where Ivanov was, he had to believe Kit was headed there, working with SVPD, and now, FBI. The man he'd tried to shoot looked like FBI. Typical American jerk. The other option, that she'd suddenly disappear, go into witness protection, wasn't something Mishka could look at. It was too frightening. It would put an end to all he'd anticipated since the day he'd found out she'd divorced Vadim.

Mishka wouldn't rest until he had Kit under lock and key. And maybe under him, too.

"Come as soon as you can, son. I am a lonely old man here."

"Goodbye, Father."

He hung up and flipped through television channels, looking for some afternoon porn to while away the time until he had another idea of where she might have gone.

There were two possibilities:

He'd assigned his minions to watch Kit ever since the ungrateful bitch sent his father to prison. Vadim had given the peasant bitch from Ukraine a beautiful home, all the designer labels a woman could want, and still she'd turned him over to the American authorities.

Vadim told him that he should let it go, let the woman who called herself Kit Danilenko go. They'd rebuild their corner of ROC in Silver Valley without her to mess things up again.

But Mishka could never let her go. He'd wanted her the moment his father had brought her home, when he'd foolishly believed Vadim would give her to him, his only son, as a fatherly gift for all the grunt work Mishka did at the pawnshop and keeping the ROC honchos off their backs. He'd been thirty years old at the time and she was sixteen. A far better match than his father, who was fifty-three and old enough to be her grandfather.

It had been a direct kick to his balls when Vadim had invited Mishka to the courthouse wedding, enabled by the fake IDs he'd had produced for Kit to show she was eighteen and of legal age. His father hadn't shown any sign of comprehending how foolish he appeared. For Vadim, it was a show of Russian power and sexual prowess to wed a young, beautiful girl.

Kit, for her part, had been a frightened little kitten, like her name. Her fear had turned to bitter resentment within days, and she'd never given Mishka the respect he deserved.

Mishka had offered to help her out, to ease what he knew had to be less than satisfying sexual encounters with his drunk father. But she'd spurned him at every turn, refusing to give in to the chemistry that he felt between them.

It only made sense after his father went to jail, taking the blame for both of them and protecting Mishka from prosecution, that Mishka would seek her out and make up for how rough Vadim had been on her. But she'd completely changed not only her name but her life. At first it had been hard to track her down. He'd panicked, thinking she'd gone into the witness protection program. But then fate interceded, in the guise of one of the ROC operatives who'd been arrested for money laundering in Silver Valley's big-box stores.

The ROC man had been in the pawnshop years before and remembered seeing Kit at one time. He recognized her standing with a group of SVPD cops right after he'd been busted in a sting against the local ROC, and told Vadim, already in jail.

That was over a year ago. With his abilities to continue regular ROC ops severely limited, Mishka had scraped out a living at the pawnshop and found a new hobby.

Keeping tabs on Kit.

Crap and double crap. Luther wasn't immune to the constant tension that flowed between him and Kit, nor was he beholden to it. He'd been here before, but it had been a very different situation. When Evalina had betrayed him to her drug-loving mob boss, it had seemed too easy. And it had been. It'd been a setup, one in which he could have easily been killed. As it worked out, it was Evalina who'd lost her life. He'd gained another ROC defendant, one who was going to jail for at least thirty days. Not as reassuring as the lifelong sentence Kit's ex-husband had received, but close enough. He'd take the odds.

Still, playing bodyguard to the civilian equivalent of a noncombatant wasn't in his arsenal of favorite assignments, either.

He stood in his apartment, prepping the last of the supplies he'd load in the Jeep before they left. It was thirty minutes until he knocked on Kit's door and told her to be ready. He'd had her sleep in the one bedroom, while he took the pullout sofa. He, Colt and Claudia had all agreed it was the smartest thing to do, with the shooter still at large. No one could count on the perpetrator being random.

Soft footsteps alerted him that Kit was awake right before she entered the tiny kitchen and eating area. She looked no worse for wear, which didn't raise his spirits. It'd be easier if she were an aloof jerk, and not exactly his type. Athletic and down-to-earth, with a good grasp of logical problem solving skills. The way he'd watched her emotions play across her face last night as they'd discussed their options with Claudia and Colt—Kit knew her stuff and wasn't afraid of doing the next right thing.

Going with him into the woods proved that.

"Good morning. I'm packed and ready to go." Fresh scrubbed skin sans makeup with her hair pulled up into a long ponytail took him aback. The professional woman with her hair twisted up yesterday had vanished and in her place was this very young, very vulnerable-looking duplicate. Her eyes sparkled with intent. "What's the problem?"

"Problem? There's no problem."

She sniffed. "That's right, there isn't a problem. I'm not in uniform like you've been for a good part of your life from what I can tell, but I'm not going to weigh you down. I'll keep things running in the background so that you can do whatever you need to do."

"That's great, Kit, except that my job is your job until we determine we're onto Ivanov. I'm not going to be using any of the weapons we're bringing along unless the situation flips on its head."

Kit's eyes widened and he realized with a jolt that the deep blue depths were definitely the kind he'd be able to get lost in.

Stop. Mission first.

"Yeah, I thought so." He moved to the counter and

slapped together the toast and egg sandwiches he'd laid out for them. The coffee shop would be open; nothing he made here would be better than that. Plus it'd start their alibi that they were going off for a hunting weekend, if ROC was watching them.

"Thought what?" Instead of backing away, Kit walked up next to him at the tiny counter.

"Please. Don't insult either of us. We both know this will be a very boring, routine mission if it goes as planned." With long hours together in a small cabin, waiting for Ivanov's cell phone to light up on the comms gear laptop.

Kit's mouth spread into a wide grin. "You're kidding, right? I thought you were an ROC subject matter expert."

"No one's a complete expert on ROC, but yeah, I know a good amount."

Her grin, mesmerizing as her pink lips framed it, morphed into a sardonic twist. "Then you should know above all else that you always have to expect the unexpected with them. Sure, we know that if they sniff us out, we'll spook them and they'll run. But ROC, like my ex, doesn't like to leave any trace behind, including any cops that were after them. Trust me, this mission is anything but routine."

As she spoke, he watched her, heard her voice, recognized the words. And he didn't disagree. ROC was a fearsome opponent, and its members, especially its leader, Ivanov, didn't tolerate any kind of LEA who'd discovered them. The stakes were even higher now with Ivanov basically running on empty financially. Save for the missing billion dollars that they all thought Markova might be connected to in some way.

"You're quiet, agent." Kit's eyes tilted up as she smiled. It wasn't a sarcastic or mean comment, simply collegial.

"I'm listening. I know when someone has a good thing to share."

No, he hadn't been surprised by anything she'd said. It was how he felt as he stood next to her, watched her, absorbed her presence. Kit Danilenko was a woman unlike any he'd worked with before.

"You're smiling now. Why?" She'd caught the grin on his face.

"I'm laughing at myself. You've put my assumptions of you on their asses."

He left out one thing. She'd knocked him on his butt, too.

Not something he normally let a woman do. As if he had a choice with Kit.

Chapter 8

If someone had told Kit just two days ago that she'd be sleeping in a relatively strange man's apartment with such ease, she'd have cringed. Yet not only had she fallen asleep with ease, she hadn't experienced an iota of anxiety upon waking.

Until she remembered the shooter, and the sounds of the shot followed by breaking glass. Sounds that were unfortunately not new. She'd survived more than being illegally trafficked from Ukraine at the tender age of sixteen, more than being forced to marry Vadim only a month later, claiming she was eighteen as her forged passport and driver's license claimed.

A vision of who she'd been, the young girl forced into womanhood at the hands of a man three times her age, flashed across her memory as she used the bathroom for the last time before they left. She'd cried buckets for that girl, for the lost innocence, the repeated sexual and physical abuse that she'd endured for the next six years. Yet every now and then she appeared in her mind's eye. It used to be a harbinger of danger— maybe a new man in her life that she needed to be careful around, like the college professor who played fast and loose with all of his students. He'd incorrectly assumed she was just another naive coed, looking to solve her daddy issues in his bed in exchange for advanced exam information. For that warning, she was grateful her younger self had reappeared.

Today it wasn't about being warned or afraid. It was a reminder of how far she'd come, and that she was stronger for it.

She brushed her teeth and then packed up her toiletries, noting the bright butterflies printed on her makeup bag. The zippered pouch was a gift from Annie, a reminder to embrace the new woman she'd become, who she was today. Her caterpillar days were long past, as was the long journey of metamorphosis while she processed her pain. The group therapy room as well as her counselor's office were her chrysalis, the safe spaces where she'd shed the shame and guilt that she'd carried for too long.

Kit placed her hand on the doorknob and had the sense of anticipation she used to as a girl in a village on the outskirts of Kiev, when her mother promised they'd visit her favorite park. The slide was the most fun to her, from the long climb up the steel ladder to the giddy excitement of sitting at its apex, giving herself time to take in the surrounding playground. The best part was seeing her mother or father at the base of the slide, waiting for her, smiles splitting their weathered faces. They couldn't have been much older than her present twenty-six, and yet her memory saw them looking like the average fifty-year-old in America. Life in Ukraine, a former Soviet satellite, had been difficult for them. She saw that now.

And yet, they waited at the base of the slide, ready to catch her after she shrieked down the long tin surface, knowing their arms would wrap around her and prevent her from landing in the deep mud puddle at the base.

Kit turned the doorknob and left the bathroom. Yes, it was like throwing herself down that slide, but this time she'd be the one to catch herself.

What she didn't know was if she'd be laughing at the end of the ride.

Kit's surprise at having no fear with Luther, none of the usual trepidation she did around a strange man, continued through the morning.

Last night she'd fought with Colt over needing to stay anywhere but her apartment. The shooter had shaken her up, yes, but with SVPD placing a patrol officer in charge of surveillance of her apartment building, she didn't worry about a reappearance right away. Still, when her bosses told her to stay with Luther, she'd finally complied. Colt and Claudia had offered up their guest room, but staying with a superior wasn't something she was going to do. She didn't want to act like a quivering baby and was determined to be the woman she wanted to be. Confident, sure of herself, fearless.

"You've been quiet." Luther was driving. They'd cleared town and were on the highway that would take them into the mountains and open hunting areas.

"You have been, too."

He grunted, shifting in the heated leather seat. "I like to get my thoughts together before an op."

She savored the warmth of her car seat on the cold day.

"We went over it pretty extensively yesterday, and again last night." She looked between the seats to verify for the fifth time that her equipment was loaded.

"You're as OCD about checklists as I am, I see." His voice grumbled next to her ear and she straightened, embarrassment forcing a stiffness into her joints.

"I'm not OCD, not in truth."

"I don't mean as a medical diagnosis, Kit. It's a compliment. You're a professional and you're making sure you have everything you're going to need."

"I'm used to working with SVPD and TH in their different comms vans. I don't normally have to worry about the equipment being there or not—it's part of the vehicle."

"Understandable." He continued to look straight ahead at the road, and she saw that his gaze took in the large hawk perched on a bare tree.

"As long as I've lived here I've never gotten over the birds."

"There are a lot of hawks, eagles and falcons, that's for sure. Most people don't notice them." He cast her a quick look. "But you don't miss much, do you?"

"I, ah, I've had a lot of opportunity in my life to learn that details are what make the difference."

"I suppose you have." His voice was upbeat, but she heard the thread of compassion.

"They told you about my past, didn't they?" When he remained silent, she pressed forward. "It's okay if they did. Why would you agree to work with someone you didn't know anything about?"

"Claudia and Colt each briefly mentioned that you've got the experience to handle the language translation that we're going to need. You're from Ukraine, and you were brought here on false assumptions when you were still a kid, a teen. That's all I really know."

"Come on, Luther. They told you who my ex is, I'm sure."

Silence descended in the front seat as effectively as a wet blanket. Kit couldn't have spoken another word if she wanted to, and waited for his response.

Finally, she heard Luther's long exhalation.

"Kit, you've had to endure more than most people do in a lifetime. As for your ex—to me, an ex can only be a former spouse or lover, whatever, if it was your choice to be with them in the first place. As I see it, that criminal didn't count for anything but a source of pain in your life."

He understood. She'd never spoken to another man about her torturous marriage, the sham of a relationship that had nearly broken her. Had, in fact, at different points. Until she'd summoned the courage to take Annie up on her offer for help.

"Thank you."

"Nothing to thank me for, Kit."

"No, there is. Thank you for understanding, and for your willingness to work with me."

"Okay, that's not going to work." His eyes met hers before looking back at the road.

Her breath hitched. This was what she'd feared. He'd find fault, figure out why she wasn't up to this task.

"I knew this would happen." Her voice sounded so

damn weak, and if she'd been alone, she would have thrown a pillow across the room, screamed and gone to take a long hot bath.

But she was with Luther, the stalwart undercover agent who saw through her with each glance. Keeping her tears to herself, she lifted her chin and prepared for him to turn the car around.

"Drop me at my apartment. I can go stay with Annie and Josh if I need to."

"What. The. Hell." Luther's voice boomed in the car and she involuntarily jumped.

Luther wanted to kick himself in the mouth, except his foot was already there. Both feet, actually. Kit had shown nothing but total courage and professional detachment since she'd walked into Colt's office and heard their mission objective. Through the brief and somewhat frenzied planning and shopping she'd stayed cool. When the bullet tore through her skylight, she'd jumped—out of the way, following standard evasion tactics.

To see her face white and pasty now, because of something he had or hadn't said, filled his mouth with the taste of bile.

"Kit, you misunderstood me. Let me try again."

He saw her shake her head vigorously, in his peripheral vision. If he could grab her hand, look her in the eyes, he would. So that she'd see his sincerity. But they'd started to climb and the highway had gone down to two lanes, winding around the first cluster of mountain foothills.

"No need. Just take me back home." This version of Kit was not the woman who'd greeted him this morning. Great, just great. It'd taken him, what, fifteen minutes to make mincemeat of her self-confidence? He felt like the lowest bird on the food chain, unable to escape the raptor that was his big mouth.

"I'm not taking you home, Kit. We're going on this mission, together. I'm sorry if I pushed too hard on your history—it's none of my business. None of it." He needed to hear the words as much as say them. The reminder that she was a mob operative's spouse, albeit an ex, would keep him from seeing her as anything but his work colleague.

She's nothing like Evalina.

The memory of how the ROC mob honcho's wife had used him, how stupidly he'd fallen for her sexual charms, made his self-disgust all the greater. It was one thing that he'd allowed himself to be duped and his heart dragged through the ROC crap. It was another to cause Kit, a true victim of her circumstances, any pain.

"Are you sure you can trust me, Luther? Did you know that I've had years of therapy and medical help for what I went through with Vadim?"

The mention of her ex made his skin tighten, the tendons in his hands taut with the need to get vengeance for her.

"Which is why you're perfect for this job, Kit. You're a survivor. I wouldn't have agreed to come out here with some amateur who might know the Russian language but is clueless about the idioms and colloquialisms. You've got a special gift. The fact that Claudia and Colt are willing to send you out in the field speaks for itself."

She didn't reply, and he risked a look at her profile. The stoniness was still there in her face, but her posture had eased the tiniest bit. Her teeth gnawed at her lower lip and he saw his opportunity.

Let her know you care, but not too much.

"Look, I've been working organized crime ops for the better part of a decade. I was in the FBI before, and spent a lot of time analyzing the movements and habits of ROC thugs. After I signed on to Trail Hikers I learned even more and became imbedded with ROC gangs on three different occasions." The last had been what he'd thought of as his last undercover with ROC, and yet here he was again, heading into the fray.

"So why do you need me?"

"That's what I'm trying to explain, Kit. Even with all that experience, I still missed the signs during my last mission, and it almost cost several agents their lives." "My partner came in and at the last minute saved my life, because he's a native speaker like you." Like Kit, his partner had also been trafficked here and forced to perform sexual acts as a minor. But that was his story to tell, not Luther's.

"Where's your partner now? Wouldn't he be better to go into the woods with?"

"No. He's been assigned to another op." His partner was in Silver Valley too, but working a much bigger issue—cybercrime on the Navy base. Silver Valley boasted one of the few landlocked Navy bases in the States, and it happened to be the headquarters of many different military commands. Commands that had access to the highest classifications of government secrets. The thought of working inside buildings and cubicles, either inside a government agency or monitoring for an enemy hack, didn't appeal to Luther. He preferred to be out in the world of more tangible enemy targets and goings-on.

"Too bad for you." Her voice was stronger and he let himself relax a smidge. The Kit he'd met a week ago and gotten to know this past week was coming back.

Just in time.

The morning passed quickly as Luther drove them through miles of pristine Appalachian Mountain scenery. The direct route to the hunting cabin wasn't more than a twenty-five minute drive, but he'd explained that he couldn't take a direct route to the hideout, and she understood. Basic evasion tactics were always enforced with SVPD and Trail Hikers. After being targeted by the mystery shooter, ensuring they weren't followed was all the more important.

Luther was a pro at the wheel and she wasn't tense around him, until the woods became more than passing scenery. The twisting roads cut through heavily treed areas, often with precipitous shoulder drops.

Kit found herself fighting the urge to tell Luther she'd changed her mind about going undercover with him. It wasn't the undercover part, or being with Luther, which is what she'd expected to cause her some trigger issues. Instead it was a bit of motion sickness, combined with being surrounded by the dense trees as the truck climbed higher into the mountains and the forest surrounded them.

"It's hot in here." She shrugged out of her overcoat, wishing she hadn't worn long thermal underwear in preparation for the predicted below freezing temperatures. The cabin couldn't be trusted to have a steady heat source, and her clothing choices had seemed perfectly sane this morning.

"You can lower the heat on your side. Here." He reached over and turned off the seat heater. She'd been so busy paying attention to Luther and her reactions to him she'd forgotten about the seat heater. "Go ahead and open your window. We're almost there, anyhow."

"Claudia wasn't kidding when she said it was in the middle of nowhere." Trail Hikers had several safe houses available throughout the world, and in Pennsylvania they tended to be of the more rustic variety. Although she'd heard that there were some very modern shelters that TH agents used when in deep undercover, she'd never seen them. With TH, everything was on a need-to-know basis. As an unsworn SVPD employee who provided similar support to Trail Hikers, her information access was limited mostly to communications for specific ops.

Kit didn't think she'd ever want to be a full-fledged agent, as she'd seen too much violence while being forced to live with Vadim. Agents like Luther had to clean up the dirtiest, most vile corners of the planet, which often included eliminating the bad guy.

Bad guy or not, Kit didn't want to be the one pulling the trigger.

"Your face is red. Do you feel okay?" Concern etched his query as Luther turned into what looked like an overgrown underbrush, but in fact was a dirt road that gave "off-road" new definition.

"I-I'm fine, just need some fresh air." She held tight to the handle above her window and tried to lean into the jarring bumps as the undercarriage hit rut after rut. The cooler outside air fanned her face through the window crack. It was impossible to close her eyes and do her usual breathing exercises.

"How much longer?"

"Three minutes, tops."

She gritted her teeth and tried to distract herself with the feel of the plastic handle under her palm and fingers, the sight of so many tree trunks and the bright green of the pines. A flash of black and white on the forest floor just feet from the vehicle reminded her of childhood cartoons that she'd loved in Ukraine, featuring a skunk.

"I just saw a skunk."

"We're going to see a lot more than skunks this weekend. Here we go." The bumping stopped as Luther pulled around a small, nondescript wooden building. It was barely discernible from the woods that surrounded it, and she knew the road wasn't anything marked on a map.

"Thanks. I'm okay—I just need a minute." She opened her door the second he put the car in Park and relished the feel of solid ground beneath her feet, the brisk pine-scented air cooling her cheeks. She braced herself for Luther's concern, ready to urge him to give her some space.

The sound of a door closing and the matching reverberation through the auto's steel frame vibrated against her back as she leaned against the car. Another *thump* as the back hatch opened. Eyes closed, she kept breathing in the fresh, clean air and expelling what she envisioned as her anxiety and impending panic attack. If she could just have a little time to herself, she'd get through this.

The problem was explaining to Luther what the heck

was going on, and that wasn't something she ever enjoyed. His footsteps sounded on the ground, crunching leaves and pine needles with his sure stride.

It's no one else's business, unless it affects your work.

Annie's assurance echoed in her memory, and she opened her eyes. She could tell Luther whatever she wanted. He knew enough about her past—if he was concerned she wasn't reliable, he wouldn't have brought her out here. Would he?

As she eased off the car and took a few steps, her anxiety evaporated. It had been motion sickness, a too-hot car. Not a PTSD flashback. Relieved, she realized she'd made it through a rough spot.

Luther wasn't anywhere in sight. She looked around. Besides the hut of sorts, there was nothing but trees. Kit closed her door and walked around the perimeter of the tiny clearing. Luther stood with one foot on a small stoop as he methodically lifted boxes and equipment off the ground where he'd placed them and into an open door. She noted that the door looked like nothing more than plywood on the outside, but in truth was four inches thick, probably steel. "Nice door."

He grinned, a quick flash of levity she didn't expect. "It really passes as an old, beat-up hunting stop, doesn't it?"

"Let me help." She walked up to him and peered into the dark interior. "This is a whole lot of shack and not quite the cabin I expected."

Luther grunted. "We're 'hunting,' remember? All we need is a place to sleep and maybe warm up each night. We'll be outside most of the time."

"Not really, though, right?" She handed him one of

the boxes, filled with dry goods. They'd planned for up to two weeks, just in case, but it was a foregone conclusion that they wouldn't be out here longer than the holiday weekend.

He stopped and stared at her. "Yes, really. A little less talk and more getting unpacked." The grim expression on his face reminded her that she wasn't here as a simple assistant or even comms expert. She was part of their team while they waited for Ivanov to show up.

"Sorry." Annoyance flared the moment the word left her tongue, and she stood and looked at him. "Wait a minute—no, I'm not sorry. This is the first time I've been out on a mission like this. I'm still learning, Luther."

"Again, less talk while you're at it, too." His glance was noncommittal, as if she were no more than a new teammate who'd need more instruction.

"Fine." She got the message. He'd sent her all the signals that this was going to be business-only, no small talk or getting to know each other's astrological signs. If Luther wanted her to be the stellar comms expert she was, as well as maintain total professional demeanor the entire time, which in this case meant behaving like a hunter, she could do it.

Only after they'd unloaded the back of the car as well as the gear on the back seat, did she enter the tiny dwelling.

"I suppose we're lucky to have that." She pointed at a single electrical outlet that was situated near the minuscule sink and counter. A table stood against one wall and held a propane camping stove and several pieces of comms gear, from walkie-talkie to disposable cell phones.

"It can handle the entire load of our equipment, plus we have a portable generator if need be. The gas for it is buried in a tank outside."

"Where do we sleep?" She looked around the rest of the space. A beat-up sofa and two chairs she assumed had been part of the set with the table were all she saw. And a woodstove. "The floor?"

"Ye of little faith." His teasing comment caught her attention after his "we are undercover, darn it" spiel. She watched as he walked two steps to the far wall and reached up to what she'd thought was nothing more than a paneled wall. His fingers moved. She heard a loud click before he lowered the panel and she saw that it held a double mattress, as well as two pillows. It rested on the back of the sofa, which made the bed angle back.

"That looks a little uncomfortable."

"We'll move the sofa out of the way."

"So you get the bed and I get the sofa." She reached down and grabbed her sleeping bag, tossed it on the sofa as if to claim it.

"We can alternate."

"So you're generous, are you?" The teasing comment came out of her mouth without her thinking about it. As if she'd known Luther longer than two days, as if she had no history of being anxious around men. An immediate rush of something warm and wonderful washed over her, and she tugged at the collar of her flannel shirt.

"Still hot?" He'd meant it with the most polite intention, she was certain. But his eyes held a small light in them that she either hadn't noticed before or hadn't wanted to see.

Luther Darby was the hot one here.

No, no, no. Why did her libido and need to be with a man decide to appear now, when she had such an important job to do? And when the man in question wasn't someone she could ever count on. For her life and protection during this mission, sure, no doubt. But for the first man to get involved with, to be there to help her navigate new-to-her feelings?

Nope.

It was a good thing, really. Luther wasn't someone she had to worry would want anything more from her than she was willing to give. He hadn't pushed her on any of her past during their conversations so far. She'd revealed only what she was comfortable with.

His hand on her shoulder jolted her from her self-examination. Kit jumped, her calves hit the sofa cushions and she landed on her butt.

"Oof."

"Whoa, sorry about that. Here." His hand was in front of her, the offer to help her up like an olive branch. She grasped his hand and did her best to ignore how incredibly strong his grip felt, the calluses on his finger pads evident and hallmarks of a man who wasn't afraid of hard work when necessary. Nothing like the soft, pudgy hands of her ex. The only time Vadim's hands had been hard was when he'd hit her.

As soon as Kit was back on her feet, she scrambled to the side, standing near the open door. She rubbed her upper arms. "I'm going to get my coat—I left it in the car."

"Sure." To his credit he didn't ask her what her problem was, or why she was so damn jumpy around him.

Why would he? He knew what he needed to know about her.

Her jacket was on the passenger floor, where she'd left it. The chill of the day settled around the mountain and she shrugged into it, wishing she could text Annie that she'd had a flash of anxiety but had managed it. Her friend would text back an encouraging response or funny GIF. But they weren't to do anything with their personal cell phones while out here, unless it was an emergency. It was too risky they'd be intercepted by ROC.

While Ivanov and his hostage Markova appeared to be operating separately from the main East Coast ROC collective, the LEAs couldn't be certain. And being on their own didn't mean the ROC bigwigs didn't have their own comms equipment. One thing ROC's heroin and human trafficking trade had done, besides almost decimating Silver Valley's teens as well as the entire Harrisburg area, was bring in untold amounts of money. ROC's technology was often more advanced than any legitimate LEA's.

As she made the quick walk back to the cabin, she spotted a separate building, farther back in the woods, behind a grouping of large boulders. Curious, she walked toward it, wondering if it was an outhouse, or maybe storage facility.

To her delight it wasn't only a bathroom with what looked like two real toilets as opposed to an old-fashioned outhouse, but it had a generous shower room with both hot and cold handles. Still suspicious, she turned one of the hot water dials and was rewarded with a stream of warm, then hot water.

"Do you need a shower already? We haven't even

gone on our first hike yet." Luther's voice made her jump, and she banged her hand on the piping before she calmed herself down enough to shut off the water. Turning on her booted heel, she faced him as her hands itched to shove at his chest and knock him off his feet.

"You really need to stop sneaking up on me." Anger rushed in where she'd normally be fearful. "It's not fair to put me in a place where I have to constantly explain why I'm such a nervous mess."

Chapter 9

Luther wished he had the ability to turn back time, about thirty minutes or so. Before they'd arrived at the stakeout.

Before he'd put Kit back on edge.

Working with a partner who had combat-related PTSD wasn't new to him. But a woman whose mental health had been so deeply affected by a husband who'd been forced on her while she was still a kid?

Nope, no experience to draw from there.

Her eyes were still on him, burning through to his soul.

He took a step back and held his hands up. "I'm sorry, Kit. It's only natural for me to be extra quiet when working. I'll try to let you know I'm coming next time."

"I'd appreciate it." She slapped her hand against

the wall of the shower. "I hate being the person you have to worry about, when you're working something so important."

Her bottom lip jutted out, and she immediately bit down on it, her teeth in sharp contrast to the ruby red. Out here in the natural light she was more beautiful than she'd appeared at SVPD when they'd met, when she'd been in a business suit and had minimal but still detectable cosmetics on her skin. Now he saw how luminous it was, and understood why his fingers itched to touch her.

It's more than her skin you want to touch, man.

He let out a long sigh, hoping to demonstrate that he wasn't frustrated with her but with himself. "We have to get this clear right now. You're totally within your wheelhouse to ask me to not go stealth when I come up to you, if you don't make eye contact with me. But you need to do me a favor."

"What's that?" The wariness was back in her eyes, her breathing more shallow. Crap, no matter what he did or said it seemed to put her on edge.

"Stop playing the 'terminally unique' card. You're not the first colleague I've had who's dealt with the residual effects of traumatic events. In fact, I struggle with my own 'old tapes' of past takedowns and conflicts I've been in."

"Oh." He watched her digest his confession. And swallowed. He'd never told anyone about his own struggles with anxiety after his involvement with and the murder of Evalina; how he'd thought she'd died at the hands of one of the ROC players he was tasked to bring in. A year and a half later, Luther still had nightmares.

"To this day I have flashbacks. They're not nearly as rough as in the beginning and don't last as long. Now, I'm in a place where I can actually use all those tools they give you when you first get diagnosed. The deep breathing, staying in the present moment, grounding to an inanimate object, or the best—petting your dog or cat."

A smile spread across her face. Finally, he'd hit home plate with something. "You saw my cat, Koshka. She's gotten me through an awful lot these past couple of years. I wish I could have brought her with us."

He nodded. "I get it. Although the coyotes out here make it too much of a risk, if you ask me. Did you have her when you were still with your ex?" He genuinely wanted to know. It was almost a need, the way he tried to figure her out. He held the bathhouse door open for her as they made their way out.

"Heck no. Vadim wasn't a fan of animals as pets, unless they were stuffed and hung on the wall." She pushed past him and walked to a large tree, placing her hand on the bark. "I'd asked for a dog at one point, and he'd agreed as long as it was a guard dog, his words for a vicious attack dog. I passed. All I ever wanted to do was go to the local shelter and rescue a puppy." She rubbed her palm against the rough bark as if it were a dog or cat. He figured the motion was soothing to her. "After I escaped, and was on my own for a while, I realized that my current lifestyle and small flat wouldn't support a dog. But a cat—that was perfect. Annie knew a neighbor whose cat had unexpectedly had a litter, so I met Koshka when she was only a week old. Even then I knew she was mine, by the way she snuggled into my palm." Her eyes were on him, looking at him with open speculation. "You think I'm crazy, don't you?"

"No." He took a step toward her but stopped himself before he crossed into her personal space again. From the slight smile that curved her lips, he knew she didn't miss it—that he'd paid attention when she'd asked him not to crowd her.

"It wouldn't be out of the ballpark if you did."

"That's a strange way to use that expression, and I already told you, I'm familiar with anxiety and depression that's caused and triggered by trauma. It's not crazy or insane to react to a life-threatening event. It's what makes us all human."

"'All' of us?" Her brow rose and the skepticism was back, even after what he'd told her about his own experiences with PTSD.

"Yes." He turned toward the cabin, their home base for at least the next twenty-four hours, unless by some tactical miracle they intercepted and located Ivanov before then. "I'll finish setting up. Take your time out here. We'll be spelling one another—ah, I mean taking turns being on watch, awake, as soon as we get started, so count this as your first break."

Leaves and small twigs crunched and snapped under his feet but they weren't loud enough to keep her reply from reaching his ears.

"Aye aye, Captain."

Good thing he wasn't facing her as the grin on his face probably made him look far from the competent agent this op required.

He looked around the room and decided to set up the kitchen area. Kit would handle the comms equipment when she came back in. After a quick look out the small, side window to make sure she was still within shouting distance, he got to work. The minifridge was cold so he shoved their dairy and other perishables on its shelves, then moved it aside and under the table. The portable comms rack set up quickly, the half-a-dozen electronic units stacking vertically.

Next, he focused on setting up the handguns and rifles he'd checked out from the TH weapons locker. Only two items were legit hunting gear: the crossbow and slide-bolt hunting rifle. The rifle met his standards for elk hunting, but the cartridges they'd brought were the best for deer. Not that he intended to take down any animals on this trip, save for Ivanov or Markova if he had to. But he and Kit might be out here for a long while, and it was imperative they keep up their cover. As hunters with deer season opening on Monday, they'd be faced with actually hunting if this op went longer than the weekend.

He'd brought his grandfather's vintage rifle for Kit to carry when they conducted their faux hunting activities.

Work kept his hands occupied, but since he'd done so many similar ops, he couldn't keep his mind from wandering, alert for Kit's return. He knew the basics; she'd been lured to the States by some bad guys, forced into an arranged marriage to a man old enough to be her grandfather. Anger steamed his thoughts and he clenched the rifle barrel as he set it next to the door.

"You look ready to kill a bear."

He snapped his gaze to her face. "Your turn to sneak up on me."

"I wasn't sneaking. Just practicing. How do you

walk so quietly when there are dry pieces of wood everywhere?" She motioned at the ground. A puff of her breath crystallized in the air.

"Practice." He stepped aside and motioned for her to enter. "Come on in. The sun's on the other side of the mountain and the temps are dropping." He ignored the scent of her hair—strawberry something?—as she moved inside and took stock of his quick work.

"You've done a lot in ten minutes."

He shut the door and put the barrier beam across it. "We don't have a lot and there's not much room, so…"

"I'm going to need a place to sit with the laptop. I can used the sofa, but do you have any problem with me taking up some space on that table?"

"I have something better." He pulled a beat-up TV tray from under the couch. "As long as you don't mind eating from paper plates on our laps, this is yours."

She took the pale pink aluminum apparatus from him and looked at it as if it were an alien spaceship. "What on earth is this?"

"A TV tray. Let me guess, they didn't use these in Ukraine?"

She shook her head. "No, we lived in an apartment that wasn't much bigger than this." He must have looked confused because she set the tray down and gave him an understanding smile. "I lived in a very large house—you'd call it a mansion—with my ex since I came here almost ten years ago. But before that I grew up in a block apartment building left over from Soviet times. It's what most people in the cities in Eastern Europe still live in."

"I've seen one or two." He couldn't explain those missions, not to anyone. They'd been at the highest level of security clearance with need-to-know limited to him, Claudia and the highest levels of government. Because of his limited Russian skills he'd worked with another agent. An agent who'd been killed as they'd freed an American agent held hostage by the Russian mob in St Petersburg, Russia.

"Have you?" She nodded. "Of course you have. You wouldn't be working against the ROC in this particular op if you didn't have that kind of experience with them. So you really understand their global reach." Kit wasn't asking a question; she seemed bemused, maybe even impressed.

"I do."

"Wow. Few Americans do."

"I've found that unless you're working in the military, law enforcement or cyber intelligence, there's no reason to know what all the threats are. That's the burden we accept when we take our oath."

"I didn't have the same oath as you."

"Just because you're unsworn doesn't make your role any less important. You know that."

She nodded. "I do. I just wanted to make sure you did, too." Her saucy grin made that unfamiliar thing happen in his chest again—the start of a belly laugh. As he let the mirth out, he met her sparkling gaze. A zap of awareness, right to his crotch, reminded him of the potency of their chemistry.

And they'd never so much as kissed.

Luther's grin caught her off guard, even though she'd been engaging in banter with him just like she would with fellow SVPD and TH officers and agents she worked with. Kit's breath caught, and that warm swirly sensation lined her gut again.

Did Luther know how attractive he was?

"You're complicated, Kit. I like it. Let me set up your laptop tray and then we'll figure out what to eat."

As he snapped the frame together, she decided she liked the femininely styled table. Although it was a bit rickety and rocked when she put the laptop on it.

"This will do, thank you."

"Why don't you get everything going, and I'll heat up our meal?" He fiddled with what looked like a brief-case but was in actuality a propane powered ministove.

"There's a microwave in the corner over there, under the bedding on the shelves next to the bathroom." She motioned to the far side of the cabin, past the wood-stove. The bathroom was in name only, with a tiny sink and toilet crammed into a closet. The minimal privacy made her grateful for the bathhouse.

"A microwave is a lot easier, and safer." Relief reflected in his tone and she smiled at this uncharacteristic side of him. Super secret agent, concerned about how to make a camping dinner. "Why didn't you mention it sooner?"

"I forgot. We were too busy bringing everything in." As her screen lit up and the comms software launched, she cracked her knuckles. "It doesn't look like there are a lot of hunters out here yet." Her screen reflected no more than a dozen blips, indications of cell phone use.

"There won't be until Saturday, Sunday night. The season officially opens on Monday. Everyone's with their families for Thanksgiving tonight and tomorrow."

That's right. It was only Wednesday night.

"Last year Annie and Josh had me over to make pumpkin pies on Wednesday night. Colt and Claudia had all of SVPD who were alone on Thanksgiving to their place for turkey dinner on Thursday." She hadn't told him she'd baked them a pumpkin pie for tomorrow. Thanksgiving was one of the American holidays she'd taken to since moving here. She wished she could be with her family today, but this was more important, to ensure their forever safety. They'd accepted that her work schedule wouldn't allow her to visit New Jersey this Thanksgiving.

"That sounds…cozy." He removed the bedding and dumped it on the sofa next to where she sat. "The microwave is over there because it's plugged in to the only other outlet."

"You could use this tray for it—I can operate the laptop on—"

"Your lap?" A silly play on words yet it made her giggle as if he'd pulled a dozen balloons from his pocket.

"Yes, my lap." She noted the various markers on the screen hadn't moved since she'd launched the tracking software. "This could be a long night."

"You can put an alert on your computer so that it'll wake you with any new activity, right?"

"I can, and will, when it's time to sleep. But I like to get a feel for what I'm up against when I work these kinds of ops."

"Claudia mentioned that you have your own way of doing things."

"Did she? As in, I'm not as well trained as all of you

who served in the military, or worked for FBI or CIA before you came to Trail Hikers?"

"No, not at all. She said you're the best we have against ROC, that it's to your benefit that you never served. You overlook nothing, don't assume something's not worth your time."

She snorted. "I admire Claudia, and I'm grateful to work for both SVPD and TH, but she's a little too generous with her praise at times. I know I'm capable, but I can't hold a candle to someone who's worked in intelligence or cryptology, from a global perspective."

He emptied something in a plastic container into one of the two pots she saw near the portable stove. "Ah, but just like politics, big crime usually gets taken down at the local level."

"What? I don't get it."

"They say political action, what's important, happens at the local level first. Higher-level politics can sway one way or the other, but your life will be most affected by what's going on in your small part of the world. In your case, Silver Valley Township."

"I get that. I pay income tax to the township, and expect my garbage and recycling to be taken care of, the street and lots I have to park on cleared when it snows, that kind of thing. Is that what you mean?"

"Yes. And don't forget who gets voted in at the township council level picks the Chief of Police. The County Sheriff gets elected. So your safety hinges on local politics."

She let her gaze rest on him. There was more to this undercover agent than his good looks, practical knowledge and lethal capabilities as evidenced by the array of weapons she'd watched him unload and set up. He looked up from stirring the mystery meal in the pan. "What?"

"I wouldn't expect you to be thinking about things like this—you're an operative."

He paused, and she wondered if it was from her words, or if maybe Luther had more he wanted to say but didn't know her well enough to share yet. "There's more to life than law enforcement."

"You're in a lot deeper than the average LEA officer, Luther."

"So are you. Which brings me back to you not accepting well-deserved praise. Claudia's not one to be effusive about anything. If she says you're the best, you are. It's not really about what you think or your insecurities."

Heat shot up her throat and she placed the laptop on the cushion and stood up. "I'm not insecure about my skills. I meant that I don't have anything to compare them to, whereas someone who's been in a war or other situation would be able to bring that to bear on a TH mission."

"Fair enough. But my other point, about crime being local, stands."

She crossed her arms in front of her and nodded. "I get it. Ivanov brought his ROC headquarters, or hoped to bring it, to Silver Valley. It affected the town like nothing else ever has, really. Sure, the opioid epidemic had already brought heroin here, but it ramped up to a level that necessitated an entire new hospital and trauma center being built. And he's brought in some ugly characters, including my ex. Yeah, it's local."

He didn't reply as he measured rice and water into the second pot.

"Can I help, with dinner?"

"No, not tonight. If we're here for longer than we expect, we'll trade off."

"You're taking a bigger chance on my cooking than my ability to do my comms work." She worked as she spoke, sneaking glances at his backside. Luther had broad shoulders that tapered to buttocks that she was certain his hiking trousers only hinted at.

"I do all I can to avoid chances in the field. I'm willing to take a risk on your kitchen skills."

He looked over his shoulder and smiled at her, nothing more than collegial agreement. Certainly not flirtatious. A warmth spread from her heart to her entire body, infusing her with a sense of well-being. And intense desire.

Kit looked down at her screen, breaking the moment. She'd worried that her test this mission would be managing her anxiety and stress levels, preventing an unwelcome PTSD flashback. Instead, she saw the next hours and days with Luther as a way to learn new tactics. How to keep her heart safe as she grew to know this multilayered man.

And how to keep it all professional, sexual needs safely tucked away until she was in a more appropriate setting with a man she didn't have to worry about being taken from her with each op.

Great. She was already concerned about losing Luther to his work.

For once she was grateful for ROC and her mission to help take them down. It was a legitimate distraction that would keep her from making a huge mistake.

Falling for Luther.

* * *

Markova watched Ivanov walk off from the mountain house they'd been holed up in on and off for the last several days. She needed time alone to think about what he was up to.

There was no question he wanted this meeting with what remained of East Coast ROC, his last-ditch effort to regain his throne. He relied on her for funds, and she relied on him to make the meeting happen. No way would the remaining bosses meet with her. She was persona non grata after stealing the IDs and passwords for all of Ivanov's overseas accounts. No matter that the authorities now had all but one of the accounts' security data, the one she'd kept on her person, and hadn't buried. There had to be at least one or two ROC accounts she wasn't aware of, however, or ROC would have ground to a halt after US LEA seized the lists she'd stolen.

Markova wanted, needed to become the ROC boss, just for a short time. But she couldn't do it without the man who posed the greatest threat to her plan—Ivanov. Not for one minute did she believe he didn't intend to kill her after the meeting. Either he'd be the number one again, or he'd make an escape back to New York, maybe even Russia if the FBI got too close for comfort.

When he'd made her his captive and took her on the run with him, they'd had to leave Pennsylvania and the East Coast completely for a short while, and she had to keep up the ruse that she would give him the codes to imaginary remaining offshore accounts. Since they'd come back to Pennsylvania, he'd been cagey. She'd assured him that she'd already transferred the money to several separate banks in many different countries, via a dark network of digital money laundering. That part was true. What she hadn't told him was that she'd combined all of the funds by depositing them into one American account, in her future assumed name. The new identity she'd planned to take when she left ROC, which was still her total focus.

Except it wasn't going according to her preferred timeline. She couldn't escape into her new life even if Ivanov was dead, because LEA was all over ROC at the moment, as if they had nothing else to do but take down this particular crime organization. Ideally, she'd fake her own death, to ROC and US LEA.

Ivanov's latest habit of taking phone calls on the burner phones made her nervous because it meant he was in contact with, and vulnerable to, influence from another ROC operative. She needed to maintain her manipulation of him by being his single source of comfort and reassurance.

Her other concern was that he increased their chances of being found by LEA with each phone call. She'd escaped from prison once; authorities wouldn't be so stupid a second time. Ludmilla Markova knew that if she went back to prison it would be maximum security, for life. She'd rather be dead.

Ivanov abruptly turned from the bunch of trees where he'd leaned against one and spoke, his breath puffing out in white against the dark bark. She stepped away from the window and went to the kitchen area.

His footsteps made hardly a sound on the wooden deck before he opened the door and stepped inside. Ivanov had aged; the alcoholism had ruined his liver, but in his midsixties he was as lethally diabolical as ever. She'd found that out when he'd taken her captive in the headstone factory during a shoot-out with local LEA. Markova knew she was lucky she'd convinced him she was still on his side and hadn't meant to try to usurp his authority in ROC. A lie, all of it, but he'd believed her.

"You making us a meal?" His gruff words were heavily laced with his Russian accent. He'd never shaken it, which she supposed didn't matter since he was the head of East Coast ROC. Or had been, until it looked like he'd taken all the funds and absconded with them. The higher-ups still didn't trust him.

"Starting it." She pulled beets and cut venison out of the refrigerator. They'd happened upon an Amish farm stand, a boon as it kept them from going into a regular grocery store and increasing their chances of being spotted on a security camera.

Ivanov still had his appetite for authentic borscht, which she'd learned at the elbow of her babushka. Her mother had been too busy working on the Communist Party committee she belonged to. Part of keeping Ivanov in her pocket was keeping him happy with food. As much as she resented using the gift of her babushka's recipe on him, she'd do whatever it took. It had gotten her this far.

"We're stuck here through this weekend. The American holiday of turkey." He spoke as if telling her a piece of news, shucking off his jacket.

"We expected that. We're here until we know where to meet the group." Waiting to make sure he was seated and looking a little more relaxed, she chopped the beets. The bloody red juice stained the worn wooden counter and seeped into the lines on her hands. How many people's blood was on her hands, invisible to anyone but her?

"Who were you talking to, Dima?"

"My son."

Her spine stiffened. Ivanov's son Vlad was known for his particularly cruel torture methods. Vlad was efficient and got the business of running a criminal organization done with little to no fanfare, but Markova never trusted him. She had a gut feeling that Vlad wanted his father's position and would stop at nothing to achieve it. It was prudent to consider him as much of a stumbling block to her attaining power over ROC as Ivanov.

If Ivanov was talking to Vlad, the chances of him trying to kill her were increased. She was working him, establishing the bonds that were needed to execute her final plan of escape and freedom from all she'd ever known in FSB and ROC. Her stomach tightened at what poison against her Vlad had planted in his father's psyche.

Of course, her FSB training had taught her to not rely on gut instinct as much as the facts. But the facts validated her intuition when it came to Vlad Ivanov.

"Don't look so grim as you make the borscht." Ivanov walked near her and made himself a cup of tea. "You'll spoil it." His old-world superstitions surprised her, as she knew he'd come to the US as a young adult. Apparently it had been too old to shed the peasant thinking.

"You're almost out of your buckwheat honey." There hadn't been any at the roadside stand. She'd had to pretend to be an interested customer as she filled up a small basket with root vegetables and other produce staples. The Amish family didn't bat an eye at her all-black clothing, and seemed excited to have customers this close to the holiday.

"You'll find me more, I'm sure."

Goose bumps ran down her forearms, and Markova wasn't frightened by much. Ivanov's words, spoken like a threat, confirmed that Vlad had told him to remain on guard around her, to make sure she understood he was in charge, not her.

If only she could take the butcher knife and kill him right now. But that would only lead to being chased for the rest of her life. She didn't have the time, money or other resources to stage her own death at the moment. And she didn't want to have to look over her shoulder for the rest of her years, for either ROC or American LEA.

Patience had been a key skill learned during her FSB training.

Markova continued to slice the beets, relishing the weight of the knife in her hand. Soon, with persistence and a bit of luck, she'd be free. But not yet. She could put up with this ruse for the time being.

Chapter 10

Kit stared at the contact she was listening to over headphones. It appeared as a dot on the laptop's screen, and it was a woman's voice. It could be Markova. Whoever it was spoke English with no discernible accent, and they were talking about getting the big feast ready for later tonight. Since it was now Thursday, it made sense. It could be just another hunter, though.

A hand grasped her shoulder and she jumped. It wasn't from surprise, as she'd seen Luther's shadow on the screen as he walked up behind her. Her startle reflex was a result of the warmth of his hand radiating through her merino sweater and long underwear, reaching across her chest and then up her throat and onto her face.

The man was an enigma to her. She wrenched off her headphones.

"I'm listening here." His eyes widened and he took a step back, holding his hands up in a surrender position. The exaggerated action made her laugh, and she realized how shrill her words were.

"Sorry. I go into another place when I'm working."

"I can see that. I'm the one who's sorry—do you have something we can use?"

She shook her head. "Not yet. It's difficult to find a contact we can build a search net around, as I'm sure you know. And right now I'm only intercepting people who seem to want to get drugs delivered in time for their Thanksgiving dinner tonight." Kit waved her hand at the screen. "I'm hoping it's like you said—we won't have a chance to find Ivanov and Markova until the hunters head out for opening day."

"Right. They're not going to feel comfortable talking, even on burners, until they are sure they're part of a cluster of comms."

"I did catch the end of a conversation that was in Russian, but I didn't recognize the voices and all they were talking about was buying an expensive purebred guard dog."

"That could be Ivanov."

"Maybe, but the contact never appeared on my screen. I heard it and by the time I started searching, it disappeared."

"ROC likes to use obtuse code when they're talking, especially if they're not using any kind of encryption."

Her hackles went up. "Um, I'm aware of that." She was an unsworn, not incompetent.

"Hey, I didn't mean to question your abilities."

"Then don't." She saw his brow raise but ignored it.

People-pleasing was something she left behind with the woman who'd been a victim of her ex's abuse.

"Why don't you take a break?"

"Don't you need one, too?" As soon as the words slipped out, she felt her face flush. "Wait, I'm sorry. It's none of my business what you do with your time. I'm here to support your ops, period."

Luther surprised her by laughing, a deep belly laugh that had a greater effect on her than watching a sexy actor in a love scene. "I'd be wondering what I was doing too, if I were you. You've been at it since you woke up this morning, and it probably looks like I'm not doing much but walking outside every so often."

She stood and stretched, her hips complaining with audible pops.

"Is that your back?"

"No, my hips. I sit a lot in this job and they get tight. Exercise helps. I swim a couple of times a week."

"I like to swim, too, but I prefer surfboarding."

"Really? I peg you as more of a bodybuilding type." She looked at him, saw how the muscles fought against the shirt he wore, how his thighs filled out his camouflage hunting pants. And they were supposed to be loose fitting. Saliva filled her mouth and she looked away, desperate for something else to rest her gaze on. The window with short frilly curtains caught her eye. "I could use a walk."

"Fine, but you can't go out there alone. I'll stay behind if you want me to, by several strides, but you're unprotected out here."

She eyed the gun he lifted, watched as he checked the chamber. "I'm not allowed to fire a weapon in the line of duty, but I know how to use one."

"Firing a handgun isn't the same as using a high-power weapon against a superbly trained ROC operative."

"When I was married…to my ex…" She trailed off, her chest suddenly tight. Breathe. In. Out. "I had to do something to feel like I was in control. The yarn shop, downtown, was a good escape for me, as was taking classes at HACC." At his blank expression she elaborated. "Harrisburg Area Community College. It's how I got my certification to work as an unsworn at SVPD so quickly, and why Claudia okayed me to be part of TH. Plus, the fact that I'd learned to fire every type of weapon Vadim owned, on my own without him knowing, didn't hurt." She offered him a wide grin.

Luther didn't smile back. "I'm going to wave the bs flag on that one, Kit. Claudia and Colt don't hire anyone unless they're highly qualified. Your language abilities are top-notch."

"I won't argue that." She wasn't full of conceit or arrogance—she was grounded in a place of truth, of solid self-esteem that she didn't have before she'd divorced Vadim. "But this job also requires a thorough knowledge of law enforcement and criminal justice. I loved learning about it all from the minute I began, five years ago. Way before I ever dared to hope I'd escape Vadim or his dealings with ROC." It was before she knew she'd be able to do it and come out alive. Something she wasn't ready to share with Luther.

"Was weapons training part of your criminal justice program?"

"No, but I made it so. I spent a lot of time at the firing range on the other side of the river. I couldn't do it at the range near our home, near the Appalachian

Trail. That's where Vadim and his thugs went to have a good time. They'd brag about all the weapons they'd fired, and thought I had no clue what they were talking about. But I'd fired the same guns and rifles, learned everything I could about each weapon's capabilities."

"Vadim had weapons in the house." He'd read the intelligence reports, knew the arsenal the man had.

"Sure, in a safe that he never told me the combo to. He wasn't stupid—he must have known on some level that if I had access to his weapons I'd try to kill him for what he'd done to me."

"That had to be hard."

"It wasn't easy. But it made me who I am."

Luther could listen to Kit's sultry voice all day, stay inside this tiny cabin with her and never leave. She didn't behave like any other woman he'd ever met. Of course, she was unique, having survived an arranged, human trafficking marriage to an organized crime leader.

"I admire how well you seem to have overcome what you've been through."

"There's nothing to admire when you understand that I'm lucky to be alive. Vadim would have taken me down with him, but more than him, his son would have killed me if either of them found out I was working with SVPD and then TH to bring Vadim in."

"His son, who may have been the shooter at your apartment." Luther vaguely recalled that Vadim's son had been mentioned in the reports, but he'd focused on the human trafficking ops that Vadim had facilitated, and how TH and SVPD had interfered to end the evil cycle of abuse through Silver Valley.

"Yes, Mishka. He's about forty years old now, and always saw himself as some kind of heartthrob. Mishka never made it a secret that he was interested in being more than my stepson."

"Did he ever—" It was hard enough to know Vadim had abused her for years, but to think that his son had, too, made Luther want to knock their heads together. Hard.

She shrugged as if they were discussing hunting season. "He tried, a few times, when Vadim was at work, or passed out drunk. All I had to do was remind him of the security cameras Vadim had throughout the entire house and he backed off." A flicker of vulnerability crossed her expression and he had what he thought of as operational insight.

"Mishka should be in jail, too."

She nodded. "Yes, but Vadim made sure that wouldn't happen. Someone had to be on the outside to watch the pawnshop and keep things going."

"They didn't shut down the shop?"

"At first, yes, the prosecutors put a halt to all financial dealings in Vadim's name, and some in Mishka's, too. But ROC has a lot of money and slick lawyers. The pawnshop and all of its accounts were actually in Mishka's name, a smart business move on Vadim's part. When Mishka didn't get indicted, his lawyers fought to get the pawnshop in the clear and running again."

Anger tossed around in his gut. "You're sure Mishka hasn't approached you more recently, besides in the diner?" Colt had told him about Kit seeing Mishka in the diner. He didn't want to scare her by bringing it up, but he'd been with her in her apartment, seen the flash of fear in her eyes and how she'd gone rigid after the shooter tried to take him out.

She shook her head. "No. I honestly think he didn't know where I went for a long while. I changed my last name and have kept a really low profile."

"Why didn't you consider witness protection?"

"I did, for a second. But I can't do that, because I'd never see my parents again. They're safe and enjoying life in New Jersey, closer to the city. It wasn't necessary to go into hiding, in the end. Vadim wasn't ever high-level ROC. While he provided a huge boon to their human trafficking racket, it was only a portion of their profits. Once heroin hit the market, it became their focus."

"ROC is known for revenge killings." He couldn't, wouldn't ignore the protective feelings he had toward her. ROC played for keeps.

"They're not interested in coming after me. I'm too low on their food chain. I'm not even on it, as I never participated in Vadim's dirty business." A shudder ran over her, moving her shoulders and rib cage. His arms ached to pull her to his chest, to comfort her.

Yeah, right. That's what his erection wanted, to comfort her. He mentally cleared his mind of visions of her naked. It wasn't fair to either of them, not with this op, and not now that he'd heard how rough she'd had it. A man wasn't someone she needed, it sounded like.

"I was afraid that the shooter might be Mishka, and I told Claudia we need to be watching him. I've seen him here and there, in downtown Silver Valley, over the last few months. I hadn't seen him until recently, so all I can figure is that either I'm more relaxed about my comings and goings, or he's found out where I live but is afraid to approach me because he knows I work for SVPD."

"It's probably a little bit of both." He had to let his logic take over his thoughts or he'd pack Kit up in the Jeep and head for the hills—anywhere but these hills, this mountain. The sudden streak of protectiveness stunned him as much as Kit's composure as she opened the door to her past torture.

"Yes. Mishka's an arrogant, spoiled, entitled brat at heart. He's never been told no by Vadim, and when he couldn't get what he wanted from me, he pouted. He's still got his lower lip jutting out because I refused his advances, not just when Vadim was my husband, but after. He told me to come see him at the shop as soon as the divorce was final."

"When did he do that?"

"He came up to me and my lawyer as I left the courtroom, right after I'd testified against Vadim." She looked at the window over his shoulder and squinted. "Huh. It's snowing. Kind of early for winter in Central Pennsylvania."

He followed her gaze and watched huge, fat flakes swirl in the daylight. "It's supposed to get cold, but the snow should be gone by tomorrow."

"They don't know what's coming next with the weather around here." She grabbed her camo jacket and shoved into it. "I adore snow, and I need a break from this tiny place. With or without you." She tugged a knit cap onto her head and the dark olive color emphasized her eyes. He swallowed, knowing that if they were just a man and a woman on their way for a snowy walk, he'd be tempted to kiss her.

You're already beyond tempted, man. Okay, so he'd be kissing her if she weren't a colleague.

Not true. You've enjoyed time with a colleague or two.

He had, when out in the field for months on end. It had always been a mutual release of sexual tension, with no strings attached.

Kit was a ball of twine, the epitome of entanglement.

You're not the man to make it better for her. Who was he to think she needed a man, namely him, in her life?

"I'll be waiting. Take your time." Kit went out the door, and he gave himself the time it took to put his outerwear on and to shake out of the hormone haze he'd been in the last several hours. Kit was an attractive woman, and her wry sense of humor matched his—not something that happened often. She'd be the perfect person to develop a relationship with, if... If he wasn't an undercover agent who never knew where he'd be from one week to the next. If she wasn't the survivor of an abusive marriage and human trafficking. He didn't know Kit very well, but he knew enough.

Kit needed a man who'd be there for her through thick and thin. He wasn't that guy.

You want to be.

He zipped up his jacket and reached for the cabin door. Now came the tough part—following through on what he'd decided, ignoring the constant thrum of tension between him and Kit. And his unexpected attraction to the woman who'd survived a life that had been a death sentence for so many others.

"You really don't have to be my babysitter. I hike the Appalachian Trail—the AT—all the time on my own." She stayed several strides ahead of Luther, more for her own sanity than to show him that she was in great shape. Nothing she was boastful about, but Kit took her physical fitness seriously. Strength and being capable of handling herself in stressful situations was part of her PTSD therapy.

Luther had stayed close behind her the entire hike. They made it to the top of a rise that gave them a sweeping view of Cumberland Valley, and she couldn't ignore the warmth from his body heat through both of their quilted down hunting jackets, even at several inches apart. At this point she was so turned on by him she didn't know if it really was his body heat she felt or her own need.

"Your sexual awareness will awaken when you least expect it."

Kit ground her teeth, wishing she were alone so she could scream out in frustration.

"This is stunning." Luther looked at the valley below as if he'd never been anywhere as beautiful as Cumberland Valley. The frosty cloud of his breath parted the snowflakes, and his chest rose and fell in a mesmerizing rhythm. His ski cap covered most of his wavy brown hair, save for a few locks at his nape. Most of the TH and SVPD agents she'd worked with sported military cuts.

"Is your hair long because you've been undercover recently?"

His eyes were steely in the dim light, and snowflakes clung to his crazy long eyelashes. Why was it that men were awarded with what she'd paid good money to get at the local salon?

"I'm rarely *not* undercover, in a sense. Especially the last couple of years."

"ROC?" Colt had said as much, but maybe Luther had done other work.

He didn't answer right away, and his full lips looked ridiculously soft amidst his day-old stubble. Did he affect that look for their hunting cover or was it his regular grooming standard?

When his mouth curved, she forced her gaze back to his. Amusement folded the lines at the edges of his eyes like the accordion her Uncle Slava used to play at family gatherings. An ache that she'd only ever associated with being homesick welled up, and she fought to stay in the present, to not allow her melancholy to rule her life as it once had.

"Yes, mostly ROC. Exclusively for the last two years." He looked away, and she fought to keep her hands from reaching for his face, forcing his attention back on her.

But the tension between them was nothing less than excruciating. Did she really want that back, want to be in the whirlwind of emotions that he stirred?

Yes.

She forced her gaze back to the valley, which, through the snow, looked like a gently smudged version of itself. If she followed Luther's lead, she'd get through this. He didn't appear to have anything tugging at his instincts other than tracking down Ivanov and Markova. Luther knew how to stay on point.

"So many agents have done the same, sacrificed too much." She thought of the dozens she'd met and worked with in only the past couple of years. "I can't wait to see ROC completely dismantled."

"Do you believe it will ever be wiped out? We both know how far and wide their web is, as you mentioned."

"I'm Ukrainian. Was. For a long time, I couldn't imagine life without the constant threat of ROC. Now that I'm American, by choice, I have hope we'll finish this op and wipe them out. It's a matter of time."

"You weren't brought here by your own will." He'd decided to ask now, to dig deeper. Fair enough. She had nothing to hide from him. And curiously, Kit wanted Luther to understand her better.

"That's not true, about being forced to the States. At first, I did come here on my own. I signed up for an au pair training course."

"Your parents agreed to it, when you were underage?"

"Spoken like an American. Even with all of your ROC experience and knowledge, you don't get how clever they can be. The course was supposedly a two-year affair. We attended workshops on Sundays for three hours each. At the end of two years we'd be certified to be au pairs either in the UK or North America." The wind picked up and she wiped snow off her face. "My parents thought it might be a wonderful opportunity for me. I learned German and English in school and already knew Russian and of course Ukrainian."

"When did it go wrong?" He spoke quietly, as though he knew it was tender ground.

"The second month. Looking back, I know that they 'sorted' us all that first Sunday. Figured out who would go where and when. I was one of the luckiest girls— I got to come here sooner!" She heard the sarcasm in her voice and pulled back. "Sorry. It's not a time I really enjoy discussing."

"Then don't." His hand grasped hers, and her fingers automatically curled around his. Through the layers of his leather and her knit gloves there was an indisputable sense of security. Like she'd been waiting for this kind of closeness with another human being forever. "Let's keep walking. We have about another two hours of daylight."

This time she followed him, winding through the tall pines, climbing over the multitude of rock outcroppings that were ubiquitous in Pennsylvania. She figured Luther to be maybe eight years older than her, tops. Yet he was as agile as a man younger than her.

"How old are you, Luther?"

He stopped and looked over his shoulder at her. "Thirty-one. Why? How old are you?" He was younger, closer in age to her, than she'd thought.

"Twenty-six. But I feel like I'm one hundred."

"That's fair. You don't look much older than twenty-seven."

She stared at him, shocked that he was actually making a joke at her expense. Laughter escaped her, and she let go of the ugliness of their earlier conversation and the memories it scraped up. "I have enough life experience to satisfy an old woman, that's for sure."

"Ah, but Kit, you forget the gift from your sufferings." He was serious again, and he backtracked the few feet to stand in front of her, no more than a foot between them.

"Gift?" Was he about to tell her she was strong, a survivor? Because she'd heard it all during her therapy and group sessions. And yes, she knew she'd had to dig deep to get through it all. Especially toward the end of her marriage, when she'd played both sides. She'd

Loyal Readers
FREE BOOKS Voucher

We're giving away THOUSANDS of FREE BOOKS

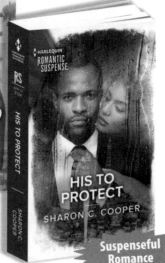

Suspense

Suspenseful Romance

Don't Miss Out! Send for Your Free Books Today!

Get up to 4
FREE FABULOUS BOOKS
You Love!

To thank you for being a loyal reader we'd like to send you up to 4 FREE BOOKS, absolutely free.

Just write "YES" on the Loyal Reader Voucher and we'll send you up to 4 Free Books and Free Mystery Gifts, altogether worth over $20, as a way of saying thank you for being a loyal reader.

Try **Harlequin® Romantic Suspense** books featuring heart-racing page-turners with unexpected plot twists and irresistible chemistry that will keep you guessing to the very end.

Try **Harlequin Intrigue® Larger-Print** books featuring action-packed stories that will keep you on the edge of your seat. Solve the crime and deliver justice at all costs.

Or **TRY BOTH!**

We are so glad you love the books as much as we do and can't wait to send you great new books.

So don't miss out, return your Loyal Reader Voucher Today!

Pam Powers

LOYAL READER
FREE BOOKS VOUCHER

YES! I Love Reading, please send me up to 4 FREE BOOKS and Free Mystery Gifts from the series I select.

Just write in "YES" on the dotted line below then return this card today and we'll send your free books & gifts asap!

➡ YES ⬅

Which do you prefer?

| ☐ **Harlequin® Romantic Suspense** 240/340 HDL GRHP | ☐ **Harlequin Intrigue® Larger-Print** 199/399 HDL GRHP | ☐ **BOTH** 240/340 & 199/399 HDL GRHZ |

FIRST NAME   LAST NAME

ADDRESS

APT.#   CITY

STATE/PROV.   ZIP/POSTAL CODE

EMAIL ☐ Please check this box if you would like to receive newsletters and promotional emails from Harlequin Enterprises ULC and its affiliates. You can unsubscribe anytime.

▼ If offer card is missing write to: Harlequin Reader Service, P.O. Box 1341, Buffalo, NY 14240-8531 or visit www.ReaderService.com ▼

BUSINESS REPLY MAIL
FIRST-CLASS MAIL   PERMIT NO. 717   BUFFALO, NY

POSTAGE WILL BE PAID BY ADDRESSEE

HARLEQUIN READER SERVICE
PO BOX 1341
BUFFALO NY 14240-8571

NO POSTAGE
NECESSARY
IF MAILED
IN THE
UNITED STATES

given TH and SVPD what they needed in order to capture Vadim and his cohorts and free the women he'd most recently been involved with trafficking. At the same time she'd pretended to be happy with Vadim, as if nothing was amiss. Other than the usual sense of foreboding, knowing that with his next binge he'd put his hands on her again, beat her, threaten to kill her.

Vadim had been a mean, mean drunk.

"Stay here with me, Kit. In the now." His gaze was intent on her. "I'm sorry I asked about your past—I didn't mean to stir it all up or upset you."

"You didn't do anything wrong. It's fair for you to want to know more about the person you're working with. Especially on such a critical op."

"So let me tell you what I see in you, Kit. The gift you received."

She sucked in a breath and was surprised that her lungs shuddered as she did so. As if what Luther was about to say was going to make all the difference in her life.

"What, Luther?"

"You know who you are. No one is going to tell you what you want, where you want to go. Some people go their entire life and never figure that out."

His words touched a chord she'd left protected, hidden under layers of her heart's scar tissue. She blinked against the swell of tears, hoping he'd think it was from the snow.

She let out a short, humorless laugh. "I think I wouldn't complain if I hadn't had to figure out who I am so soon, if ever."

Luther regarded her with a look that she could only interpret as honest. Not pitying, not patronizing, nor detached. He'd listened to her, heard between the words she'd spoken. Had he ever thought about becoming a therapist?

"I know. And if I could change what you'd been through, I would do it in a heartbeat." He'd taken a half step closer, or maybe she had. Gloved fingers wiped the tears from her cheeks. "I don't know a whole heck of a lot, Kit, but I've come to understand that while I can't change most of the world's ills, if I get a chance to make a difference for one person or one community, it's worth it. You're doing that—you've channeled what happened to you into a career of service."

"Did I have a choice?" Her voice fell to a whisper. Standing this close to a man who read her better than anyone else ever had, after only knowing him for forty-eight hours, seemed like more than a work assignment to her.

It felt like fate. When Luther placed his forehead to hers, their breath intermingling, she didn't resist.

"I've been through my own hell, too, Kit. Nothing like what you've faced, but I've seen things most people would never imagine. It can be lonely in that place of dealing with your own reality."

"Yes." She sighed out her response and her body swayed toward him. Tired of fighting her desires, she placed her gloved hands on either side of his face and forced him to look into her eyes. "Thank you for letting me know I'm not alone, Luther."

His answer was immediate and not of the verbal variety. When his lips touched hers, she was still looking into his eyes and saw something deeper than curiosity or commiseration. Before she could figure out what it was, his lids lowered and she followed suit.

Tentative, feather-like touches to her lips with his tongue made her mouth tingle and sent the sensation down her throat, deep into her core. The warm, insistent pulse between her legs let her know that this wasn't a chaste, conciliatory gesture. On either of their parts.

"Kit." He spoke against her mouth, giving her a chance to pull back. Kit wrapped her hands around his neck and tugged his face closer, standing on tiptoe to press her mouth firmly against his. When she opened her mouth, he groaned and his hands reached around her waist, pulling her in close by pressing on her lower back. The throbbing in her most private parts turned into an all-out need.

Her gasp escaped the kiss, and Luther's head lifted. It took all of her willpower to not cry out at the loss of his heat, the sheer pleasure of this moment, more powerful than anything she'd ever experienced with a man before.

"Kit." He crushed her head to his chest, and they stood together in the forest, their breathing uneven and audible as snow fell around them.

Kit didn't know what to do. She'd had plenty of training from her ex in how to sexually please a man, but she'd never had to be concerned about her own response. With Vadim she'd done what she'd had to, putting her satisfaction on the back burner. Even in the midst of the worst days with her ex, she'd retained enough self-respect to not look for sexual release with him. He was a pig, pure and simple.

Luther was everything Vadim could never be. Which made him all the more dangerous, because in one short kiss Luther had made her more vulnerable than ever.

Chapter 11

Luther took the few moments he needed to get his thoughts back in order after kissing Kit.

What the heck was wrong with him? He never, ever veered from his mission plan. Kit wasn't a seasoned undercover colleague who had no problem with a quick fling. With her, the stakes were high. Kissing her hadn't been on the table. He'd told himself as much before he walked out of the cabin.

The pressure of her hands on his chest snapped him back to cold reality, and he let his arms drop from where they'd held her tight. Kit's face was beet red, and she looked like a kid who'd stolen the last cookie from the jar. Guilt tore at him, knowing he'd somehow made her feel embarrassed about her response to him.

"Kit, let me apologize. I crossed way too many boundaries here."

She met his gaze with clear eyes that sparked with the vitality he'd noticed in Colt's office. "Yeah, I'd say our professional boundaries are about three miles back, over your left shoulder." Her sardonic smile was like a mirror—he'd given this same kind of response to other women. But Kit was the woman and he was the guy. He had experience, life lessons about intimate relationships she'd yet to explore.

And yet she was treating him like he was the in-genue.

"It won't happen again." The words were automatic, and he fought to ignore the erection that didn't compre-hend the meaning of *mission first*. "You shared some deep memories with me, and I don't want you to think I was taking advantage of your vulnerability."

"My vulnerability?" She shook her head like he was a beginner in the game of life. "Luther, my vul-nerability ended the day I decided to get out of my slave-marriage with Vadim. I haven't gone through years—yes, *years*—of counseling and medical ther-apy to not know the difference between sharing an intimacy with you and being weak or naive. Trust me, you didn't take advantage of me. In fact, how do you know I wasn't using you to get what I need?"

"Wh-what you need?"

"Yeah. Just as I thought." She shook her head. "Women have needs, too. We're out here in this god-forsaken place with nothing to do but track down the bad guys, except the bad guy hasn't shown yet, and probably won't until Saturday or Sunday. Did it ever occur to you that I'm just as able as you are to have a no-strings relationship?" Her spine had to be made of steel and he felt himself losing purchase, falling for the very woman he couldn't. Kit needed more than he could ever giver her, deserved more.

"Except we both agree that we can't do this. Not during this op. And…and how do you know that I have no-strings hookups?"

She guffawed. "Please. You're still single at thirty-one—you're undercover most of the time. How else are you going to get much-needed physical release?"

He stared at her, a quick response on his tongue, but despite her candid talk, he couldn't shake the need to use his manners around her. He couldn't bring himself to explain, in succinct detail, how he took care of his "needs" when lacking a woman to share themwith.

But Kit already knew, he had no doubt.

The large sprawling prison complex stamped a grim snarl on the rolling hills of Northern Pennsylvania. Mishka lowered his visor against the sun as it glinted off the concertina wire, coiled on top of the eighteen-foot barbed wire fencing. He reminded himself that there was no busting his father out of here. Markova's escape from county jail last year had been an anomaly that would be impossible to repeat. Vadim could have gotten out of the county jail, maybe, with a lot of help from ROC or at least a couple of very expensive lawyers.

But not after his trial, not from this fortress.

The federal prison facility was going to be Vadim's home for the rest of his quality years. His sentence had been for twenty-five years to life, but even if he came up for parole in fifteen years, he'd be an octogenarian. Mishka didn't think his father was going to make it that long. He'd never been one to take care of himself in the first place, and prison living hit him especially hard.

Mishka showed the requisite identification and went through several checkpoints before being led to a utilitarian area that had a dozen or so tables scattered with visiting family members. Picking a table farthest from an occupied one, he slinked into a cold plastic orange chair and waited for Vadim to be led in.

The man whom the guards released into the reception room was a shadow of the ROC operative who'd kept an iron fist on Silver Valley just a couple years ago. Gaunt and unshaven, Vadim's dull gaze lit up when he recognized Mishka.

"Son!" The guard placed him in the chair across from Mishka. Mishka knew the rules—no touching, no hugging, not even a handshake. He knew that the average American wouldn't understand, but in their Russian culture, the custom of three cheek kisses, followed by a bear hug, was central to the expression of affection.

"Dad." He hoped just being here would cheer the bastard up. Not that he cared that deeply, as Vadim had been as tough on him as he'd been on Kit. But it was hard not to have compassion for the broken man who sat across from him. "I brought you some treats—the guards will get them to you."

"They didn't give me the vodka last time."

Mishka swore. "I brought enough for a New Year's party."

Vadim shrugged. "The staff had the party, not me, and certainly none of the other inmates."

"Are you doing okay, considering?"

"I'm stuck in this hellhole until my dying breath. How do you think I'm doing?"

"I haven't found Ivanov yet, but I will."

At this, the light in Vadim's gaze returned, reminding Mishka of how tough the man was. "Damn right you will. We need him to bring in the big guns and get me out of here."

"Dad, you know I want that more than anyone. But even the best lawyers might not be able to help you with your time."

"They will. ROC always wins."

Mishka bit back the reply that Vadim wouldn't listen to, anyhow. Ivanov wasn't winning at the moment. Not if no one in ROC knew where he was.

"No one has seen Ivanov in months, Dad. They think Markova is with him, but he may have killed her by now."

"Why would he kill his best agent?" Vadim rubbed his stubble jaw. "No, you mark my words, Markova is still here, and she's the key to Ivanov's survival."

"Why do you think that?" This was the first Mishka had heard of this. The word amongst lower-level ROC workers like him was that Markova had stolen funds from Ivanov that left the East Coast ROC frozen, hurting for cash flow.

"Markova is the most violent, lethal agent ever seen outside of Russia. She escaped the FSB and used the oligarchs to protect her—several of them are tied into New York ROC."

"So?"

"You are too American, Mishka. You only know the stories of KGB and FSB. You never saw how effective, how brutal they are when it comes to business." Vadim emphasized *brutal* so strongly that his spittle hit Mishka's lips. "Markova is the one with the power now, not Ivanov. Find her, let her know you're obedient to her, and you'll have whatever we need to get me out of here."

"She escaped from prison, that's certain." Mishka had been as stunned as noncriminals when the reports of how she'd smuggled heroin laced with fentanyl into the county prison and had made sure the packets had fentanyl on the outside of the plastic wrapping. The drug had entered the guard's systems through skin contact and disabled an entire shift in a matter of minutes. Markova had used the window to escape and she was still on the run, after attempting murder and conducting random thefts for petty cash.

"She's the one you need to find, my son, not Ivanov. Although he'll be with her, it's true. He has no choice."

"Do you have any idea where they are, Dad?" He knew his father still had sources both inside and outside who kept him informed. Mishka had a rough time getting anything out of anyone in ROC anymore. Since Vadim went to jail, it was as if the ROC on the outside didn't trust Mishka anymore.

"I might. But you have to be very, very careful. If Ivanov knows that you've discovered his one ultimate hideout, he'll kill you on the spot. You're going to have to get to Markova first, pledge your loyalty to her, not Ivanov. Remember this, Mishka."

"I will."

Over the next several minutes they talked about random everyday things. It was to throw the guards and listeners off their scent. They'd said nothing that LEA didn't already know. Although Mishka doubted they had any clue about where Ivanov's fort was. He'd have read about the ROC leader's arrest or seen it on the news.

"It's going to be open hunting season in a few days. Will you get a deer for the year like we used to?"

Mishka and his father had never hunted only for deer. This was his father's code for letting him know he was about to give him the clues about Ivanov's hideout.

"I hope so. It's always much more economical than shopping for beef in the local grocery stores."

Vadim laughed but it sounded like a snarl. "Remember when we took down the buck near the hunting village?"

Mishka knew this was the part he had to listen to. He leaned in and memorized everything Vadim told him. By the time he stood up to say goodbye to his father, he was certain he knew where Ivanov hid.

"Goodbye, Dad."

"See you next month?" A guard held Vadim's elbow, and his father's pitiful expression made Mishka think for a nanosecond that the man had been dealt too harsh a hand. By the time he said so long and ambled out to the visitor parking lot, memories from when he'd been born thirty-nine years ago until now came flooding back.

He turned the key in his sleek sports coupe and headed for the highway. While he didn't live in a prison and had a much softer bed than his father, Mishka had always felt like his heart was imprisoned. He'd never known his mother—she'd been Vadim's only other wife besides Kit and had died shortly after his birth. Vadim told him to never ask about it. As a kid he'd thought it was because it was too sad to talk about. But once he realized he was part of the ROC, under his father, he learned the truth from another operative. Vadim had killed Mishka's mother when he'd found out she'd had an affair with a local police officer. It'd been an unforgivable offense. Once married to ROC, you knew you'd die with them.

Vadim had gotten away with it because of his learned expertise in wiping out evidence. It was the hallmark of an ROC member.

Mishka used to hate Vadim for killing his mother. Even if she'd been a cheating bitch, she'd been the one to give him life. But now that he understood Kit was working with SVPD, he knew she was around men all the time. It would be natural for her to become involved with a police officer. Just like his mother.

He didn't know who the man was who'd been in her apartment and he didn't care. All that concerned him was that he hadn't been successful in killing him. He'd had a contact watch her building the rest of that night and the next morning.

Kit had left with the man the next day. His contact hadn't been able to follow them—the strange man had driven and had evaded the ROC man. Which made it pretty clear to Mishka that Kit was with a cop, but where?

He had to find her. Whatever she did for SVPD, it was probably about ROC, which right now meant it had to do with Ivanov and Markova, as the entire LEA community seemed to be after them. How many times in the last six months had he and his employees at the pawnshop been questioned, warned that if they had any contact with either Ivanov or Markova they were obligated to report it?

Mishka figured that wherever Ivanov was with Markova, Kit and the man were close by. Were they holed up in a tent, or in an unmarked police vehicle? Images of the jerk's hands on Kit made Mishka's blood boil.

Good thing his contact had managed to place GPS emitters on all the vehicles in the parking lot behind Kit's apartment, and on the vehicles parked in the street in front of the building. It was a matter of time before they figured out which vehicle hadn't come back and then traced it to where Kit was. He'd have her back in no time. And kill the police officer she was with.

His hands tightened on the steering wheel and he turned his music on. Heavy metal crashed through state-of-the-art speakers, crowding out his angry thoughts. But not enough to keep him from focusing on one thing.

Kit.

"Did Colt or Claudia have anything new?" Kit spoke to Luther from her laptop station next to the rack of comms equipment. They'd gotten back to work as soon as they'd returned, leaving the kiss and its aftermath on the trail.

After a few hours, Luther had gone outside and used an advanced piece of technology that was TH's version of a burner phone, with a signal scrambler, to call in.

He took off his jacket and placed it on one of two hooks near the door. "Not specifically, no. We still don't know where Ivanov is."

"But?"

He paused, his mouth a thin line. "We have agents in place in the prison where Vadim is, up north. We know that he's still in comms with some of the ROC operatives, including his son."

"The federal prison, I know." She took her headset all the way off. There had been no new movement on any of the contacts on her screen for the past hour. "It's okay to bring Vadim up, Luther. It doesn't turn me into a puddle."

"Of course it doesn't. But he can't be your favorite topic."

"If it helps us catch Ivanov and bring down ROC, it doesn't matter how many times we have to talk about him." Surprisingly, she wasn't putting on a face for professional reasons. She meant it. "So what about my ex?" She didn't have to say his name, though.

"He's been visited most regularly by his son. They bribe the guards with vodka, but that's standard. So far we have nothing extraordinary to report." Luther's concern vibrated off him, and she wanted to stand and put her hand on his arm, or his shoulder, but that wasn't possible. Not if she wanted to avoid another embrace. Or more, if her body's heated response to his presence was a precursor.

"Mishka has always been loyal to his father." She spat the words, knowing that the same loyalty was probably all that had kept her from being raped by the man. Plus she suspected Mishka had suffered at Vadim's hands as a boy. Mishka, like her, had a healthy fear of his father.

"They are planning something. We're not sure what, and there's no way Vadim can ever expect to escape his sentence. A breakout is out of the question, and no lawyer will ever get him off early, on appeal. He's truly locked up for life."

"And?"

"That leaves Ivanov. Mishka was there today, at the prison, and the agent thinks that Vadim gave him a clue as to where Ivanov is."

"So we wait for Mishka to go there, and then move in?"

"That's just it. If our agent figured this out, there's a good chance another ROC operative will also and let Ivanov know he's being watched."

"And he'll run, disappear again."

"Right." Frustration etched deep lines on either side of Luther's mouth. She'd turned the single bare bulb lamp on, and the woodstove had a glass front that gave off a decent glow that helped light the small single room.

"I've been up against tougher odds before, Luther, and have found the bad guy. Ivanov and Markova are bound to start talking at any point after the other hunters show up. As soon as they do, we'll catch them."

His brow rose. "Are you always this positive?"

"Annoying, isn't it?" She gave him a grin, and was rewarded with an answering twinkle in his eyes. But his mouth remained downturned, the weight of their mission clearly affecting him.

"Hey, why don't we take a break and get some dinner? You said you already cooked the turkey?"

He nodded. "I did." Leaning down he flipped open one of the coolers and pulled out a large aluminum foil–wrapped tray. "I was going heat this up on the woodstove."

"You—you weren't kidding? You really made a turkey?"

"Why would I joke about Thanksgiving? I brought

both sweet and mashed potatoes, too. They'd be too difficult to cook here and I didn't want to settle for just one kind."

Her mouth watered and her stomach rumbled. "I'll help. Tell me what to do."

They worked side by side in the cramped area for the next half hour, heating up the food.

"If you go in the cooler, there's some dressing and sweet potatoes." Luther was opening a can of cranberry sauce.

"Is there nothing you didn't do for this meal?" She'd never experienced a sense of holiday festivity since she'd left Ukraine. Memories of working around the lumbering stove in her babushka's dacha flooded her mind, and she sank onto her haunches, her hand on the cooler lid.

"You okay?"

"I'm good. Just reminiscing about my childhood." She had to stop letting her thoughts roll off her tongue around Luther. But again, she didn't experience the feeling of vulnerability or shame she would have with another stranger. It wasn't just because she'd taken the time to heal from her ordeal.

Luther was different.

"It's natural to do that on a holiday, even when you're working." He moved pans around on the woodstove. "Have you ever seen your family again?"

"Oh, yes, of course! I even got to bring them over after I married Vadim. He allowed me to do that, at least. Of course he threatened to kill me if I ever told them I hadn't married him willingly. Plus I was afraid he'd hurt them. He said he'd kill all of us if I ever tried to run."

"Is that why you didn't you try to escape, tell the authorities, go back to Ukraine?"

"Partly. It's the paradox of being in an abusive relationship. I feared Vadim, and I also got into the victim mentality that was as much my bond as was his abuse."

"I'm sorry, Kit."

She walked the two steps to him and handed him the foil-covered sweet potatoes. "About what? It's not your fault."

"I'm sorry you ever had to go through that. That any woman has to." Regret and frustration mingled on his expression.

"That's why you, I, we do what we do. Right?" She looked from the hands that had taken the sweet potatoes from her to his eyes and immediately took a half step back. Being this close to his rugged face, the eyes that told her so much more than his words, was as dangerous as the piping hot woodstove. More so.

"I suppose." He looked away, and when he lifted the foil off the potatoes, she saw the marshmallow topping. "I didn't get pumpkin pie. Time ran short and I forgot. These sweet potatoes will be our dessert." He sounded as if he'd failed her immeasurably, and she couldn't help but giggle.

"Oh, please. Stop being so glum. I brought pie."

His turned to her, eyes widened. "You did? Pumpkin pie?"

"I did. Of course I thought I was being so clever, slipping in a Thanksgiving treat to enjoy between our canned soup and beans. I had no idea you were such a homemaker."

His smile was tempered by seriousness. Did he ever let go and chill? "Not a homemaker. I'm a decent cook and I enjoy it. But a home—that's not something I've had for the last decade. Nothing permanent, anyway."

"Aren't you tired of the constant moving?"

"Sometimes. Actually I never felt the need to settle down. It seemed like a boring choice, something that would interfere with my career."

"It sounds as if you're reconsidering?"

Luther stilled, as if she'd told him something life changing. "Not on a conscious level."

Kit let his statement stand, naked and honest, without reply. She understood needing to figure out what was best for herself. How many times had her therapist or Annie discovered a part of her changing before she was ready to acknowledge it?

Luther lifted a fork to his mouth and tasted the mashed potatoes. Without missing a beat he added salt and pepper and stirred with the single large wooden spoon.

"You even brought over-the-top cooking supplies."

He shrugged. "One spoon can do a lot of things."

"I don't believe you, you know."

Blue eyes directed at her, wariness in their depths. "About what?"

"Not wanting to settle down. Sure, I get that you like being on the go, and traveling is probably in your blood since you do it so much. But you don't get as far as you have in life and not find someone special. Have you ever been married?"

"You don't mince words, do you?" The frosty overtones returned to his voice. She'd overstepped.

Just when Luther was showing his human self.

Chapter 12

Luther hoped that by puttering at the stove he'd hide how much Kit's query shook him.

Puttering? For freckles sake, he didn't *putter*. Ever.

"I'm sorry, Luther. Forget I asked that. It's absolutely none of my business. It has to be the long hours and isolation that's bringing out our inquisitive natures. Let's stop and focus on our Thanksgiving feast." She was at his side, but left a foot between them, enough room to demonstrate she posed no threat.

A strangled laugh lodged in his throat. How had this woman, Kit, turned him upside down in the space of a day or two?

"It's a fair question." He moved back to the small propane stove, the door to the cabin open a crack to facilitate ventilation. It gave him a bit more space, keeping the temptation to hug her to him at a minimum.

Funny how just a bit ago it would have been him comforting Kit, but now he needed, wanted, her comfort.

You can't entertain the thought.

No, he couldn't. Like cookies, that one kiss had him craving a dozen more. He'd never stop at a kiss with her again. He leaned against the doorjamb and faced her.

"I've had a few fairly serious relationships, but only one that made me think I was going to seek a different kind of job with TH. Not so much undercover work, maybe do intelligence analysis or training for them. I'd always thought that if I ever met someone I wanted more than a night or a couple of months with, I'd get out of this part of the business."

"Why? What if you met someone who also worked undercover?" *Zing.* She'd hit eerily close to the truth.

"Do you already know my past?" Claudia and Colt had given him a brief rundown of what Kit had dealt with, leaving out the more intimate details that she'd later filled in, of course. He couldn't expect them to not let her know a little about who she was assigned to spend time with, alone, in the woods.

She blinked and shook her head as if he was silly to even consider she knew his past. It made the weight of his need to protect her heavier. Claudia wouldn't have mentioned Kit's past if she didn't expect him to look out for his new colleague.

"Not at all. Why would they tell me anything so personal?" The tiny lines between her brows appeared, and he swore he saw her wheels turning, the cogs of her mind falling into place. "Wait—they told you about me, didn't they? And Vadim?"

He went to her then and led her to the sofa, where he tugged her down next to him. This wasn't a conversation to have standing up, as if they were talking about the weather. "They didn't say a lot, just enough to let me know that you weren't a rookie when it came to ROC."

"I feel so stupid. Why didn't you tell me when we talked about it?" Even in the dim light he saw the red on her cheekbones and keenly felt her embarrassment for the second time.

"Please don't look at it that way. I wanted to hear your part of it, whatever you were willing to tell me. I still do. But I don't want to pry, or stir up parts of your past that you've put to rest."

"They didn't tell me anything about you." She bit her lower lip.

"Colt might not know. Claudia does." He looked at her eyes, luminous in the lamplight. Even after all she'd seen and been through, he felt the waves of innocence coming off her, as if she'd somehow, through her fathomless strength, saved a precious part of herself. The part that Vadim's abuse could never touch. A deep, honest part of himself wanted to be the one she shared that with.

"What does Claudia know, Luther?"

"That I was in love with a woman I never should have looked at twice. The wife of one of the ROC targets I went undercover to take out."

"Did you get him?"

"Yes. But she was killed in the firefight that ended the mission."

Kit gasped and compassion immediately flooded her eyes.

"I'm so, so sorry, Luther."

"Don't be. The heartbreak isn't that she died. We

were over before that. I found out that she was playing me, and it almost cost me my life, and my team's. We were imbedded with the gang in New York for the better part of a year. There were four of us. I thought she was the real deal, and maybe, for a brief time, she was. But she'd been a mob wife for too long. Unlike you, she'd known what she married into, had searched it out, in fact. Some people like the thrill of the power and status that money brings no matter where it comes from. She had learned to lie out of both sides of her mouth, too easily. When push came to shove, she didn't trust me to get her out of there, and in the end, she didn't want to leave. She died next to her husband of twenty years."

"She was older than you."

"By only six years. As you know too well, ROC thugs like to marry younger women, girls."

"They do." Her agreement came out on a breath. He looked at her, but the pity he expected was nonexistent. Kit watched him with the understanding only a woman who'd been involved with ROC could have. "It's not your fault, you know. That you loved her. We don't get to pick who we love or don't."

"You sound like you've loved and lost, Kit."

"I've felt the loss of my childhood dreams, and it was a heartbreak a day living with Vadim. But unlike you, I've never met that one person who made me think there was no one else for me." She let out a harsh laugh. "I have to admit I don't believe in one person for everyone. Not after what I lived through."

It was the first time he detected any regret from her about what she'd survived. "That might change with time. You're still so young."

"I've lived more lives in my years than most do in fifty." She stood and brushed her hands along her thighs as if trying to sweep away the intimacy that continued to grow between them. "Let me check the comms before we sit down to eat."

"You've got the alerts set, right?" He'd used the same equipment before, although he didn't have the depth of expertise Kit did with it.

"Yes." Her face glowed from the blue-green screen. "I always keep an eye on it when I'm in the middle of an op, though. You're right—we're probably not going to get anything useful until Ivanov's comfortable that there are enough hunters in the area to cover his conversations. But we can always hope. He might think he needs to talk to someone at any time."

"True." He stood. "I do want to say one more thing, Kit. While I've figured out that my future doesn't include settling down and finding that special someone, that doesn't mean I don't believe it's not possible for others. Look at Colt and Claudia. Their relationship is legendary."

Her lips moved into a soft smile. "They met later in life. Long after the time most folks fall in love, or think that romance is even a remote possibility."

"What does that have to do with anything?"

"You think you're done with finding someone, Luther, but maybe you just have to wait another twenty years."

A sense of uneasiness shot through him. Followed by a strong jolt of lust.

Luther didn't want to wait twenty years to find a woman who made him feel this strongly after only knowing one another such a short time. He turned to the woodstove, removing the heated ceramic dishes from the surface to the tiny tray table and rickety kitchen counter. It would be disastrous if Kit saw his expression, as he was certain his regret glowed like a neon sign.

He'd regret not having more with Kit than a shared mission in this tiny cabin.

"Do you think that's such a good idea, Dima?" Markova hated playing the good little Russian woman, but it was her greatest tool against Ivanov at this point. He'd grown moody and petulant as the hours went by, and his boredom had reached a peak as he pulled out yet another one of the burner phones from the black plastic bag.

"They're not going to expect we're here, and if they do, good luck finding us because this place is about to be loaded with hunters from all over the state."

"The majority of who will arrive beginning tomorrow through Sunday. Not tonight."

"I can wait until tomorrow morning to make my next call, but that's it."

"We're closer to the meeting, then?"

His dark, deep set eyes landed on her as if he, too, were beyond tired of being with her. "*Da*. No more than a week away, at most two. We'll have it all back to how it was."

"Finally. As it should be." Markova's jaw hurt from clenching her teeth against what she wanted to say, what she wished she could do. Kill Ivanov and head for the hills. But she'd still have the entire ROC after her if she did that. No, her escape had to be when it was best for her, after Ivanov was taken out by his own.

She'd be in charge for only as long as it took to be able to disappear for good.

Until then, she waited.

Never the outdoors type, Mishka surprised himself with how much fun driving into the wilder part of Central Pennsylvania was. At night, on Thanksgiving. Most people were sleeping off turkey and vodka on the sofa. He was on his way to his destiny.

It was too easy. He'd had to make three calls, promise fifty percent of the payout for the heroin and fentanyl shipments due in next week to his contact, but he'd found out where Kit was. His contact gave him the GPS location of a Jeep and texted him a photo of the vehicle taken when it was parked near Kit's apartment building.

Stupid SVPD and the FBI. They thought they had the ROC nailed down and driven out of Silver Valley. Just wait until he had Kit at his side, and they picked up Vadim's pieces.

LEA had caught his father, sure, but Vadim wasn't the brightest candle in the window. Even though he'd never met his mother, Mishka credited his intelligence and ability to stay calm under any circumstance to her. It sure wasn't from Vadim.

He parked his car in the pullout marked for hikers and backpacking campers. There were few vehicles tonight, but he knew the deer hunting season began Monday. This lot would be full by tomorrow morning, but he and Kit would be long gone by then.

Kit and that bastard were supposed to be no more than three miles from here, according to his contact. He snorted in the darkness. Thanks to him, SVPD had a mole who had no problem taking Mishka's money in exchange for information on who the cops were watching, and for information like where Kit was holed up with some strange man. She'd have to pay for her disloyalty to him, of course, but after he captured her.

Mishka tightened the backpack's straps over his bulky frame and began walking, a headlamp guiding him through the dark forest. He'd have to go all dark once he found their campsite. Supposedly it was a broken-down hunting cabin that SVPD gained when the DEA finished using it for a safe house. His contact told him to leave no trace of being there, and he'd assured him that he only wanted to check it out.

What he wanted to do was scare Kit and make her realize she still needed him. He'd promise to keep her from Vadim—easy since his father was locked up for life, basically. She might be upset with him, and he'd reassure her that he forgave her for all she'd done. It'd all be worth it if they were together in the end, wouldn't it?

Mishka heard a rustle off to his right and froze.

"Who's there?" Crap, his voice was shaking and had the edge of the Russian accent he'd learned as a child from Vadim. This was crazy. He had a rifle slung over his back, a pistol and a knife strapped to his calf. He'd bought the best money could buy at the outdoor store. All except the firearms—those he already had, from the stash the authorities hadn't ever found, hidden in the storage facility they didn't know about.

A groundhog lumbered across the leaf-strewn path, and Mishka grabbed his handgun, ready to fire. Then he became aware of the silence and how far the gunshot would travel.

No, no. He couldn't. Not until he reached Kit.

"You look tired, honey." Claudia's blue eyes pierced through Colt as effectively as they had the first day he'd met her, all those years ago when she'd moved to Silver Valley. They'd met as a matter of course, as he was the Chief of Police and she'd been assigned to be the Director of a new government shadow agency that was headquartered in Silver Valley. The location, at the time, seemed the perfect cover. Why would there be a state-of-the-art undercover agent training and intelligence center in one of the most bucolic places in Pennsylvania?

"I'm good." He shoved the seared salmon around on his plate. Claudia had insisted on them eating together, be it at home or in one of their favorite restaurants, every night that a mission or police work didn't keep them apart.

"Colt."

He sighed and sat straighter in his chair. "I'm losing it, Claudia. I think it might be time to retire."

"That's not news. We're both looking at a change in the next year or so. We spent last vacation talking about it."

"I know. That's not what I meant." He fiddled with his napkin before meeting her calm gaze. "How can you stay so grounded when you're in the middle of the ROC case?"

"It's not easy, but all I have to do is remember why I do this. We're getting these bottom suckers out of our community, and if we're lucky, wiping out their East

Coast operations. Just think of all the people we'll be saving. You know that better than I do, Colt."

He did. Hadn't SVPD seen the brunt of the opioid and heroin epidemic in Central Pennsylvania? They were finally turning the tide, only to have ROC's heroin shipments find another way into the area. But if they were able to take down Ivanov, and along with him Markova, ROC would be brought to a standstill for at least several months. Enough time to clean them out of the entire Cumberland Valley, as well as New York and Florida and in between.

"The deal is that there's been a few things going on that don't add up."

"Such as?"

"When the shooter was at Kit's apartment, and Luther didn't catch him—didn't you think that was strange? That a shooter outran Luther, your best agent?"

Claudia nodded. "I chalked it up to Luther being more concerned about Kit and wanting to come back to her."

"Agreed. But then my officers have noticed that there have been the same thugs around crime scenes, and Kyle King says he's noticed jerks hanging around downtown in front of the coffee shop. As if they're watching."

"You think they're monitoring Kit, in her apartment?"

"Yes. And the worst part is that I think I have a leak in the department."

"Oh. Ooooh." Claudia's eyes widened and she nodded. "Now it all makes sense. No wonder you've been so distraught."

"I haven't been distraught." Though his stomach had been churning more than usual, as if he'd been eating greasy pizza every day instead of Claudia's well-planned homemade lunches.

"Who do you think it is?"

"I have no idea. I mean, I can eliminate my entire department by virtue of how much I trust them. But too many things have happened to chalk it up to coincidence. And I'm really concerned about Kit and Luther's security."

"It's an awful feeling to think someone has betrayed your entire team." Claudia reached for her phone. It was her special secret weapon—a phone like no other, with the capability to send encrypted messages that no other agency, be it their country's or a foreign government's, could break into. "I'll send Luther and Kit a message that they need to be on the lookout for any extra players. But it's unlikely that someone would find them out at that old place, don't you think?"

"I have no earthly idea. Everything I used to count on has blown up or gone the way of the dinosaurs over the last decade."

"Except one thing." She'd finished tapping out a message and placed her phone down. "You have me."

"I do." He opened his arms and she sat on his lap. "I don't want anything to happen to you. It'd kill me. You're my life, Claudia."

She kissed him and he kissed her back, wishing his troubled thoughts could take a break so that he'd have the focus to make love to her like he wanted to.

"You're mine, too." She rested her forehead on his. "We're going to beat them at their game, Colt. And then we'll turn over our jobs to the young'uns." They laughed, and for a moment Colt allowed the warmth of what they shared to wrap around him and make the sharp edges of the ROC threat blur.

Chapter 13

The turkey meal made Kit drowsy, and she had to catch herself from nodding off in front of her laptop. She needed to move, so she set alerts and stood. Moving into a long stretch, she saw that Luther appeared equally beat as he sat by the comms rack, the stack of portable equipment they'd brought to find Ivanov with. He constantly monitored the various units for power variations.

"I'm going to take a shower before we call it a night. I've set the alerts to sound, and if your guess is right, hunters will begin arriving early tomorrow morning."

"Ah, you can't go to the bathroom shed on your own."

"Excuse me?"

"You can't go there alone, neither can I. It's protocol." It hadn't come up yet, as they'd used the tiny bathroom closet in the corner of the cabin. But she needed more than hand sanitizer at this point.

"It's also protocol to not leave this kind of equipment unattended." Even in a building that was in truth a vault.

"Which is why I carried the most important components in my backpack when we went for our hike."

She sighed, not relishing putting it all back into their backpacks, showering, then unloading it again. As small and portable as it all was, it meant time away from monitoring the signals and precious sleep. Still, she'd heard Claudia loud and clear about taking care of herself whenever she could out in the field. There was time for a shower now; there might not be tomorrow.

"I'll take the laptop and two of the other units. Can you manage the bigger box?"

"Let's not disconnect it all. We can roll it on this rack to the bathhouse, and keep it in the dressing area, where it'll stay dry."

"And take turns showering and watching it?"

"Yes."

The thought of seeing Luther's body without the layers of cold weather fabric made her sleepiness dissipate as quickly as if he'd poured ice cubes over her. The shot of heat to the area between her legs reminded her that Luther could easily become more than a work partner. Something they'd promised one another to stay away from, after their kiss in the woods.

Ah, but that kiss. She'd never been touched like that before. As if she were precious, Luther wanting to savor each and every nuance of the gesture. A memory she'd always cherish.

But that was all it was. A memory.

"It's not rocket science, Kit. We're moving the equipment along with us. It's how I manage when I'm out in the field on my own."

"So you never, ever leave the equipment alone?"

"Nope. I end up stinking to heaven by the time I'm done, especially on the longer ops, but we get our bad guys behind bars and keep the security of our comms gear intact."

"ROC has a lot of money and resources. From what I've read, they are capable of owning and operating far more sophisticated equipment than any government."

"Too true. But Trail Hikers isn't the US government, not officially anyway. And unlike the government, TH has an unlimited supply of cash and technological access. I've no doubt ROC's equipment can match most of ours, hit for hit."

"But?" She heard the doubt and the pride in his voice.

"They're missing a critical element—good people with fire in their bellies to do what's right regardless of the consequences."

"Now you're talking like a Marine."

"I am. You know Claudia was a two-star General in the Corps, right? It's what got her this job, and has made Trail Hikers a force to be reckoned with."

"An anonymous force. The ROC around here, at least the people I knew who worked with my ex, only know about SVPD and FBI. They mentioned DEA and CIA from time to time, too. But in actuality they lump all LEA together. And if or when they've seen a TH agent at work, they assume it's FBI or another agency. It's beyond them that there could be something they don't know about."

"That's a little odd, isn't it? I mean, the Russians are known for subterfuge and underhanded tactics. Why wouldn't they expect it from us, too?" Luther was genuinely puzzled if she read his expression correctly.

"Ah, but here's where so many of you undercover agents mess up. You think ROC is the same as Russia and the Russian government, her people. But ROC is more a function of some oligarchs gone rogue, combined with the thousands upon thousands of former Soviet nation refugees who landed in American in the nineties. ROC evolved as a way to protect a culture while providing money laundering for the oligarchs who were gobbling up the profits of the new capitalism in Russia."

"You learned a lot in history class." He jested, but she knew it wasn't mean-spirited.

"And we lived it. My parents were ecstatic when Ukraine was freed from Soviet rule, and they've been enraged since Russia claimed the Crimean Peninsula in 2014. They're so appreciative to be Americans now, but the ties to Ukraine are in their blood."

"I get it—I do. Not that I've personally experienced it, but I've operated in plenty of countries where the citizens are under constant threat from their government or another's. Did your parents come over as political refugees?"

"No, but they could have, it turns out, after 2014. I brought them over as part of a deal I made with my ex." She didn't want to talk about it, but she'd agreed to put up with Vadim's abuse after she'd figured out she could get out and leave him, and he'd appreciated that she had choices. It was her bargaining chip to have him pay for the visas and travel costs for her parents and sister. "I got him to fund my family's visas and travel to New York. They're all citizens now, living in New Jersey." The familiar taste of bile hit the back of her throat as her stomach churned. "I hated using Vadim, and working the system, to get them here. But I love them. My family is my life. Their visas were legit and they applied for citizenship immediately when they arrived." It had been situational ethics at best, morally repulsive at worst. She'd spent long hours in counseling sessions talking about it. Her therapist assured her that she'd been in survival mode, and reaching out for her family was natural, no matter the cost. And in fact, she'd saved all of them, in the end, from a very hard life. They'd all achieved the American dream, for which she was forever grateful.

"Why didn't you run away to them, when your ex was abusing you?" Luther's query held no judgement, and he was looking at her as if she was his hero or something. It made her happy and regretful all at once. If only her life had been more straightforward.

"It's not that easy. He threatened to have the entire ROC wipe out my family the minute I showed my unfaithfulness to him. It was a big risk to work with SVPD on bringing him down, but I'm glad I did it. So is my family."

"They can't be happy about you working in law enforcement." His words made her freeze as she gathered up her shower supplies, now that they had the comms gear racked and strapped in place. "Let me guess— you haven't told them?"

"They think I'm a receptionist at the police department. Working to save money so that I can get my law degree."

"Are you still in school?"

"No, but I have considered law school. There are many very good ones within driving distance."

"You'd be a great victim's advocate, that's for sure."

She warmed at his compliment. "I do some volunteer work for victims of domestic violence, and I'm in a support group with other survivors. We meet weekly. I would relish the opportunity to help them legally, but for now this kind of justice works for me, too. Where's that tarp we brought in? It'll be good to drape this with, in case it starts snowing again."

"Here." He reached under the sofa and produced the camouflaged plastic sheet.

"Thanks. I'm ready when you are."

"Then let's go." He zipped his jacket and opened the door to allow her to roll the small rack of equipment out onto the stoop and then down the two short steps onto the snow-dusted ground.

Neither of them spoke but instead made their way quietly up the steep embankment to the hidden bathhouse. Kit had to admit that the planning for this setup had been genius. No undercover agent or cop wanted to be caught unawares in the shower, and keeping the cabin minimalist made its cover as a hunting lodge more believable.

It also made her wonder what it would be like to be with Luther in more comfortable surroundings. If they'd conducted their surveillance out of a fancy hotel room, complete with a bath, would she still have paid enough attention to him to figure out she was attracted to him more than ever? Or was it just the Spartan surroundings and total lack of anything to do but watch her laptop screen that made her take a second glance at Luther?

You took thirds and fourths, too.

So she had. As she gingerly hauled the tech equipment up the base of the mountain, careful to avoid jutting branches and sharp rocks, she braced herself for being naked with only a shower stall separating her from Luther.

Mishka wanted to shoot someone for how difficult the pain in the ass climb to where Kit stayed was. What the hell was she doing out here, in the middle of nowhere? And what did this have to do with her work at the Silver Valley police station? He figured she was a secretary or at most did some kind of filing work. He remembered that Vadim told him she was going to the community college for courses, but didn't know what she'd studied. He assumed some kind of nontechnical work. Kit had never shown a talent for anything but keeping his father well-fed and happy in the sack.

His contact couldn't tell him if the man she was camping with was the same one who'd missed his bullet or not. Mishka figured it was better if he didn't know—he'd want to kill the guy first, and that would put Kit at risk of being hurt or running away. He wanted her safe and sound, with him.

He stopped when he saw the red scarf his contact had left for him, attached to a tree he'd said was only "one hundred paces from where they're camping." Since when did Kit spend a night anywhere other than in a warm bed?

Mishka slid out of his backpack and placed it on the ground. Using his flashlight he pulled out the device he'd had one of his father's former colleagues make for him. It was cell phone activated. Once he got the bomb in place either inside or under the car Kit had used to get up here, he could be as far away as half a mile and make it blow. It'd be enough to let her know she had to come out of the woods, enough for him to grab her. He'd wait on the other side of the cabin for her to come out. If the man came out with her, he'd warn them to leave. Or use his weapons on them.

Whatever it took to get Kit back to him.

The bathroom building was no more than fifty yards from the cabin but appeared to be carved right out of the sheer granite rock that comprised the side of the mountain. To a passing hiker it wouldn't be immediately noticeable, and even if they saw the entry door, it looked like a utility service box for a very large transformer.

Kit followed Luther into the main changing area, a tiled room with high, narrow windows for ventilation. They worked together to remove the tarp and place it across the wooden mats that reminded her of a chic spa.

"Who built all this? Trail Hikers?" She'd seen some of the agency's safe houses and they were far more comfortable and modern than the hunting cabin. This bathhouse appeared more fitting to a TH hideout.

"My understanding is that it was a combination of LEA. FBI and DEA used the cabin as a safe house for more than two decades. They were unloading it and Claudia decided it was a perfect location for TH agents to disappear to as needed, while undercover or otherwise."

"Are TH agents ever *not* undercover?"

"Touché."

"Who goes first?" She looked around the room, giving it more attention than she had the first time. "Where does that door go to?" She noticed a wooden door with a glass window that she hadn't noticed before.

"It's a sauna. I'll turn it on, so that you can use it after your shower. This whole setup was designed to support agents who might not have remembered to bring a towel along for their ops." He grinned at her, and she had to remind herself to stay centered on getting a quick shower and then taking their equipment right back to the cabin.

"Why so serious?"

"I, um, I don't like having our work interrupted for too long. I'll take a quick one."

"Relax. We're the ones doing the surveilling. It's not like we're the prey. Take your time. As I've learned time and again, you don't know for certain when your next shower will be."

"I thought we'd be going back by Monday at the latest. You don't think it'll take that long to locate our targets, do you?" She'd never needed more than minimal time to give either SVPD or TH agents the GPS coordinates on a suspect, once she established solid hits. If she was doing analysis of conversations, that could take longer.

"No telling. While I'm willing to buy into the theory that Ivanov won't risk a phone call until the area's more populated, I wouldn't bet on it. As you know, when ROC wants something, they ignore the rules."

"What would he want that badly to risk capture,

after he and Markova have successfully eluded LEA for so long?"

"Access to whatever she still has on him."

"You think Markova still has remaining accounts of his?"

"What else would it be? Whenever we follow the money, we track ROC's activity without a hitch. The government has frozen all of the accounts we discovered on the password lists Markova buried in the old barn's keystone. If she'd given us everything, why would Ivanov keep her alive?"

"Maybe he hasn't. Or maybe she didn't turn over everything." In Kit's experience, ROC never let a betrayal go. By taking all of Ivanov's account information and changing the passwords, she'd been the first one to freeze East Coast ROC operations. Once the US government had the information and the accounts were legally frozen, ROC's bankroll was effectively gone.

"What?" Luther must have seen the thoughts coming together in her eyes.

"There has to be more money available, at least one of the accounts that she didn't put on those lists with the user IDs and passwords."

"That's above my pay grade. I'm paid to take out targets, and right now we have two to establish a location on."

"Will you be with the team who brings them in, then?"

"Depends."

"You want to be."

"Of course I do. For reasons you have no idea…" He turned to his small duffel bag. Did he remember that he'd told her about the ROC wife he'd fallen for?

"I'll get my shower." Kit knew when someone needed breathing space. And Luther wasn't alone in that requirement—the longer she spent with him, the more she knew it was going to be hard not to work with him. As much as she'd enjoyed comfortable working relationships with her fellow TH and SVPD colleagues, she'd never fallen into a routine with another so quickly.

Nor had she ever told them, save for Annie, about what she'd been through with Vadim. And now Luther knew, the emotional parts if not actual abuse details.

Stripping to get in the shower, she realized she didn't feel as naked as she had when telling Luther about her past.

It was also the safest you've felt.

The shower was huge, big enough for five people. It reminded her of the master bathroom in the mansion she'd lived in with her ex. But unlike the ostentatious, over-the-top fixtures, these were stainless steel with contemporary lines. She imagined that it had served for groups of agents as needed, and practicality made it so roomy. When she turned the handle she heard a flash heater fire up and nearly groaned with gratitude. It was going to be a hot shower, something to ease the tight neck muscles she'd incurred from hours of staring at a laptop screen. The slip-proofed tile floor was warm under her feet as hot water streamed over her head, her breasts, her legs.

If she kept her eyes closed, the water could ease her anxiety at being in such a close proximity with a man like Luther. A man she'd actually be interested in getting to know better, spending much more personal time with, if they didn't have the definite boundary of working together. More than that, Luther made it clear that he wasn't interested in anything more than what he currently had. His work. The one woman he'd cared for had betrayed him, then been killed.

Kit understood betrayal. And Vadim wasn't dead, nor had she loved him, not even briefly. The bastard had gotten all she'd ever give him—the better part of six years of her life.

She was grateful for the fancier bar she'd grabbed from her apartment as its lavender scent filled the shower. Only recently, secure in her steady income, had she allowed herself these little luxuries. Lathering it against her skin, she recalled how she'd had to rely on friends and handouts when she'd first been free from Vadim. He'd left her nothing, as the government seized all of his assets. The only reason the pawnshop still existed was that it'd been put in Mishka's name, and she'd never, ever considered asking him for a dime.

She laughed, the sound open and louder than she expected with the echo of the flat ceramic walls. The truth was that she'd have paid Mishka to leave her alone if necessary.

Here, in the middle of the woods with Luther and their operation against ROC, Kit felt more secure and grounded in her life than she had since she'd read the advertisement in the local paper for an au pair while sitting on her parents' sofa in Kiev.

Maybe this was what Annie had meant when she'd told her that she'd gradually realize she'd healed from her traumatic time with Vadim.

And if her skin hummed, and her insides trembled

when she thought of the man on the other side of the wall while she stood here naked, that was simply part of being a healthy human.

Luther tried not to smell the feminine scent that emanated from the door to the shower room. It wasn't a TH supply; of that he was certain. The last time he'd used a TH safe house, the soap had been plain white bars, not whatever was making the shower steam smell like a woman.

Not *a* woman. *Kit*.

He opened the sauna door and sniffed, willing the cedar and steam to erase the thoughts of Kit, naked, standing under running water. He'd almost convinced himself, or rather his dick had, that it would be okay to relieve the tension with Kit. Until he heard her speak so openly and honestly about her abusive marriage. Hell, it hadn't been a marriage, save for the legal piece of paper. She'd been an unwilling captive of a very bad man.

His throat and face began to burn and he shut the sauna door. The last thing he needed was to get emotionally involved with a woman with Kit's past. And she would need a man to help her heal from whatever that monster had done to her, if it was even possible. She'd require a man who'd always be there for her, at her side, patient, compassionate, understanding.

He could admit to himself that he was capable of patience and understanding. But being there for the long run? Not happening with any woman. Luther had learned his lesson the night he'd realized his life was about to end because of his mess-up. He'd trusted the wrong woman.

A laugh sounded in the shower, followed by a soft humming. Kit was enjoying herself. No reason to rush her. They were safe out here, conducting nothing more than a surveillance mission. If, like other ROC ops, this turned into something more lethal, he was prepared. Luther would take care of them, but most of all, he'd protect Kit.

Sinking onto the wooden bench that lined the bathhouse wall opposite of both the shower and sauna doors, he relaxed his back against the cool tile and closed his eyes. A bit of meditation might keep him from doing what he really wanted. Blame his erection, but the truth was plain and simple, and not so biological.

He wanted Kit Danilenko far more than a work or bed partner.

"Your turn!" Kit padded out of the shower room, glad she'd thrown her terry robe into her bag. She could have dressed in the shower, but the sauna beckoned. Plus, it'd help dry her hair more quickly.

Luther opened his eyes but remained still on the bench as he watched her. He wore his same clothes, no doubt ever mindful that they could be called into dangerous action at any time. "How was it?"

"Great. Did you take a catnap?"

"Something like that." He stretched his arms overhead, stood and cracked his neck. "I like to meditate when I can. If I'm not on an op, I do it regularly."

"Which means rarely."

"Pretty much." He leaned down and grasped his small backpack. "The sauna's ready. Feel free to adjust the heat as you see fit."

"Thanks." They had to walk past each other, and Kit wanted to slap her cheek to snap out of the cloud of awareness Luther's presence wrapped her in. If she were honest, she was in need of sexual release, but it wasn't possible. It hadn't been while she'd worked through her trauma—she wasn't ready. And now, feeling more ready than ever, the very man who'd awakened her deeply protected natural urges was off-limits. For reasons far too numerous to have her mind tick off.

She lifted her chin and aimed for the sauna door. One step, two, passing him, ignoring the wonder of how he'd look without his jeans on, almost there—

His hand reached out and gently grasped her upper arm.

"Oh!" The skin under the terry cotton reacted with heat and a sense of urgency that spread through her and coiled in her pelvic floor, making her legs as wobbly as the old coffee table in front of her sofa. She looked up into the danger zone—Luther's face, especially his eyes, and the gray heat was scary and a relief. Scary because this was new territory for her, and relief because it was validation to see he felt it, too. It wasn't a casual attraction that had led to their kiss. Some kind of fire had been lit between them and dang if she knew how to put it out.

He immediately dropped his arm. "I'm sorry, Kit. I would never hurt you. This job can turn on a dime, and if it does, I'll do whatever it takes to keep you safe."

"I know that." She saw the concern in his eyes and needed to convey that she wasn't afraid of him. "It's not you, Luther. It's me, one hundred percent." She was screwing this up so badly. She knew she should have gone straight into the sauna, out of arm's reach of him.

Except Luther deserved the truth.

And the truth was, she wanted him too badly to stop now.

Chapter 14

He tried to turn away, but this time her hand on his heart stopped him.

"Kit—"

"Let me explain something, Luther. I have to get this out in the open. It's only fair. I'm not afraid of you. It's this…this thing between us. I get that it's probably one-sided for the most part. I haven't been with anyone since I left my marriage, and it's only natural that I'd become interested in a single man I spent so much time around, don't you think?"

"That sounds logical." His arm thrummed where her palm touched his chest and it took years of training for Luther to keep himself from bundling her close. He'd never had his protective instincts triggered like this before. Nor his desire.

She smiled, her skin rosy from the shower. All he

saw was her face and the top of her throat, the rest was left to his imagination. "One thing my experience with trauma and healing has taught me is that I can't rely solely on my brain anymore, Luther. Logic and common sense are important, as are instinct and self-awareness. But it's okay for me to have my feelings. And that's just it. I'm having all kinds of inappropriate feelings for you, and I owe you an apology. I'm sorry if it's making your work space uncomfortable."

"Oh, babe, it's not the wrong or bad kind of discomfort, trust me."

She scoured his face with her gaze, and to his surprise her response was to place her hands on his chest, stand on tiptoe and press her lips to his.

Luther froze. Then he grasped her shoulders, leaned back, breaking the connection. "Kit, are you certain?"

"I'm beyond sure, Luther."

He waited for her to come back, to kiss him again. This had to be her call. It was his desire to empower her, let her know how desirable he found her. Yet it had to be at her pace.

Kit's lips were sheer magic on his, their softness enticing his mouth to answer with a fierce kiss filled with all the need he had for her.

Not yet.

"Babe." He breathed into her mouth, wrapping his hands around her waist and gently nudging her, inch by inch, up against him. When her body was flush with his, he deepened the kiss, allowing his hands to grasp her buttocks.

"This is spectacular." She kept kissing him, her tongue licking his lips and teeth. He couldn't stop the groan that growled from his throat, and finally let himself kiss her like he'd dreamed since seeing her in Colt's office. When she thrust her pelvis against his, he opened his eyes to see her arousal on full display in the blue depths of hers. Her half-closed eyes opened fully, meeting his gaze as her breath hitched and the rosy flush turned into a full bloom.

"Can I touch you?" He moved his hand to the side of her rib cage, stopping short of where her breast pressed against the fluffy robe.

"Please, yes." Without preamble, Kit untied her robe and let it drop.

"Whoa, wait—" He grabbed it before it hit the floor and moved to the side to hang it on a hook. And to give himself a second to check himself. This time was going to be about Kit's pleasure. She deserved that .

"I don't care about my robe, Luther." She stood before him with total confidence, her body taut and soft in all the right places.

He cupped her face. "You are so beautiful, Kit."

"You make me feel beautiful."

"Tell me if I do anything you don't want, babe."

"I want it all with you, Luther. You're the right man for me, right now."

"I'll buy that." He couldn't wait any longer and lowered his head, longing for her kiss.

Kit had never experienced the sensations Luther's kiss and touch sparked. She was helpless with desire and bursting with the knowledge of what her body, her touches did to him. Luther let her know each time a caress affected him, and she was positively giddy knowing she brought him pleasure.

He held her breast in his hand, gently squeezing and

caressing while kissing her thoroughly. She reached between them and stroked him through his hunting pants, the nylon fabric leaving little to her imagination.

"Yeah, babe, that's it."

"You're so hard, hon."

He pressed her up against the wall, where her robe hung, so she wasn't chilled by the tile. "You okay?"

"I'm wonderful." She could hardly talk around her breathlessness. Never had she truly understood the fussiness of love scenes in the movies, not in her past life. Now, with Luther, she understood why her girlfriends oohed and ahhed when the leads got together. This was… Beyond.

"We're just getting started, babe." He kissed her deeply, slowly, before trailing his mouth over her throat, his hands taking their own journey on her waist, over her hips, lower, until his hand was between her legs and his fingers stroked her, her wetness saying everything she couldn't articulate. Her legs quivered and her knees were close to giving out. When his mouth closed on her nipple, she cried out.

"Hang on, babe, we're getting there."

Getting where? He'd already made her feel things she'd never dreamed of. The tight coil in her pelvic floor threatened to reach a breaking point, but she had no clue how to get there.

Luther showed her.

He sucked her nipple and did some kind of secret finger maneuvers in her most private parts. A sheer wave of pleasure welled up in Kit. She grasped his shoulders, grinding her hips in sync with his fingers. Oh, his magic hands.

"Luther, I'm… I'm—"

"Go with it, babe. Let it take you." He moved from her breast back to her lips, and when his tongue met hers, he pressed into her with his fingers. The sensation of a wave broke into an explosion of ecstasy, and it took her several breaths to realize the woman screaming his name was her.

So this was an orgasm.

Luther couldn't get enough of Kit's every expression, the way she soaked up each stroke of his fingers, every kiss, as if it were all new to her. She still clutched his shoulders, her gasps slowly easing into a regular rhythm as he held her against him. Her scent surrounded them, and if they weren't in the Trail Hikers' hideout he'd take her to his bed and show her how very little they'd explored.

"Luther."

"Kit." He kissed her closed lids, her lashes long and full. She opened her eyes and he was gifted with her glow of pure sensual satisfaction, making her eyes a deeper hue than usual. "I take it that was okay?"

"Okay? It was like nothing I've ever—but you, Luther. We must take care of you." She became almost businesslike in her countenance, and he grasped her hands, holding them against his heart.

"Are you kidding? You just gave me the biggest gift ever, Kit. You opened up to me, shared your most intimate self."

"You don't understand, Luther. I owe you big-time. I know this is going to be hard for you to believe, but that was my first orgasm with…with someone else."

He sucked in his breath. Of course. Her bastard ex wouldn't have bothered to pleasure her. Vadim was one of many loser ROC operatives he'd crossed paths with over the years, from what he'd read of his files when he'd found out he'd be working with the woman he'd abused.

"You think less of me?" Vulnerability laced her tone, but he saw the steel in her gaze. Kit was a survivor.

"Babe. I can't think of anyone more incredible than you."

"Can I do something to please you now?" Her offer to reciprocate was genuine, but he couldn't shake the truth of what she'd survived, how she'd never had her needs met before.

"Not this time, sweetheart." He kissed her forehead, then the tip of her nose. "I'll take a rain check, though, when we're in a more comfortable spot."

"Deal." She gave him a shaky smile and a tear slid from the corner of her eye. He kissed it away, cupped her face in both hands.

"You're beautiful, Kit." He couldn't tell her enough.

She raised her hand to her face and swiped at her eyes. "I have to admit, I'm feeling a little vulnerable right now."

"Here." He removed the robe from the hook and wrapped it around her, helping her with each sleeve before closing the front and tying the belt. "I'm sorry that our first time together was in such a challenging—"

"I'm not." Her fingers covered his mouth and he reflexively kissed the tips. Luther stood up straighter. He was definitely not the kiss-on-the-fingertips kind of guy.

You're getting in too deep.

"But it wasn't as good as it's going to be, babe." He

kissed her, hard. "Next time." Reluctantly he took a step back, then another, grabbing his stuff. "It's my turn to shower. You head into the sauna and I'll meet you there in a few. But if you get too warm, get out. Dehydration is not something we can afford."

She nodded and he saw her more professional demeanor come back, which was actually hilarious since she was naked under her fluffy robe and her cheeks were still rosy from her orgasm.

That she'd let him bring her to. White-hot heat went straight to his groin, and he made a quick exit to the showers. Thank goodness this part of the ROC surveillance and takedown would be over soon. He wasn't sure how much longer he could wait to make love to Kit the way she deserved, for as long as they both wanted .

Mishka grunted as he stood in front of the Jeep that matched the photo his contact had provided. Anger swelled at having to hike the last two hours, in the dark, through this freaking wilderness. Screw his original plan not to grab Kit as soon as the car exploded. What had he been thinking, that he'd frighten her and the man she was with, drag out the scare tactics a bit?

No way. Since he'd had to come this far and go through this much effort, he was going to get what he wanted now. Besides, once he had Kit, he'd have more bargaining power with Ivanov and Markova. Unbeknownst to his father, he'd established contact with Ivanov, promising the ROC East Coast leader that he'd not only pick up where Vadim had left off, but was willing to provide far more services to the organization than his father ever had. Ivanov hadn't promised him anything.

Mishka figured Ivanov was gun-shy after Vadim got locked up and concerned that Kit would say more to implicate additional ROC operatives. But Kit didn't know anything past Vadim's world, and had known very little of that. His father had kept her in a bubble, giving her enough leash so she wouldn't go to the authorities.

Until she had.

Anger flared again, and his hands shook as he placed the explosive devices on the undercarriage of the Jeep. His remaining ROC contacts had told him exactly where to put the bombs to guarantee maximum damage and effect. He detested crawling around on the ground like an animal. He expected his underlings to do this kind of work, the ones who'd stayed loyal to Vadim and him after Vadim was sentenced.

A rock cut into his knee and he jerked, the meaty part of his upper arm hitting the car body. A shrill, deafening car alarm rent the air.

"Damn it!" He scrambled to his feet and ran to the shelter of the surrounding trees. If Kit or the man came outside now, they might see him before he had a chance to activate the bombs. It would ruin his plans, or at least delay them during the extra time it would take to put down the man. The feel of the handgun under his hand, still holstered, boosted his confidence.

He hid behind a large tree and waited, but no one appeared. The siren continued, and he began to wonder if anyone was in the cabin. Maybe they'd gone hunting. He snorted. Kit was no hunter.

He fingered the burner phone and weighed his options. It seemed a waste to have such a major explosion without anyone to witness it. Yet today was the only time he could get away with it, before the hoards of hunters drove up into the mountain area in preparation for open deer season on Monday. And taking Kit's only viable means of quick transportation away was important.

What was that stupid saying? In for a ruble, in for it all?

Mishka depressed the cell phone button that ignited the explosive and plugged his ears.

Kit breathed in the sauna's cedar-scented air, relishing the hot wooden wall behind her back. When was the last time she'd been in a sauna? Only once since she'd left her sham marriage, when the girls went to Hershey Spa to celebrate Annie's marriage to Josh last summer. It had been okay then, since she was with a group and felt safe.

Vadim had kept a monstrous sauna in the pool room on his property. She knew most folks thought she'd lived in luxury in the mansion on a beautiful estate adjacent the Appalachian Trail, but to her it had been no more than a prison. Her entire life had been with a beast in a steel cage, having to watch every step around the beast that was Vadim, especially when he drank.

But this—this time with Luther was revelatory. She couldn't think of a time when she'd felt safer, except maybe when her ex had finally been locked up for good. Even then she'd always feared a reprisal from ROC or Mishka for what she'd done, providing evidence to take down a key criminal in Silver Valley and in fact Pennsylvania. Vadim's many human trafficking crimes were documented and listed as charges in his indictment.

She moved to rest her back against the wall and stretched her legs in front of her on the cedar bench. The sauna was dry but had a bucket of water next to the heater. It made her smile, knowing Luther had taken the time and forethought to fill the pail and get the sauna to the right temperature.

None of it matched the heated exchange they'd shared, though. As much as he'd made love to her, ensured her extreme pleasure and forgone his, she still recognized that it had been a couples event. His eyes had reflected emotions she was afraid to label, and she was certain hers had, too.

Impossible. They'd only known one another for what, ten days? A memory of Annie telling her how Colt and Claudia knew they were destined to be together after only knowing each other for a day flitted through her thoughts.

It was highly improbable, but definitely within the realm of possibility to fall for someone she'd just met.

You've fallen for him?

She shook her head, loosened the belt on her robe a bit. It had to be the postclimax effect, to be thinking this way. It was only normal after her first shared orgasm. Vadim, besides being abusive, had never once considered her response. She'd learned to fake it, to make him think he was giving her pleasure. It kept their most intimate interactions to a minimum, especially as he aged and the progression of his alcoholism took away his ability to have an erection.

Kit blinked. Having the orgasm with Luther wasn't the only first for today. She was actually looking at her ex and that horrific excuse for a marriage with a detached, clinical eye. Her therapist had been right.

*One day, when you least expect it, you'll wake up
and realize that the life of trauma you survived is no
longer running your life.*

Tears brimmed, and unlike the many she'd shed
during her years of therapy and healing, these were an
outlet of the joy that welled in her chest and squeezed
her heart.

Life was good, indeed.

On the other side of the wall the shower's running
water stopped, and she allowed a smile to stretch across
her face. Luther was on the way to the sauna. Despite
his insistence that they'd be together in a more appropriate place after the op was over, she thought that
maybe it was time to see how far she'd healed. Was
she ready to be sexually assertive with him?

A high-pitched noise sounded from faraway, and
she stilled, thinking it could be water running through
the pipe or maybe she was misinterpreting a hawk's
cry. But an animal's sounds wouldn't pierce the walls
of the bathhouse.

When the noise continued, she swung her legs down
and stood. As she reached for the sauna door, the floor
rose up under her and she flew back through the air, her
bottom hitting the floor of the sauna as a loud *boom*
percussed. The building shook, and the back of her
head hit the low bench, sending stars across her vision.

"Kit!" A deep bellow, as though a mountain lion
were on the other side of the door.

"I'm here." She shouted back, but her words were no
more than a hoarse whisper. Luther would never hear
her. Fear started to break through her pain.

The door burst open, bringing hope and a surge of
cold air.

Luther.

"Kit." He knelt next to her in the dark, and his breath washed over her cheek. "Can you hear me?"

She blinked, slowly grasping that she was resting on her elbows, her legs spread wide, her robe gaping. "Y-yes. I hit my head. I'm fine." She moved to rise, and his hands, which had been feeling her head, her neck and back, helped her up.

"Easy." She stood, and to her relief her legs hadn't betrayed her. They were as sturdy as ever.

"I'm good." She met his gaze and nodded, then winced. "My head's going to hurt later, but I didn't lose consciousness."

"You've got a bump, so you should be fine."

Another smaller explosion sounded and she gripped his arm. "What is that?"

His mouth was in a straight line. "I'm afraid it's the Jeep. We've got to get out of here." With no preamble he half carried, half pushed her out of the sauna, and they walked the few steps to where her clothing hung. "Are you steady? I need you to get dressed and get ready to go."

"Go where?" Fueled by adrenaline, she was already putting on her underwear, followed by her pants, socks and hiking boots. Luther had impressed the need to always have good sturdy footwear even if only going to the bathroom.

"Away from here." He moved next to her and she heard the scrape of cloth, his zipper, the stamp of his feet into his shoes.

"Okay." She put her jacket on and zipped it, felt inside the pockets for her gloves. All she had were thin knit; she'd left her heavy-duty pair in the cabin. "I'm ready."

"Here." His hand hit her arm in the inky darkness, and he felt down to her hand, pressing something hard and metal into it. "It's a .22. You can handle it no problem. If anything happens to me, don't hesitate to fire at whoever's out there, and then get out of here. Go down the mountain but keep in the woods, out of sight of the road and anyone driving on it. Wait for SVPD or TH to show up and make sure it's them before you reveal yourself."

He fired the orders at her not unlike how she'd heard Colt brief SVPD before they went into a dangerous house, or when Claudia gave her elite agents a briefing before an ROC operative takedown. What was unusual was to have the words aimed at her.

"You're forgetting that I can't do this, Luther." She held the gun out to thin air. "I'm not licensed, I'm unsworn, I—"

"You're a target. Keep it out for now, then put it in your pants waistband once we get going. Do you know how to fire it?"

"Yes." She didn't elaborate but knew he'd trust her. All those hours with Vadim, practicing his favorite hobby, had made her an expert shot. Vadim had his own firing range in the basement of the huge house they'd occupied, and she'd found respite there. Firing a weapon gave her a sense of control in a situation that was out of control. At one point she regretted not using her expertise on Vadim, to escape her life. But she'd vowed not to break the law to gain her freedom. And it had worked out.

"Come on." He grabbed her other hand with unerring accuracy and held it up to his backpack, already securely strapped to him. "Hang on to the pack, or my jacket, feel along the wall, follow my voice."

They moved faster than she'd thought was possible in total darkness and all she heard were their steps and her heartbeats. Within minutes that felt like hours they stood behind a copse of evergreens, judging from the scrape of needles against her face and the pine scent. The night air bit through her clothing and she longed for her ski cap. Wet hair and freezing temperatures didn't mix.

As they waited, her eyes adjusted and the sliver of moonlight that cut through the treetops began to illuminate the property right behind the cabin. The Jeep wasn't visible on the other side of the building, but she smelled an acrid odor and saw flashes of light that were undoubtedly flames.

Someone had blown up the Jeep.

Her insides began to shake from the severity of the attack against them, but she forced her core muscles to tighten around her center, the antianxiety and calming skills she'd learned kicking in on autopilot. Kit knew to remain silent, as she'd participated in plenty of surveillance ops. Of course before this, she'd been safely ensconced in an unmarked van or truck, monitoring comms on her screen.

Her laptop. Mentally she thought about where she'd left it and then remembered Luther had packed up the most essential comms gear into his backpack, including her small laptop. The stress of their situation was affecting her. At least she recognized it.

The sound of heavy feet on wet leaves alerted her,

and she strained her eyes to make out the male figure walking around the back of the cabin.

Mishka.

He walked up to the door, climbed the two steps and pounded on the door. "Come out, Kit! I know you're in there."

She fought against the gasp that worked past her lips, clapping her hand over her mouth. How had he found her?

Luther reached back and gave her forearm a reassuring squeeze. Relief flooded her, but her body remained poised to run at the drop of a pin.

More door pounding. When he tried to open the door, she couldn't help grinning to herself from their hidden post. Like her, Mishka must have thought the door was nothing more than a flimsy piece of wood. He'd never get through the four-inch-thick steel door, and short of blowing up the cabin like he had the Jeep, the cabin would remain off-limits to him.

He left the stoop, swearing loudly in Russian and she tensed. Mishka's voice sounded eerily similar to Vadim's, and it would be easy to believe she was back where she'd started all those years ago, at Vadim's mercy.

No. You're here. Luther is right next to you. You are safe.

A giggle snaked up her throat and she squashed it. While her usual affirmations proved helpful, the safety of her or Luther wasn't totally clear.

The sound of something hard hitting a window brought her back from her thoughts, grounded her. Mishka was attempting to break in through the tiny window, which his hulking form would never get through. As she watched, the glass didn't even crack. Kit hadn't thought to ask Luther about the window, but now realized it was made of bulletproof and Mishka-proof glass.

"I know you're out here, Kit!" he screamed, and she startled, taking a half step backward. A branch snapped under her sole and she froze, praying the sound didn't break through Mishka's frenzied fit.

Luther raised his arm to her chest, as she continued to hold her breath.

"Who's out there? I hear you, Kit!" Mishka's voice cut through her. "Come on out, Kit. I'm not going away and you'll never get into the cabin again. I forgive you for being with this stranger. Who is he? FBI? Don't listen to whatever they've told you to do. Come out to me now and we're cool."

"The only person here has a hunting rifle aimed at the target between your eyes. Get the hell off my property." Luther's voice rang out and if Kit were Mishka, she'd already be running.

"I'll never listen to you." Mishka's snarl made bile rise, burning the back of her throat. Without preamble Mishka fired into the trees where they stood.

Kit screamed.

Chapter 15

As long as he lived, Luther would never forget the sound of Kit's scream as bullets hit the trunks near them, sending bark flying and he and Kit to the ground.

A piercing heat flooded his upper thigh and he swore under his breath.

"You okay?" Kit was right next to him, but he knew she didn't know he'd been hit. And he couldn't let her, or she'd become an easy mark for Mishka.

"You need to go now, Kit." He spoke through gritted teeth as bullets flew and Mishka had what sounded like a mental breakdown. The jerk wasn't going to go peacefully, and he didn't want Kit near this. "I'm going to keep talking to him, keep him behind the cabin. Head out to the front of it, then use the road as your guide. Go!"

He expected her to start running and moved aside to

let her pass. Her hands reached up and grabbed his face, and she planted a firm kiss on his lips. "Be safe, Luther."

She disappeared through the trees, and he turned his attention back to Mishka. The man was still yelling.

"Kit! I know you're here."

"She's not." Luther stepped closer, still leaving enough room to duck behind a tree if needed. The moon's glow kept the area behind the cabin lit up almost to daylight proportions with the reflection off the thin layer of snow, and his enemy was smart enough to stay in the shadow cast by the building, but not quite genius. Luther saw the outline of the man, and more importantly, his weapon, against the fresh snow on the shrubbery.

The unmistakable profile of an AR-15 made his blood run cold. He and Kit were lucky they hadn't been killed by the spray of bullets Mishka had already fired. He could only hope the shot his leg had taken was a graze, but from the deep fire in his thigh, he doubted it.

Kit.

She'd be safe—that's all that mattered. He clenched his teeth against the pain. He'd been through worse.

"Come on out, Mishka, and let's talk this over, man-to-man."

"Only if you send Kit out first." The coward thought he was dealing with a stupid ROC operative.

Luther heard the desperation that trickled into the jerk's voice. And he hadn't fired again, which Luther hoped meant that he hadn't had a chance to reload. He'd gone through a clip's worth of rounds, or close to it.

"I can't do that because she's not here." Luther moved closer, keeping his eye on Mishka. A loud thud sounded to the left of the building and he held his breath, know-

ing Mishka heard it, too. Luther had given away his location with his voice, so Mishka knew it wasn't him.

Run, Kit, run.

Mishka fired into the air. "Kit! Stop this nonsense."

Luther wasn't about to allow Mishka a chance at
getting Kit. The thought of what the bastard would do
to her wasn't a place he could allow his mind to go and
remain sane. Sweat began to pour from his temples
and into his eyes; he knew it was a sign of shock—his
body had done this before.

But he'd never had a woman who'd meant so much
to him, in so short a time, also be at risk.

Save Kit.

"You don't want her, Mishka. You want me." Keeping his weapon ready to fire, Luther stepped into the
clearing. Anything to distract the madman. Anything
to save the woman who meant more to him—

"Put your weapon down, lawman." Mishka's weapon
was pointed at him, but Luther saw that his face was
still pointing toward the trees where they'd heard Kit
trip. Luther had heard her feet when she rose and was
confident she'd gotten at least to the edge of the clearing but couldn't be sure.

"I'm a sure shot, Mishka. Drop your weapon." Luther prepared to fire, but the ground swelled beneath
him as Mishka's image dipped. He blinked, willing
back the nausea and black dots that closed in on him.

Luther pulled the trigger but never heard the shot
go off as he dropped to the ground, unable to maintain consciousness.

Kit.

Kit half ran, half limped through the trees, on the
path she and Luther had found yesterday when they'd

begun their hike. She had to fight every instinct to run back to Luther, to tell him to stop talking to Mishka. Her former stepson was a maniac, just like his father, and would kill Luther if given the chance.

More shots fired and she kept going, knowing that her and Luther's survival depended on her getting to the road and then doing as Luther had instructed—keeping to the trees but following the dirt road back to the main highway. It'd take her all night.

She sent up a prayer that the quiet behind her was because Luther had neutralized Mishka, and nearly cried in relief when she saw that she was past the cabin, beyond where the Jeep was parked.

Had been parked. Flames still burned, on what she could only guess was the upholstery. The frame glowed in a few places, and the stench of the burning vehicle was worse here, making her eyes water.

She knew she was visible but took the chance to cross the small clearing and headed toward the dirt road. It was a small victory but she'd take it. The sense of accomplishment when she recognized the road through the smoke and moonlight spurred her forward, her bruised hands and knees not so painful.

As soon as she got to the road, she'd climb back into the wooded area—

A harsh yank on her still-damp hair forced a scream from her lips, and she found herself flat on her back, looking at the tip of a rifle barrel.

"Did you really think you'd be able to get away, Kit?" Mishka's profile against the pale moonlight was more sinister than the demons of her worst nightmares. Because, unlike his father, Vadim, Mishka wasn't in jail. He was here, and she was certain he was going to kill her.

* * *

"How much longer?" Colt rode shotgun as Claudia plowed her Hummer up the side of an Appalachian mountain, her driving skills only hinting at her well-honed fighting skills.

"Five minutes, tops." Her face, illuminated by the dashboard, reflected her distress. "It's not like either of them to not check in."

He ran a hand over his face. "I know." If Kit was hurt, or worse, at the hands of ROC, he wasn't sure he'd forgive himself for sending her on this op. She'd suffered so much at the hands of ROC and one of its members, to have to face the end like this...

"Stop it, Colt."

"What?"

"I know you. You're blaming yourself. This isn't our fault. We're up against it, about to take ROC out of Silver Valley and dismantle all their East Coast operations. Whatever it takes to get the job done is the deal, my love."

"And this is why I knew I had to marry you. Who else can make facing a deadly adversary sound so sexy?"

Their phones sounding alerts cut off her answering laugh.

"Keep driving—I've got it." Colt checked his phone and his stomach dropped when he read the SOS.

"It's from Luther. He says the Jeep's been blown up. He and Kit are evacuating."

"There it is." He looked out the dashboard and heard both their shocked intakes of breath. All that remained of Luther's Jeep was a burning pile of steel, approximately a half mile from their location.

Claudia screeched to a halt, grabbing a rifle from the back seat and handing it to Colt. She took one for herself. They both wore holstered handguns.

"Ready?" She looked at him and he nodded. "Let's do it." Claudia exited and followed suit on his side.

They walked away from the Hummer, weapons drawn.

"How do you want to proceed?" He was a member of Trail Hikers because he was the Chief of Police and needed to be able to work closely with the clandestine group. Claudia was the expert and boss on any TH ops, and right now TH was running the show on the push to bring down ROC. FBI was in the mix, too, and would get a lot of the credit when they succeeded, but anyone who was briefed on the entire mission knew the deal.

Claudia Michele was the lynchpin that held it all together.

He watched his wife, the love of his life, assess the situation in the moonlight. "We could drive the rest of the way there, but it'll give us away. It's no more than a half mile from here."

"Let's go, then."

Claudia was a faster runner than he was, but Colt could pour it on when needed, and kept up with her, the urgency to get to the cabin palpable.

After five minutes, he noticed the shape of a building next to the reddish glow, which was growing larger as they closed in.

Claudia's breath hardly hitched. "Yes. It looks like a beat-up shack but it's practically bombproof."

He said nothing. If Claudia, the director of the most elite government shadow agency in the world, said it was "practically" bombproof, it meant it was one of the safest places on earth.

They drew closer and slowed to a quick walk. Claudia motioned for him to stop. The stench of what he recognized as a burning car replaced the pine scent of the woods. Colt had another familiar sensation, one he always faced with deep regret.

He'd been around enough crime scenes, come to the aid of undercover cops enough times to know a bad deal.

Fear welled, managed by years of experience. Colt had to be the partner Claudia needed. Especially if, as he suspected, they'd arrived too late to make a difference in the outcome of tonight's op.

"Stop it." Kit's voice scraped her throat, her jaw clenched as she fought against her hair being pulled by the man she never wanted to see again. Not for the first time she wished she'd worked harder to have him put away, too.

"Shut the freak up, or I'll shoot you in between your pretty blue eyes, bitch." Mishka panted, the physical exertion not in his wheelhouse. If she weren't trying to get out of his grip, she'd point out that he'd copied Luther's threat. Mishka was not original. He was the classic image of his father, allowing rich living to cause obesity and poor health.

"You don't have to make it hurt." Gasping against the assault, she held on to her hair at the root, trying to ease the discomfort of his tugs. He dragged her past the side of the cabin where he'd caught her, away from the incinerated Jeep.

Luther.

"You'll never get away with—" A hit to her cheek seared pain through her skull, already shaken from the hit in the sauna. She fought to gain balance on the wet leaves, surprised at Mishka's strength.

"I already have. I've saved you. You'll be best with me, Kit. Trust me." Fear spiked her pain as she wondered what had happened to Luther. She had to save them both if Luther had been hurt. Mishka's face was pale even in the moonlight, and she wondered if he'd not had his beer or vodka tonight. If he was in early alcohol withdrawal, he was only going to get meaner the longer she was with him.

"Use this if you have to." Luther's command cut through her fear-fueled thoughts.

The handgun was still in her waistband. It had felt like a rock when Mishka had thrown her to the ground, but thankfully it hadn't gone off. Mishka hadn't discovered it, proving he truly was a fool. He assumed she was the same girl who'd been trapped in a loveless, painful relationship by his father.

She heard Mishka's foot hit a rock and he stumbled, momentarily loosening his grip on her hair. She braced herself for another fall as he let go of her hair and she twisted out of his clutches. It was almost too easy as she found herself on all fours and quickly scrambled to standing, backing up from him.

"Don't even think about it!" Enraged, he swung out for her, his hand missing her head by no more than an inch.

"It'll be easier to go if we're both standing." She forced the words out, told herself to focus on her breathing, all the while watching his hand with the handgun. The rifle he'd used on them was slung sloppily over his shoulder and she recognized an AR-15. It made sense it was what had fired the bullets through the trees at her and Luther. At least Mishka seemed to have forgotten about the rifle for now.

A handgun could be just as deadly, though.

He loomed close, his hand just missing her upper arm.

"Get over here." He wasn't listening to reason and she kept out of his reach, unable to bolt, knowing he'd shoot her on the spot. No matter how much he said he wanted to be with her.

"Stop. Police." A loud male voice sounded further down the dirt road.

Colt.

Claudia was near, too. She'd bet on it.

The interruption forced Mishka to look away, and Kit seized the chance to grab the pistol from her back waistband. Her fingers switched off the safety and she prepared to fire, aiming at Mishka before she had time to think twice. All the hours on Vadim's firing range, coupled with the training she received from Trail Hikers on an unofficial basis, kicked in. Mostly, though, she felt the strength of Luther's belief in her.

"I'll never let her go." Mishka's voice was soaked with determination of the same intensity that she'd watched Vadim channel into trafficking hundreds, possibly thousands of girls into the country. Mishka wasn't going to budge.

"Put your weapon down and your hands up, Mishka. We can talk this out." Colt was an expert at criminal negotiations and Kit prayed he'd strike a chord with Mishka, make him change his mind.

She peered into the darkness, unable to see anyone

with the Chief, but she knew if Colt was here, Claudia had at least sent him. Somehow they'd known that Luther and she were in trouble.

Colt would never come in here alone. There had to be backup.

"Never." Mishka's response was little more than a growl and she knew Colt might not have heard him. Mishka moved quickly for a man unused to physical exertion, dropping his handgun and grabbing the rifle, aiming it in the direction of Colt's voice.

"He's got an AR-15!" she screamed as she prepared to fire.

"Shut up!" But Mishka didn't look at her as he began to swing the rifle in a sweeping motion. He was going to shoot at Colt and whoever was in the woods nearby.

Kit fired.

Mishka jerked as if he'd received a jolt of electricity to his side, then turned his head to her. His arms dropped and he let go of both weapons, wavering on his feet as he stared at her through the moonlight. Dark, troubled eyes blazed in a face lined with disbelief. "You shot me."

He dropped to the ground with an anticlimactic *plop*. Kit quickly kicked the handgun and rifle out of his reach, careful to avoid his hands in case he was still capable of reaching for her.

"Kit, are you okay?" Colt's voice halted any potential racing thoughts, and she met her boss's gaze with newfound steadiness.

"I'm okay, but Luther—"

A second figure ran up to them. "Good work, Kit. Where's Luther?" Claudia had provided backup for Colt.

"I don't know—somewhere behind the cabin, maybe. I thought he might be here, behind me."

"I'll give Mishka first aid. You find Luther." Colt spoke as he knelt next to the still figure, and Kit had no time to worry if she'd mortally injured Mishka. She had to get to Luther.

That awful feeling of something being wrong assailed her as she and Claudia ran around the back of the cabin.

"Luther!" she shouted as Claudia swept a flashlight beam across the clearing, the light illuminating the shadows that hid from the moonlight.

"We were back there." Kit ran toward the trees, fighting the panic that welled in her midsection. *Please, Luther, be okay. Be right here, safe.* As she came up against the woods, she saw him. Her blood ran cold.

Lying on his back, his upper torso atop a crushed bush while his long legs stretched out into the flattened ground, Luther was as still as a corpse.

"No!" she screamed, and ran to him. "Claudia, he's here. Luther!" Kit pounced on the ground next to Luther and grabbed his face, willed him to open his eyes. Claudia was on the other side, her slim fingers pressed to the side of Luther's throat.

"Is he…" *No, no no.* This couldn't be happening. Not to Luther.

"He's still alive but I think he's shot. We have to find out where, Kit. Quickly." They worked from his head to his torso, down his sides. At the midpoint of his thigh, Kit's fingers felt something sticky.

"Claudia, here." The flashlight illuminated what Kit feared—a large bloodstain with a single hole in the middle of his pants.

"Use your jacket, Kit." She didn't have to be told how or why. Trail Hikers and SVPD provided extensive first aid training to include bullet wounds. Kit felt underneath his leg for a possible exit wound but it was difficult with the ground already wet from the rain and snow. As she worked to stabilize Luther and stop any further bleeding, she heard Claudia calling in for emergency medical aid.

Satisfied she'd done the best she could, she held Luther's hand and looked at Claudia. "They're never going to be able to get here in time. We had first aid equipment in the Jeep but it's gone."

Footfalls sounded and they turned, Claudia with a weapon ready to fire. Colt held up his hands as he neared. "Whoa, it's me."

Claudia didn't apologize, and if she weren't so worried about Luther, Kit might have had to laugh. "Announce yourself, then."

"Mishka's out of commission, but I think there's a good chance he'll make it, if we can get him to an ER." His voice trailed off as he took in the scene before him. "Luther."

Claudia nodded. "He's got a bullet in his thigh, and he's going to need attention ASAP. I called it in, but we're going to need the board."

"On it." Colt turned and ran back around the cabin.

"You have a board with you?" Kit knew Claudia was always prepared, but this seemed over-the-top even for the director of Trail Hikers.

"We drove our Hummer. We'll fit both casualties in the back and meet the life flight at the base of the mountain, in the parking lot."

Kit shook her head. "I'll help you get them inside

your vehicle, but I have to stay here, Claudia. We can't lose Ivanov's trail over this." Though it would kill her to have to entrust Luther's care to someone else, she couldn't help him anymore.

She could, however, find Ivanov.

"You think you've found him, then?"

"Yes—did you see my last report? There's enough chatter in Russian, or at least there was, that I think it could be him. But he's smart and using a different burner with each call. By the time I get it unscrambled, he's ended the connection."

"Typical." Claudia snorted. "You can't be out here alone, though. No one can do the stakeout here. There's a good chance this was all compromised by a leak in SVPD."

That got Kit's attention.

"One of our own? Do you think it's a TH, too?"

"I don't know. We have never had a mole in TH, due to our extensive background checks. But it can happen. Right now I'm thinking it's SVPD. Either way, it's bad business."

"Who are they working for? ROC?"

"Don't know. Most likely. That's why I hope Mishka makes it—we can ask him about his plans, how he knew where to find you. He may be the person who's been following you."

"He's not. I would have seen him."

"But you might not have been aware of someone he hired to follow you."

"No." Kit fought back the nausea that threatened. She'd never felt so helpless, even in her darkest time with Vadim. Holding the cold hand of the man who'd shown more love to her in a few short days than she'd ever received her entire life, she was powerless to save him.

"You've done what you can do here, Kit. Luther's tough. He's been through much more extensive injuries. Get the comms gear together and be prepared to set it back up at a new location."

Kit nodded, followed it with "yes, ma'am." Then, throwing all professional caution to the wind, she leaned over and kissed Luther on the lips.

"Hang tight, babe. We're going to get these bastards."

Chapter 16

Luther regained consciousness in the hospital, when the prick of several needles broke through the fog he'd been in since he went down.

"What the—"

"Luther. It's Claudia. Take it easy. Here." She held a straw to his lips and he sucked the cool water down, then immediately sputtered at his dry throat.

"Where's Kit?" He focused on Claudia's face as his eyes couldn't see any farther yet. Had he taken a hit to the head?

"Funny you ask that first thing. She's safe, working."

"How many bullets did I take?"

"Only one, and it was a clear shot, with an exit wound. You're lucky. It didn't hit your femoral artery, and you'll be sore but on your feet soon."

Wasn't that the truth. He'd witnessed horrific gunshot wounds to the thigh that shattered femurs, cost the victims months of surgeries and rehab.

"When can I get out of here?"

"Maybe tomorrow, or the next day."

"I can't stay here that long." It was excruciating to talk, to think. "Did they knock me out for surgery or something?"

"It's the pain meds. They had to keep you sedated while they cleaned out your wound."

That explained why his leg burned like hell. And he knew he was only experiencing the earliest part of it. A gunshot wound to his shoulder years ago had taken the better part of two years to heal, and that shoulder still got stiff in cold weather.

"I have to be on the op with Kit, Claudia. You know that." Kit wasn't able to fully protect herself; she needed a sworn agent or officer who could keep watch while she worked the comms.

"She's safe for now, Luther." Claudia's face moved away, and he saw her sit in a chair that was pulled up to the bed. "Do you want to sit up a bit more?"

"Yeah."

She handed him the bed's controller and depressed the button with him. He let go when he was at maybe forty-five degrees, but it felt more like he was bent in two. "I hate being knocked down like this."

Claudia patted his forearm. "We all do. So do you want to tell me what happened?"

Guilt pierced his pain, the memory of being with Kit in the bathhouse pouring a healing peace through him while making him afraid to tell his boss he'd screwed up.

"Heavens, Luther, you're as red as a berry. I don't want to know any personal details about you and Kit. I'm talking about when you got shot."

"Oh." He lifted an arm to rub his face and saw that the IV needle was in the top of his hand. "We took a break from the op, since it looked like we were going to have to wait for the bulk of the hunters to show up before Ivanov would risk active chatter. Kit did think he was there, but couldn't be sure and he never stayed active enough for her to definitively trace him."

"Yes, she told me that much. When did you know there was an intruder?"

"My Jeep. It blew up. I knew as soon as I heard it that we were under attack. I was in the shower and Kit was in the sauna."

"How much time until you were in the woods, trying to get past the cabin?"

"No more than two minutes, tops." Kit had worked beside him like any other agent, keeping her cool and doing the next right thing. "Kit was a champ. She takes direction without question and never got in the way of the op, or what I tried to do. Where's Mishka?"

"He's in custody, healing here from the gunshot wound."

"You shot him? Or Colt?"

"No—Kit shot him. Took him out before he could mow down Colt with the AR-15 he was carrying. I was backing up Colt and would have shot, but Kit acted more quickly and most likely saved all four of us."

"I knew she had it in her. If she had to, that is."

"She's not going to be in any kind of trouble for using a weapon, if that's on your mind."

"No, it's not. Not at all." He rested for a minute, hating how he couldn't push through the pain and exhaustion. Claudia remained silent and he was so grateful in the moment that she had combat experience as a US Marine and had seen her share of wounded men. His current state wouldn't be held against him and she'd get him back in the field ASAP. "I messed up, Claudia."

"Hey, if you're about to tell me something personal that went on between you and Kit, save it. I'm your director, not your priest."

"Don't make me laugh. I don't have the energy."

"Is there something else you needed to say?"

"Yes. I mean it—I made a mistake. I know Kit's been through so much and it's never a good idea to get involved with someone you're working with, and yet I did. But I promise that our involvement did nothing to hurt the op." In fact being in the bath hut had bought them time they wouldn't have had in the cabin. No matter that it was a fortress of sorts, they'd have been forced to leave through the one door and been far more vulnerable.

"I implicitly trust both of you, Luther. You did an excellent job so far, but of course your cover's been blown at least with Mishka, and whoever he spoke to, so Kit's in one of our TH safe houses, working on the mission from there." She told him exactly which one. He was familiar with it from reports he'd read. "There are several TH agents coming and going from this particular location, so she's never alone. She's safe, Luther."

He had to see her, but now wasn't the time to press Claudia. It had to be mission first, and besides, he wasn't in any shape to take off and find Kit. But once he was, he'd ask about visting her.

"Claudia, one more thing—how did Mishka ever find us? I was careful to not be followed."

"You were, but some officers are better at surveillance than others."

"'Officers?'"

She nodded, her grim expression not unlike the granite outcroppings all along the Appalachian Trail. "Yes. Our forensics team found evidence of GPS trackers on the frame of your Jeep. They were still intact, surprisingly. We believe there's a mole at SVPD."

He tried to whistle but his lips were too dry. This time he reached for the water, the plastic cup on a bed table over his lap. Gulping the water down, he thought of Kit, how she'd be doing. Did she know there was a mole?

"Any idea who?"

"Not yet."

"Wait—do you think Mishka had anything to do with the shooting at Kit's apartment, that he got information from the mole?" Realization dawned and his gut swirled, but it wasn't from the pain meds, which often made him nauseous. That was why the shooter, if it was Mishka, knew Kit had someone in her apartment—another man.

"Yes, we think Mishka was the shooter. We're waiting on the ballistics from the handgun he had on him at the cabin, to match them with the shells we found in Kit's apartment. Colt thinks it's someone in SVPD that has been turned because of either a threat from ROC, or by becoming involved in the heroin trade themselves. It's not uncommon in local precincts, unfortunately. And face it, East Coast ROC is on its last legs. It needs every last helping hand it can find."

"But ROC lost Vadim Valensky when he was imprisoned. I would think the authorities would make sure his son, Mishka, had no leverage with ROC anymore."

"We all thought Mishka Valensky would find a more legal means of making a living, and on the surface it looked like he had, with the pawnshop."

"But?"

She shrugged. "I don't know since we haven't been able to interrogate him yet. His injuries were far more serious than yours."

So Kit had aimed not to injure, but kill. He knew she wouldn't have done it unless forced to, but he was proud of her for digging deep and doing the right thing, to save her life as well as Claudia's and Colt's.

She saved your life, too.

"We were so close to cornering Ivanov." He couldn't keep the regret out of his voice and closed his eyes as the weight of exhaustion tugged him down.

"We'll get him—you will, Luther. Rest for now. Kit's on the case until you're ready."

As he sank back into darkness, he thought about almost witnessing a second woman he cared about die. But Kit was alive, and had never been the willing wife of a mob boss.

Kit was her own woman. He'd best remember that, because in this weakened state he couldn't stop thinking about her and how much he wanted her as his woman.

His lifelong partner.

"Come here, sweet boy." Kit petted Koshka's silky black fur and he purred in response, curling into her lap as she worked at the comms station. Claudia had no problem with agents and analysts bringing their pets to one of the more modern safe houses.

Kit had been given half a day to gather what she needed for the next few weeks. The safe house was actually a fairly large complex, with a full operational facility located in the back rooms, apart from the main living quarters. It was as modern as her home with Vadim had been, but without the garish embellishments and constant reminders of his trophy hunting. If she lived to be one hundred, it wouldn't be long enough to never see another animal the taxidermist had preserved.

"Any luck today?" Trina Lopez-Bristol, a former US Marshal and one of the first Trail Hikers Agents who'd befriended Kit, sat in the chair next to the bank of screens.

"No. I'm beginning to think that Mishka Valensky ruined our chances of nabbing Ivanov, at least in this area. There have been absolutely zero hits on cell phones matching the burners we know he and Markova purchased."

"That was a brilliant feat, figuring out where the burners had come from." Trina referred to how Kit and the TH comms team had been able to detect frequency characteristics attributed to only one certain make of burner phone, and then trace them to one specific superstore in Western Pennsylvania, where other sporadic sightings of Ivanov and Markova had occurred.

"It's not doing us a lot of good now, unfortunately."

"Have patience. When I was a Marshal I used to think it was time to give up on a target. But just when it looked like I'd lost a trail, or they'd managed to disappear again, opportunity opened up. It will with these two."

"I wish I had your confidence."

"You have more than that. Luther wouldn't have agreed to work with you if you weren't top-notch."

"Everyone at TH is the best."

"True, but some of us are more special." Trina shot her a wide grin and Kit laughed. The mention of Luther's name, however, made the sad longing for him flare, and she wished for the hundredth time she'd ignored Claudia's order to stick to going to her apartment and then directly to the safe house. But she didn't want to get herself, or Luther, in trouble with Claudia. And Claudia and Colt were right; Kit had a big target on her head. She'd helped take their number one human trafficker on the East Coast out of commission. ROC didn't forgive and forget.

"How was your time with Luther, out in the woods?" Trina asked the question innocently enough, but Kit wasn't budging.

"Um, it was good, until the shoot-out."

"You saved the day, from what I heard."

Kit shook her head. "All I did was do my job. Anyone in that circumstance would have shot Mishka."

"It was brave of you, Kit. After all you've been through, no one would blame you if you'd frozen." Trina's frank assessment soothed Kit's concerns about whether she'd done everything correctly—had she aimed the gun higher or lower, Mishka wouldn't be here. But if she'd gone for his legs, he could have been interviewed sooner, giving up information that was more actionable.

"Everyone here seems to know what my life was

like before." She didn't confide in anyone but her therapist and Annie, but the TH agents along with several of the SVPD officers had all seen notes about her in Vadim's file. They'd been in on the operation that took Vadim out and saved countless women from becoming sex slaves. "What you all don't realize is that I'm so grateful to be working alongside you, making a difference, putting a dent in ROC and other crime organizations. I don't want one other girl to ever go through what I did. What we do here at TH matters, you know?"

Trina nodded. "Trust me, I get it. When Rob and I got back together, it was during an attempt to bring down Ivanov. We have a son, as you know, and the thought of not only ROC personally but the heroin affecting his life makes me shake in my boots."

"Pennsylvania's done a lot to enact laws to protect us all from the opioid epidemic, but we have to do our part to stop the supply, too."

"And you are, Kit. Look how much help your language skills have lent to the cause!"

"If I can get a comms hit on Ivanov or Markova, it'd make my day." Kit had complete confidence that once TH or SVPD found Ivanov, it'd be the end of the road for him and Markova.

"What's going on?" They turned to face Rob Bristol, a former Navy SEAL turned Trail Hiker. He spoke to both of them but his eyes focused on his wife, and Kit did her best to ignore the deep pang their obvious bond triggered. Since when had she longed for that kind of love aimed at her?

"Nothing, yet, but Kit's going to catch them at any moment. I'm certain."

"Ha. From your lips to the heavens." They all

laughed, and Kit knew they weren't laughing at how she'd murdered the saying. She let the warmth of being included in a group of such stellar people buoy her and told herself it was enough. It had to be.

"Ready to head home?" Trina stood and walked over to Rob.

"Yeah." They looked at Kit.

Trina spoke. "We've got to get home to take Jake to soccer practice."

"There's still soccer after Thanksgiving?"

"He's on a travel team," Rob answered, but they both beamed with pride. Kit didn't know much about the couple, except that they'd reunited several years after their son had been conceived during a combat mission, when they were in the Navy.

"Enjoy!" She wiggled her fingers at them and decided it was time for a quick cup of tea. She'd been sitting at the console for the last couple of hours with zero results. The operations center was always manned, 24-7, and during a high stakes op other TH agents worked from the locale, as well. Like Trina and Rob, they often commuted the hour to and from Silver Valley.

"Hey, Amy, will you take my screens for a few? Can I get you a cup of coffee or tea?" She spoke to the comms agent who was working until midnight.

"Sure thing. I'll have a green tea."

"No problem. Thanks for spelling me." Kit went into the community kitchen and made the tea, trying to keep her mind off Luther and how he'd be feeling by now. It'd been almost a week, and she hadn't seen or heard from him. Not that she should—he didn't owe her anything. And she had to stop thinking of him as more than a work colleague, or a man she'd happened to let bring her to orgasm.

But it was impossible. Luther was more than a TH partner or a onetime lover. They'd formed a bond out in that tiny cabin.

All those years with Vadim she'd walled herself off emotionally from him, even in the most intimate acts. She had urges and sensations, but sex with Vadim had never been pleasurable. And he was so selfish, never even asking her if she'd been satisfied.

In Luther's arms last week, she'd discovered what she'd been missing, and what she could look forward to again.

She and Luther shared undeniable chemistry, and if it were possible to date him without it being so complicated, she'd consider it. But he'd made it clear he wasn't in the market for a girlfriend, and Kit hadn't gone through all the years of counseling and PTSD therapy of the past years to not know who she was. She'd be risking her heart if she got too close to Luther. He was that kind of man.

Knowing what was best for her was a far cry from stopping the longing that assaulted her with every memory of him, though.

Chapter 17

"We still don't know who the leak is?" Luther stood in Colt's office, preferring to keep his leg straight than lower himself into the deep chairs in front of the desk. A week out and his thigh was still sore as heck.

"No. I've narrowed it down to maybe five possibilities, but you know what this is like. It's trying to find the snake amongst the brothers and sisters you trust with your life."

"Right." He winced. There had been a turncoat in one of his undercover teams in the FBI when he'd been a new agent. The sense of betrayal had hit the other agents hard, and the guilty party was still in jail for passing classified information to the enemy. "Claudia sent me over to see if you've been able to get any more information from Mishka Valensky." SVPD had jurisdiction in all that happened with the case, at the agreement of FBI, DEA and other local LEA. Trail Hikers didn't exist in practicality, and the federal agencies didn't want their presence in the area exposed.

"I was at the hospital this morning. He's still not talking."

"He will once he figures out he'll be next to Daddy in the slammer."

Colt shook his head. "I'm not so sure. One thing with ROC and anyone who's worked for them, they hold out hope of a breakout or release due to their slick lawyers. They're not the cooperating kind." Colt picked up a file from his desk and handed it to Luther. "These came in, though. I haven't been able to get them to Claudia or TH yet. I don't want to risk anyone in my department seeing them." Colt's voice was heavy with his regret over the leak.

"Understood." Luther took the file and flipped through its contents—several photographs of Ivanov and a woman whose facial profile matched Markova's, but with different hairstyles. They were in the same car, at different highway pit stops and small-town grocers. "They're not flipping cars like they were a few weeks ago."

"No. And they're being bold, stopping at some of the same gas stations more than once."

"Like they want a showdown. They're headed to the win-or-die meeting." Luther thumbed the last photo, taken as Markova got into the driver's seat of the sedan, Ivanov on the passenger side. "It's not like Ivanov to give up control, even with driving."

"I thought the same. Do you see anything different about his face?"

Luther studied the photo more closely. "If the color's correct, he looks kind of off. Yellow, even."

"Exactly."

"You think it's the ROC disease?" Luther looked to Colt for his opinion. So many ROC bosses had bitten the dust over the years not from being captured by LEA but from cirrhosis and other complications of alcoholism. It was the genetic curse of many, and especially those raised on vodka.

"Could be. But Claudia and I are certain of one thing." Colt paused, weighing his words. "We think that Markova wants to take over ROC."

Understanding hit Luther. "That makes sense. Why else would she allow him to hold her hostage this past year?"

"It's clear from the photos that she isn't being kept on a tight leash by him any longer. She goes in and out of stores while he waits in the car."

"Unlike when they first took off after the tombstone shoot-out. What do you want me to do?" He'd gotten orders from Claudia to work with Colt as a liaison between TH and SVPD. It chafed his butt that he couldn't get back in the thick of it, but his injury would put too many at risk.

"I think we need you at the safe house." Colt didn't look up from his keyboard as he typed, for which Luther was grateful. He'd wanted to race to Kit's side as soon as Claudia had told him where Kit was. "I'm printing out all SVPD has on Markova and Ivanov, so you'll know what our regular cops have. The ones who work with TH know more, like you."

"How are we going to figure out who your mole is, Chief?"

Colt met his gaze this time, and Luther saw a lifetime of weariness. "I've only had one other in SVPD,
but I've faced bad cops in two other departments when
I was younger. It's my experience that they usually do
themselves in. My one hope is that it happens without
hurting any of our people, SVPD and TH. Here you
go." Colt grabbed the reports off his printer and handed
them to Luther. "Get a good night's rest, then head out
to the safe house at dawn."

Luther nodded. It was protocol not to come and go
at the safe house during daylight unless absolutely necessary. "Roger. See you out there, Chief."

Colt leaned back in his chair, his hands behind his
head. "You will."

"You don't have to tell me all the juicy details, but
it's obvious you're different. Something happened when
you were out in the field with Luther." Annie absently
petted Koshka as they lay side by side on the leather
sofa. Kit was on the other side of the great room, clean-
ing up her meal. She and Annie were alone in the more
relaxed, living area of the safe house, and she'd told
Annie most of what had happened at the cabin. Annie
was spending time with her while Josh was working.
Josh and several dual SVPD/TH operatives were running the operations center adjacent to the safe house,
for the duration of the Ivanov/Markova takedown.

"I am different. And I know you'll think that I'm
being too hasty, but there's something between Luther
and I that I haven't ever felt."

"Why do you think I'd ever consider you as being
'hasty' about anything? You're the most thoughtful
person I know, Kit."

"I haven't had enough experience with men yet. Didn't you say I should date a lot of guys before settling down?" She shook her head. "Not that I'm thinking of settling down." She knew her red face betrayed her.

Annie got up from the couch, carrying Koshka with her. "Hold on. Yes, I think it'd be ideal to see how you feel about different men. But you have all kinds of experience, Kit. Just not the happiest type." Annie wriggled into one of the island chairs, and Koshka jumped out of her arms. "Sorry, kitty. Look, I don't want to give you the wrong impression. If you've met someone who's made this much of an impression on you in such a short time, it might be more than just the fact that he's the first guy you've ever really chosen to be with."

Kit didn't know what to think. But she knew what she felt. "I think Luther's special."

"Then you need to tell him, Kit. Life's too short—"

"Don't you think I know that? I thought he might die out there." She choked back tears, held her wobbly chin up. "I couldn't go to him in the hospital. It was too risky—if any of Mishka's men are still tracking me, I'd lead them to Luther."

"That's not really it, is it?" Annie's tone made Kit want to rage and laugh at the same time.

"Yes. No. I don't know."

"I think you do. How much time do you have until your next shift starts?"

"I'm back on at 0400."

"Come back into town with me. I'll drop you off, and Josh can bring you back when he heads in for his shift."

"I can't go back to my apartment." Kit remembered

Claudia and Colt had been clear that she wasn't safe until they had ROC neutralized.

"Not your apartment. The only condo in Silver Valley that is as fortified, electronically, as this place."

Luther's apartment.

Kit's knees shook as she walked the steps to Luther's apartment. It wasn't because she was afraid of what she wanted. She had nothing but joyful anticipation for what she hoped happened tonight. Nor was she concerned about being away from the safe house for this short time. Annie had promised that Josh would be here to get her before dawn, in enough time to make her next shift at the comms station.

It'd been tough when she'd asked Claudia for the break from the safe house. The main concern on both Claudia's and Colt's part was Kit's safety. Kit assured Claudia that she'd be escorted to and from the safe house by other TH agents and that she planned to stay at Luther's. Claudia had given her the okay, no further questions asked.

What neither Claudia nor Colt knew was that she hadn't run her plan past Luther. She'd tried to reach him all week since the shooting and he'd done no more than texted short replies, stating he was "fine" and "back at work." But he never stopped in the safe house, and she had a hunch it had everything to do with her and his not wanting to see her.

She walked up to his door and took in a deep breath. As she'd told Annie, she might be new at real intimacy but wasn't an innocent. Kit knew that what she and Luther shared was more than sexual chemistry, and wanted to prove it to him, to herself. Tonight.

She raised her hand to the buzzer. Before she made contact, the door opened and Luther was in front of her. A little paler than she'd last seen him, but far more vibrant. Standing in front of her, his gaze steady and intense as ever.

"Oh! I—"

"Come in here." His hand grasped her upper arm and in one smooth move he had her up against his chest, his back on the wall. He shut the door with his hand, the other arm wrapped around her waist.

"Luther—"

"No talking, Kit." He wrapped the other arm around her, pulled her up tight against him. "Except—how much time do you have?"

"Until four." Eight hours until she had to leave. She watched his expression as he comprehended her reply. Heat grew in her midsection, spreading to her breasts, her sex. All the planned speeches that she'd mentally practiced over and over failed her in the face of her need for him.

"We have all night." He gave her a quick, hard kiss. His lips left hers too quickly and she leaned in, but he shook his head and gently broke the embrace. "Then forget what I said—we should talk first."

He walked into the living room, and she had no idea but to follow. It was the same as she'd last seen it, before they'd gone into the field. Faced with something so tangibly a part of who she'd been just a short ten days ago, the truth hit her like a wash of ice water.

She was in love with Luther.

"I'll make us some tea, since alcohol is out." He was in the kitchen, pouring water into a small pot. "We might not have until morning, if word comes down sooner that Ivanov and Markova are on their way to the ROC meeting."

"I know." She made a slow walk to the sofa, where she sat. Space from Luther wasn't what she'd expected to need tonight, but she had to take a moment to process what she'd just discovered.

"You want an herbal or straight black?"

"Herbal's fine." She tried to make her voice steadier than she felt.

They grew quiet as he boiled the water. Kit saw that he had his security system in place, his laptop showing views from six different cameras, including the apartment's front entry and his door. No wonder he'd been right there when she showed up.

"How's Koshka liking the safe house?" He placed a mug on the end table near her and took the easy chair opposite. Now that she was under his direct scrutiny, it was more important than ever that she keep it together. She'd come here to make love to Luther, but telling him how she felt wasn't on the table. It couldn't be; it wasn't fair to either of them. Kit never wanted to burden someone with her emotions. It had to be mutual, the in-love thing. And she didn't have to love someone to enjoy great sex with them.

"She's adapted, believe it or not. The other agents adore her, except for Kyle, who's allergic. Have you met him yet?"

Luther tilted his head. "I don't know—there have been a lot of introductions since I've been here."

"He owns the coffee shop downstairs. That's his cover, for when he's not doing TH work."

"Actually, I have met him, but I didn't realize he

was LEA or TH. The first morning I was here I ran into him back by the café's Dumpsters."

"He's not going to be in the coffee shop for a while. A lot of TH part-time agents are working now. I'm surprised the people of Silver Valley don't suspect something's going on." She knew she was babbling but couldn't stop the chatter.

"Kit." He leaned over and grasped her hand. "It's okay. Calm down."

"I can't calm down! You almost died out there, and then I couldn't come see you. Claudia and Colt were insistent that I stay in the safe house, let you heal." She knew she blushed red as ever, but pressed on. "I hated not seeing you, not knowing if you'd really not been too badly injured." Her gaze dropped to his leg, covered by his workout pants. "It's still painful, isn't it?"

He shrugged. "It's sore, yeah, but not that bad. I can get around. It has prevented me from being with the team that's standing by to take down Ivanov, but I'll provide backup. It's all good as long as we bring them in."

She watched his every expression, her fingers tingling to touch him, run her hands over his face, his shoulders, his—

"Kit, we've got to talk about what's going on between us."

At least he kept it in the present tense, but she wasn't going to let that be her go-ahead to tell him what she was feeling in her heart. Not yet. Maybe never.

"Luther, that's why I came over tonight."

"Is that all?" His low timbre threw a match on her desire, and the place between her legs clamored for attention. She grasped her hands together, determined to get through this conversation before she jumped him.

"Well, no, but that all depends on you, too. I came here to tell you that I'm positive that we shared something real out in that cabin."

"And the bath hut."

"Um, yes. That was very nice, no question, but what I'm talking about is more than that, Luther. You became my friend, a confidant, someone I trust with my life."

"How foolish for you. I almost got you killed. If you hadn't taken out Mishka, we wouldn't be sitting here."

She shook her head. "No. I'm not going to let you play the self-pity card, Luther. I was able to take out Mishka only because you told me I could do it. Your confidence in my abilities did it. Yes, I have the shooting skills, but combined with your support it made me invincible."

"He's still not talking, you know." Luther's gaze was unreadable, and she wondered if he'd really missed her the way she'd missed him. When he'd just pulled her into his apartment she'd been certain he had.

"Claudia told me. But maybe it just means he doesn't have anything to say. He seemed to be focused on taking me away with him. Without me to barter with Ivanov and ROC, he doesn't have much. His father's biggest contribution to ROC is over, for good."

"If he'd harmed a hair on your head, or taken you, I would have found you. And killed him." Luther's declaration caught her short.

"I know you would have. But he didn't get either of us, not in a lasting way."

"No." He shifted in his chair.

"Is it uncomfortable to sit there? Do you want to lie on the sofa? We can switch."

"Kit, when I come over to that sofa I'm going to kiss you, and I'm not going to stop. It's best we stay like this until we're done talking. Why don't you tell me why you're here?"

"I already told you. I feel we developed a special bond. I'd like to explore that."

"Explore?" He was teasing her and she laughed.

"Well, yes. But I mean to take our time with our friendship, get to know one another better."

"I'm leaving once the op is over. And I don't do long-distance relationships."

"Why do we have to look past now? I'm willing to enjoy things just as they are, for as long as they last. Or don't." She never broke eye contact with Luther and thought she deserved a gold star for lying so well. She wasn't lying, though, not really. Just omitting the hope that this could have the potential for more than an affair.

Luther was worth the risk of one night, though. If it was all she could have with him, she was willing to accept that.

"You deserve a man to be with you forever, Kit. I'm not that guy."

She stood up, unable to remain apart from him for one second longer. "I'm not looking for 'that' guy, Luther." Holding out her hand, she beckoned for him to take it.

He stared at her for a full heartbeat before he grasped her hand and tugged until her face was next to his. "I can't have you on my lap, not yet."

"Are you okay to do…other things?" she whispered, her lips so close to his. Every nerve ending was on fire.

His mouth curved into a bone-melting smile. "Babe, you have no idea."

She stood, still holding his hand. "Then let's go."

Chapter 18

Luther didn't allow himself to future-trip into tomorrow or the day after, when the op was complete and he was headed to the next assignment. Away from Kit.

No, he remained right here, in the present with Kit. The most beautiful woman he'd ever been attracted to, because, besides her physical attractiveness, she had a brain and heart that couldn't be beat. If he were the settling-down kind, Kit would be the woman he'd want to be with.

He'd take being with her tonight, though.

"Come on." He walked her back to the small bedroom, and was a teenager again with his first love.

Whoa… Love?

They cleared the door and Kit wrapped her hands around his neck and pulled his face to hers. She was all female, from her long eyelashes, to her full lips, to the body that had possessed him in his dreams for the last week.

"You know that once we start, there's no stopping, babe?"

"Yes. Enough talking, Luther. Kiss me."

He claimed her lips and the woman in his arms was Kit, all right, but with more passion and intention than he ever imagined. Her tongue traced his lips, pushed past and into his mouth, inviting his to join the erotic foreplay. Luther's intention to take it slow with Kit, to allow her to enjoy herself fully before he took her, was impossible to honor with every piece of his body on fire for her.

Only for Kit.

"Luther."

"Babe." He worshipped her with his lips, his tongue, as he kissed her jaw, her throat. Lifting her shirt over her head, he let her finish that task and unhooked her bra, his mouth on her rigid nipple, her obvious excitement a total turn-on. He caressed her other breast as he suckled, and she ground her hips against him.

"On the bed." He eased her onto the quilted cover, and tugged her pants off. The sight of the white lacy thong against her mound nearly stopped his fun before it started. "You are a beautiful woman, Kit."

"Too much talking."

Kit lay back on the bed, completely immersed in her desire for Luther and his every reaction. Clad in only her thong, she reveled in how Luther loved her with his gaze. Watching him take his clothes off was more of a turn-on than she expected. His body was lean and finely honed. When she saw his bandage and the bruising around it, her breath hitched.

Mishka could have killed him.

She forced the frightening truth away. Luther was here, she was here and they had tonight.

Without fanfare, Luther stepped out of his underwear and she drank in his full nudity. "You're stunning, Luther."

He gave her a saucy grin. "I'm glad you approve."

She giggled as he knelt between her legs, bent forward and placed his forearms on either side of her head.

And winced.

"Luther!" She pressed against his chest, unable to bear the thought of him being in pain, especially now.

"I'm fine. It just takes time to get settled."

"No, we're not doing it this way, then." She waited for him to lean on his good side before she gently pushed him on his back.

"Kit, I want it to be perfect for you."

"It's going to be perfect for us, babe." She arched her back and slid off her thong, then straddled him. The sensation of their most private parts connecting was almost too much for her. She had to work at not grinding down on him, wanting to make sure he was comfortable. Luther's pupils dilated and his breathing increased.

"Does this hurt?" Intended as a simple question, her query came out as a series of gasps.

"Only in the best way." He ground out his response before pulling her to him. With his hand behind her nape, he kissed her with an intensity that made stars flash behind her lids. As their tongues wound around each other, Luther tilted his pelvis up and she pressed back, needing this to go to the next place.

"Babe." She wanted to tell him how good it felt, but her mind wasn't cooperating. The throbbing between her legs quickly grew into a strong, insistent pressure. They hadn't even begun to move, and he wasn't inside her yet.

Kit held her breath as she watched Luther's expression for signs of pain, but all she saw was a reflection of how she felt. Totally immersed in their lovemaking.

"We need a condom, babe. I brought them, in my purse." Which she'd left in the front room.

"I know." He gave her a devilish smile and nodded toward the side of the bed. An entire strip of protection lay next to them.

"When did you do this?" She was sitting up straight as she straddled him, ripping off one of the condom packets as she spoke.

"The minute I saw you on my laptop screen."

She laughed, the excitement building as she processed that he'd wanted this as badly as she did. "That's very good prior planning, agent."

He grasped her hands, helped her ease the condom over him. "No more talking, babe. Come here."

She leaned over him, a hand on each of his shoulders. Luther pulled her to him again for a kiss that conveyed all she needed—he wanted her, he was going to make love to her, they were going to enjoy it.

"Take me in, babe." His words, whispered in her ear, shot molten desire through her core. She eased herself over him and slowly, to make it as good for him as it was for her, lowered herself, inch by inch. Luther filled her body as he'd filled her soul since she'd met him. Fully, leaving nothing unturned, no boundaries uncrossed.

As soon as he was completely inside, Luther began to move his hips and Kit couldn't hold back any longer. She met each of his thrusts with hers, racing to meet the wave of pleasure that awaited them both. Luther gently squeezed her breasts and then lowered his hands to her back, holding on to her buttocks. The sensation of his fingers in her flesh was the last thing she felt before her orgasm hit. She heard herself calling out his name, heard his reply, but mostly Kit simply lived in the moment.

Free and joyous, with Luther.

Luther made love to her two more times through the night, and he was stoked to discover that, true to her word, Kit knew what she wanted. She took as much as he was willing to give her, which was dang near everything.

Except a promise.

He listened to her showering as he stretched out on the bed. He'd taken his shower while making love to her against the tiled shower wall only minutes earlier. The vision of Kit being completely at ease and open with him was a precious gift he'd carry always, in his heart.

Because he couldn't be with her. Not after the ROC op was finished. Luther knew himself enough to know he didn't know what he wanted after his undercover days ended. Whether he stayed with TH, or switched back to conventional LEA, he'd always want to be fighting the bad guys. Wherever in the world it took him.

Kit was settled in Silver Valley. And even if she

were the traveling type, he couldn't risk his heart again. It had been crushed by Evalina's betrayal, and he didn't believe it would ever heal. He was as close to full recovery from his heartache as possible after tonight.

But it wasn't enough for Kit.

You're being stubborn. Tell her you love her.

Luther stood and began to get dressed. He'd make sure Kit got into Josh Avery's car, and then he'd complete his part of the mission. After that, he'd be out of Silver Valley and away from the constant tug on his heart.

Kit grabbed her purse and faced Luther in the apartment kitchen where he brewed coffee.

"Josh just texted. He'll be here in five."

"I know."

"You do?"

"Yes, I heard the ding. And it's almost four. I'd expect him to be prompt."

"Yeah." She wanted to say so much, tell Luther the full truth. That she loved him. But he'd pulled back since she walked out of the shower. She'd never take another shower without thinking of how a shower with Luther went down. A blush hit her cheeks as she thought about how he'd gone down on her.

Luther turned from the counter and faced her. He cupped her face with one hand. "Kit, there's a lot that I could say right now."

"Don't, Luther. I—I knew what I came over here for. So did you. Let's not make it more than it needs to be." A dratted tear plopped onto his hand, and he wiped it away, a soft smile on his lips.

"It seems we've both learned a lot from each other."

The smile remained, but his eyes bore a sorrow she could only figure meant he still wasn't ready to settle down. To at least make a decision to be with one woman. Her.

"This isn't goodbye yet, is it? We still have the op to get through." After that, she'd have a long talk with her therapist and find a way to move forward. Because leaving Luther behind was going to hurt like nothing had before.

The one difference was that she'd had the most happiness in her life to date. With Luther.

"Yeah, the op." He leaned over and kissed her forehead, just as her phone dinged. "That would be your cue."

He insisted on walking her down to the curb, where he opened the door for her. After she buckled her seat belt, she lifted her hand to the window.

Luther responded in kind, giving her a brief wave.

Josh shifted into Drive and they were off.

Chapter 19

One Week Later

"Take this, Kit, you might need it." Claudia stood next to Kit as she loaded the last of the comms gear into an unmarked van. In her hand Claudia held out a small handgun.

"Claudia, I can't take that."

"Not as an SVPD unsworn, no, you can't. But as a Trail Hikers operative about to face down the worst enemy yet? You damn well can, and you will. Holster it to your ankle." Claudia's eyes were bright with determination.

"Yes, ma'am." After Kit found an ankle holster in the safe house supply cabinet, she quickly did as her boss had directed and then joined the caravan leaving the safe house for where they anticipated the ROC meeting was to take place. Ivanov and Markova had been tracked as they drove to an abandoned barn on the outskirts of Silver Valley. There were many such structures in various states of decay and all-out collapse, but this particular one was surrounded by acres upon acres of Christmas trees, as the current landowner rented it to a tree farmer.

With a little research, SVPD had discovered the landholder was none other than Mishka Valensky, which explained how he'd continued money laundering after Vadim's arrest. The tree farmer was an innocent civilian, a young woman trying to make a go of her new business.

It took almost an hour to get to their preestablished listening post, and once there, Kit made sure her setup was to her liking. Amy, the other comms expert, sat next to her in the cramped workspace of the van. The distraction of preparing to bring in Ivanov and Markova kept Kit's mind occupied, but not her heart.

She wanted to kick herself for not telling Luther she loved him. What harm would it have done? She'd still be nursing a broken heart after he left Silver Valley, but at least if she'd told him, it would have given him the gift of knowing he was loved. Just as importantly, she would have lived in her truth.

"Amy?"

"Hmmm?"

"Do we know where any of the other TH units are yet?"

"Um, yeah. Right here, here and here." Amy pointed to other spots that surrounded the barn. Intel had already indicated that Markova and Ivanov were in the barn, hopefully unaware of the LEA presence. The barn was in a large clearing, and the TH, SVPD and other LEA waited for the arrival of the current remaining ROC hierarchy, led by Vlad Ivanov. Kit and Amy worked in a TH van alongside the SVPD comms van. SVPD personnel who weren't also TH believed that the TH van was FBI. It allowed them to combine efforts without compromising TH's shadow profile, nor any of its agents.

Kit studied the map and guessed where Luther worked. She longed to text him but not now, during an op. Having at least an idea of where he was comforted her.

Pounding on the back door startled them both. They exchanged annoyed glances. Everyone working the op was tired and on edge. It happened during most high-stress, high profile ops.

"Keep running your comms checks. I'll see who it is." Kit stood and checked the small screen next to the door. A hidden camera revealed it was SVPD Officer Brad Morris, who wasn't part of TH. She'd have to step out of the van as non-TH couldn't see the elite technology only privy to TH.

"Hey, Brad, what can I do for you?" She jumped down, closing Amy and the equipment away from his curious gaze.

"Hi, Kit. I thought I saw you come in here. So now you're working for FBI, huh?" He acted casually but she saw the tick jerking at the side of his eye.

"You know I couldn't answer that if I was. And I'm just helping out with some of the gear setup." Lying wasn't something she liked to do but had learned at the hands of a madman, to save her life. She had no problem doing it to protect classified material or Trail Hikers.

"Chief Todd is gathering us all around to give one last briefing, and I thought you wouldn't want to miss it."

She hadn't paid attention to the SVPD schedule for the op as she was so involved with the TH end of things.

And Luther.

"Oh, okay, well, I think I should—"

"He's adamant that everyone at least listen in." His eyes shifted to the van, behind her. "Unless you can listen in there?"

She couldn't reveal any of the capabilities of the comms equipment. "I guess you're right. I should listen in. Let me tell my colleague that I'll be gone for a bit. Where can I meet you?"

"Over there, by that blue van." He pointed to an unmarked vehicle and Kit almost grinned. LEA was really going to do this—bring down ROC.

"I'll be right over."

As soon as Brad walked away, Kit cracked open the door and revealed her dilemma to Amy. "I should probably go, so that he doesn't suspect we're more than FBI." In truth, she hoped to ask Colt where Luther was located. It was important that she find him after the op, to tell him what she should have last night.

I love you, Luther.

"Fair enough. Plus you might hear something we can use. I've got it here until you come back. So far there isn't any sign of Vlad and his crew." Amy turned her attention back to her gears, intent.

"Right. See you in a few." Kit stepped back out of the van, shut the door and walked off toward Brad.

"It doesn't make sense that they'd hide out here for over a day. It has to be below freezing in that dilapidation." Luther spoke to Colt, who nodded in agreement. They sat in an unmarked sedan, the barn visible through a row of Christmas trees. He fought hard to keep his thoughts on the mission and not drift back to how he'd spent last night.

How you want to spend every night. With Kit.

"Yeah, well, has anything ROC ever done made sense?" Colt's voice was resigned. Luther got it. They'd wait out here as long as it took. At least he knew Kit was ensconced in a comms van, relatively safe from what could turn into a shoot-out.

Luther's phone lit up and he quickly read the screen aloud to Colt. "Vlad spotted on highway, ten minutes out. Driving a late model SUV." He looked at Colt. "Sounds like we're going to get this wrapped up sooner than later."

Then maybe he'd stop playing chicken with his deepest fears and tell Kit how he felt. Except how did you tell a woman you were in love with her but knew you weren't the one for her?

Frost-coated grass crunched under Kit's work boots as she made her way over to the blue van. Brad leaned against the side of it, his gaze on her. He offered her a quick, friendly wave, and she smiled in response.

"I didn't know we had another van this close." Not that she was in on the entire workings of the takedown. It would be easy to miss details here and there.

"It's going to take all of us to bring this to an end, that's for sure." Brad still looked nervous, and she saw him glance repeatedly toward the direction of the barn. It wasn't more than two hundred yards away.

"Hey, Brad, we're going to get them, you know. Don't worry."

"Worry? Oh, I'm not worried. Except I've been having some trouble with the gear that Chief assigned me."

She looked into the front of the van. "Who's your partner?" No one worked alone during an op of this magnitude.

"He's in the back. Come on, I'll introduce you." She followed him to the back of the van.

"Maybe I can help with the gear." If it was comms equipment, she'd most likely be able to fix it.

"That'd be great. Come on, I'll help you up." He grabbed her upper arm as he opened the back door wide, revealing an empty cargo area.

Confusion, chased by cold fear, made Kit balk. "No, wait—"

But Brad shoved her without deliberation into the back of the van and shut the doors tight before she could scrambled back up.

"No, stop!" She screamed as loudly as she could, banged her fists on the door. This place was loaded with LEA. Someone had to hear her. The engine started and she ran to the wall between her and the driver's seat.

"Let me go, Brad! I don't know what this is about, but you've got to stop and think about what you're doing. Your wife, your kids!" Her throat already hurt and she recognized shock.

Before she could fight anymore, the van lurched to a

hard stop, throwing her backward. Her head slammed against the metal floor, hitting her where her head had taken a hit during her mission with Luther.

Luther.

"Great news!" Claudia's voice sounded over Luther's headset. He looked at Colt, who heard the same. "FBI has apprehended Vlad Ivanov and his thugs at the side of the highway. Repeat, Vlad is neutralized. We are free to take in Ivanov and Markova."

Colt's eyes sparked with relief. He spoke into the headset. "Proceed as planned. FBI will take over from—"

"Wait!" Colt's attention was on a blue van, barreling toward the barn. "Who the hell is that?"

"Cease takedown until we ID that vehicle." Claudia's voice again, in full battle mode.

Colt looked at Luther, then back out at the van. Luther's skin crawled. It only did that when something important to him was threatened. Dread filled his belly. No, it couldn't be Kit. She was in the comms van. As they watched, a man in plainclothes got out of the driver's side and walked around to the back, where he opened the side door.

"That's Officer Brad Norris." Colt's confusion vibrated in the car. "What on earth?"

Luther's hands gripped the dash, as he and Colt sat helpless, waiting to see who came out of the van. When Officer Norris cleared the door and headed toward the barn, he wasn't alone.

He had Kit flung over his shoulder, limp and unconscious.

"No!" Luther's hand was on the handle, and only Colt's decisive "Stop!" Held him back.

"Luther, take a breath. We'll get her. She'll be okay. But we have to stay calm and figure out what he's doing first. Got it?"

"Yes." But first chance he got, he was taking down the bastard who had Kit.

Then he was going to tell her he loved her. Unless… Unless this ended like his last ROC op. And Kit ended up dead.

Kit came to as pain from a harsh blow to her solar plexus radiated through her rib cage. She coughed, wondering why the ground moved beneath her.

Brad carried her, like a sack of kitty litter, over the ground and she had no doubt where to. Oh, no, she was going to die at the hands of him, or Ivanov, Markova or worse, Vlad.

No. Stay focused. Luther. His faith in you.

The gun was still strapped to her leg. Brad's arms had her in a vice grip across the back of her thighs, and he hadn't noticed the weapon between her ankles.

Brad was SVPD and knew she was unsworn, unable to legally carry a weapon on duty. It never occurred to him to pat her down.

Each step he took made the pain in her head streak down her neck, inflaming her body. But it gave her hope, because pain meant she was still alive, still had a chance.

His grunts grew louder as he continued past Christmas trees, the branches scratching her. Something told her to remain quiet and limp. Let him think she was still unconscious.

"Come no closer!" The female voice rang out from in front of her, and she realized he'd brought them to the barn. Kit had studied enough tapes of Markova to know her voice. What was Brad doing?

"I've got what you need for your final negotiations. A gift from Mishka."

"Who is it?" Markova couldn't see from wherever she stood.

"Vadim's wife." Defiance roiled through Kit at his words. She would never be Vadim's wife ever again. But it wasn't worth expending her painful breath on correcting him.

"You have Kit?" Ivanov's voice. Deeper, but weaker than Markova's.

"Yes." Brad dropped to his knees and threw Kit onto the ground. She kept her eyes closed, but maneuvered enough so that her butt hit first and she engaged her core muscles to keep her head from snapping back again. She had to stay alert, had to do her part.

Luther.

He'd tell her to pay attention and use her weapon. But it wasn't going to be as easy as with Mishka. This time she had three adversaries, and Vlad Ivanov was inbound with countless others. Despair clawed at her concentration, and the old familiar anxiety started its persuasive chatter. It would be so easy to let go, to give it all up.

Except Kit had fought too long and endured too much suffering to give up now. If she made it through this, she'd have a chance to tell the man she loved how much he meant to her. Whether or not he reciprocated didn't matter. She had to make it, to reach Luther one more time.

As Brad continued to talk with Ivanov and Markova, she formed her escape plan.

"I can't sit here any longer, Colt." Luther had seen enough. When Kit's limp body was dumped on the ground, he clenched every muscle against the pain she had to be feeling.

"There's hope, Luther. Did you see how she didn't hit her head?"

"Her head?" Luther replayed the scene in his mind as he continued to watch Brad shout back and forth with either Markova or Ivanov.

"Yes. If she were unconscious, her head would have snapped back. But she kept her chin to her chest just long enough to protect it. She's awake, and I'll bet planning her escape." Colt's pride was evident.

"She's defenseless out there."

"She has a .22 strapped to her ankle." Claudia's voice broke his worst fear. She was in the comms loop with them.

"That's something, at least, but there's only one of her and three of them. Someone has to be backup."

"We already have three snipers surrounding the barn, Luther." Claudia was firm.

"And I'm right here, with my sight on Markova's figure in the barn window."

"Luther's right, Claudia. He has a clear shot if he gets out of the car."

"Okay, go in. But at all costs, don't distract Kit. Let her do her job, Luther." Claudia gave him the go-ahead. Luther took the rifle he'd brought and slipped out of the car. He used the Christmas trees as cover, zigzagging closer to the best spot to take out Markova, and hopefully Ivanov. Before they could hurt Kit.

Kit used every ounce of patience and self-control she had to not react too soon and risk being shot by Markova or Ivanov. She knew she could hit Brad since his nervousness had morphed into all-out panic. He'd thought Mishka's name would keep him safe, but the two former ROC leaders weren't buying it. If they killed him first, she'd have to try to kill both of them in quick succession.

"If you have Kit, you'll show Vlad that you're worthy of running ROC again."

"We don't know you. If you were important to Mishka, he'd have told us."

"He couldn't. He didn't want you to know more than you needed to." Brad's voice grew weaker, pleading. Kit waited.

"We don't need Vadim's ex alive. Shoot her now, then come inside." Markova's order made icy determination blossom in Kit's chest.

"Are you sure?" What a fool Brad was. He didn't know ROC as well as she did. An execution order was never questioned.

She quickly but surreptitiously reached for the weapon between her legs, needing only to move her arm a few inches to do so. Praying that from this distance Markova and Ivanov couldn't see her movements, she grasped the handle and tugged it free.

"Kill her!" Ivanov's voice carried across the distance.

Kit waited for Brad to turn to her, but didn't wait

for him to raise his weapon. She shot him in the chest, relieved when he fell.

And prepared to run for the tree line. Chances were that Markova would hit her before she got to safety, but she had to go for it.

"Kit, stay down!"

Luther.

Shots rang out all around her. She fought the primal urge to get up and run for her life.

Kit trusted Luther.

Chapter 20

Three Weeks Later

"Meow." Koshka swirled between Kit's legs as she finished baking chocolate chip cookies. Annie and the girls were coming over for a Friday-night chat, the first since the ROC op had been wrapped up. Everyone had been too exhausted, emotionally and physically, to consider a celebration any sooner. It was a huge relief to know Ivanov and Markova were in custody. No one had expected they'd capitulate so easily, but when Ivanov was faced with the truth that his son was going to jail, he caved and surrendered. Markova had attempted an escape, but Josh Avery shot her in the shoulder, and she survived. It was the happiest of endings for a long fight against the crime ring's hold on Silver Valley and the eastern half of the US.

In truth, as much as she'd been professionally satisfied, Kit had been heartbroken. She'd survived the shoot-out, as had every LEA agent and officer present, save for Brad Norris. Luther had found her right afterward, but hadn't allowed her, again, to say what she wanted to. He'd only pulled her to him and hugged her for several minutes, before saying he had to "go take care of business."

If she'd known he was going to leave town, as evidenced by his empty apartment that she'd visited two weeks ago, she would have spilled her heart right there in the middle of the Christmas trees. Now he'd never know the difference he'd made in her life, or how much he meant to her.

"Meow." Koshka was always in the vicinity of the oven when she had it on. Turning it off, she giggled at her furry buddy.

"No sweets for you. Here, let me get you a treat." She put the spatula down and reached for Koshka's kitty snack jar as her doorbell rang. It was wonderful to be back in her apartment, her home. Only one thing had been missing these last weeks.

Luther.

She sighed and walked toward the door. It seemed awfully quiet in her hallway, unlike the usually boisterous chatter that Annie and Portia engaged in. Plus they'd promised to bring along several other women they all knew and worked with, in TH, Claudia included.

When she looked through the peephole, her heart raced. *Luther.*

She quickly pasted a smile on her face and opened the door.

"Luther?"

His face, rugged as ever, broke into a grin the moment they made eye contact. "Can I come in?"

"Ah, sure." She stepped back, opening the door wide. "I'm expecting a group of ladies in a few minutes. I thought you were them."

He walked into her living room. Only then did she see the huge bouquet in his hands.

"Here. For you. They reminded me of you."

She took the confection of pink roses, peonies and daisies. "They're beautiful, thank you." Did he see how much the petals shook, in unison with her trembling hands? "Why pink?"

As easily as he'd given her the gift, he took the flowers from her and placed them on a side table. Stepping closer, he grasped her hands and held them between them. She felt an answering tremor in his fingers; his entire body seemed to be shaking.

Was Luther nervous? She licked her lips, searched his face for a clue to his intent. Hope flared in her belly that maybe he'd come to finish what she'd wanted to say in the middle of the Christmas trees.

"Kit, I don't want you to think you have to reply to anything I'm about to say. It's only fair to tell you, though, that I've decided to change my life for the better. Meaning, I want to be with you. I've taken a position at SVPD as a detective, and I'll still work with TH on an as-needed basis. With ROC gone, they don't need as many in their workforce right now."

"Stop!" She tugged her hand from his grasp and placed her fingers over his lips. "You told me enough when you said you want to be with me. I want to be with you, too!" She leaned up, her lips puckered.

He put his finger on her lips. "Not yet. There's one more thing."

She wasn't going to let him get to the punch line first.

"I love you, Luther!"

"I love you, Kit."

Their mutual proclamation stilled them for a second, and then Kit was done with waiting, with longing. She launched herself at Luther, wrapping her legs around his waist. He was ready for her, holding her with complete security as their lips met in their most meaningful kiss yet.

They were in love.

It was all going to work out.

Their kiss began to change into something more, heat growing in their embrace. A few coughs and *ahem*s broke through the quiet, and Kit pulled back enough to look toward the door, which they'd left open.

Annie, Portia and Claudia stood in the foyer, huge grins on their faces. And was that a tear on Claudia's face?

"Uh, Luther—"

"Yeah, babe?" He followed her gaze, but instead of releasing her, he hoisted her up higher, laughing. "You may as well all know—we're an item."

Applause and cheers echoed and Luther again lowered his mouth to hers. When they looked up again, the front door was closed and they were alone.

Together.

* * * * *

WE HOPE YOU ENJOYED
THIS BOOK FROM

HARLEQUIN
ROMANTIC
SUSPENSE

Danger. Passion. Drama.

These heart-racing page-turners will keep you guessing to the very end. Experience the thrill of unexpected plot twists and irresistible chemistry.

4 NEW BOOKS AVAILABLE EVERY MONTH!

"You doing okay?"

"Yeah. I'm fine."

Ace's gaze searched Veronica's face. "I wasn't trying to
scare you earlier."

"I didn't think that. At all. It doesn't seem real, but I
know that it is."

"I know my family has seen more than its fair share of
bad happenings around here and I'm not asking for trouble,
but there was something off about that guy. I'm not going to
ignore it or pretend my gut isn't blaring like a siren."

Ignore it? Had she been so wrapped up in her frustration
that she'd given him that impression?

"Once again, my inability to speak to you with any
measure of my normal civility left the absolute wrong
impression. I'm grateful to you."

Those sexy green eyes widened, but he said nothing, so
she continued on.

"You were watching out for me and I couldn't even manage the most basic level of appreciation." She stood, suddenly unable to sit still. "I am grateful. More than you know. I just—"

Before she could say anything—before the awful, terrible words could spill out—Ace was there, those big strong arms wrapped around her.

Just like she'd wanted all along.

"What happened?"

Her face was pressed to his chest, but it gave an added layer of protection to say what she needed to say. To let the terrible words spill out. Words she'd sworn to herself she'd never say again after she got through the horror of police statements and endless questions by drug company lawyers and even more endless questions by insurance lawyers.

She'd said them all over and over, even when it seemed as if no one was listening.

Or worse, that they even believed her.

But she'd said them each time she'd been asked. And then she'd sworn to bury them all.

His arms tightened, his strength pouring into her. "You can tell me."

"I know."

Don't miss
Under the Rancher's Protection *by Addison Fox,*
available November 2021 wherever
Harlequin Romantic Suspense
books and ebooks are sold.

Harlequin.com

HRSEXP1021